RAVE REVIEWS FOR CINDY HOLBY!

WINDFALL

"A great story with warm, likable characters."

—*The Best Reviews*

"If you're fascinated with the Civil War, Holby gives you everything you want and more."

—*RT BOOKclub*

CROSSWINDS

"Cindy Holby proves she is quite talented with an enjoyable saga that fans will relish."

—*Midwest Book Review*

"A reader who is enchanted by history and the U.S. Civil War will be sure to enjoy this read."

—RoundtableReviews.com

WIND OF THE WOLF

"A wonderful story! It captured my attention, pulled me in and made me feel like I was there with the characters."

—*Old Book Barn Gazette*

"Cindy Holby displays her talent with an insightful look at tragedy."

—*Midwest Book Review*

CHASE THE WIND

"Cindy Holby takes us on an incredible journey of love, betrayal, and the will to survive. Ms. Holby is definitely a star on the rise!"

—*The Best Reviews*

"*Chase the Wind* is like no other book you'll read, and you owe it to yourself to experience it."

—EscapetoRomance.com

THE FIRST SIGHT

Amanda leaned across his chest and picked up Caleb's left arm. She was so engrossed in her work that she did not notice the flickering of the dark lashes against his cheek. The cloth dipped into the hollow on the inside of his elbow and then swept over the curve of his bicep and over his shoulder before caressing the triceps on its journey back down to the hand. She gently returned the arm to its resting place after taking time to wash the long lean fingers. Then she moved the bed covers down past his waist.

The washcloth swirled over the ridges of his abdomen. He might not be as tall as the others, but he had to be as strong. There wasn't a part of his body that she had seen so far that seemed weak. Even the thigh that supported his wooden leg bulged with muscle, she mused as she looked down towards the foot of the bed. Her glance was interrupted, however, by the sight of another bulge.

Amanda gasped and turned to find a set of dark eyes beneath impossibly long lashes glowing up at her. She stood up quickly and dropped the cloth into the basin with a slosh as Caleb reached for the covers and pulled them up over his chest.

"I'm sorry," he said hoarsely.

Forgive the Wind

CINDY HOLBY

LEISURE BOOKS NEW YORK CITY

*To my editor, Alicia Condon,
for her gentle guidance.*

A LEISURE BOOK®

June 2005

Published by

Dorchester Publishing Co., Inc.
200 Madison Avenue
New York, NY 10016

ISBN 0-8439-5307-1

The name "Leisure Books" and the stylized "L" with design are
trademarks of Dorchester Publishing Co., Inc.

Printed in the United States of America.

Visit us on the web at www.dorchesterpub.com.

Forgive the Wind

Prologue

Virginia, July 1864

An explosion of color washed over Caleb Conners as the company of soldiers and mules entered the meadow. Pale blue butterflies fluttered around the noisy party in protest of the disturbance before taking off in a pastel cloud for sanctuary. Bright blue asters and light pink clover blooms swayed in the wake of the mules trailing through the meadow. Caleb's hands ached to draw it all, to capture the wonder of it, but he knew his simple charcoal wouldn't do the scene justice. If only there were a way for him to bring the color to life, to show the varying shades of cool blues against the deep greens while conveying the sheer beauty of the day. He really should try his hand at painting someday when the war was over. If he survived it.

"I don't know which is worse, herding cows or herding mules," Jake groused as he popped one of the mules on the rump to goose him on.

"Well, it's a lot easier than trying to get wagons over these mountain trails," Ty said as he fought with a balky mule laden with a barrel of gunpowder.

"I think our job will be easy compared to what Mr. Bishop has to do," Caleb said. Why couldn't his friends see the beauty of the place instead of the drudgery of the job? They were carrying powder down from the mountains of Virginia. Powder that would be smuggled onto a ship waiting off the coast of North Carolina and then secretly carried to New Orleans to help the Confederate cause on that front. "I'd much rather wrestle mules than sneak around out in the ocean trying to get by Federal ships."

"We all have our jobs to do," Bishop said with a smile. "And we try to do our best. My crew is one of the finest out there, and my ship has the reputation of being one of the fastest."

Caleb wasn't surprised to hear Jake snort at Bishop's comment. Jake didn't trust the man. Jake didn't trust anyone except the men he rode with, and that was only after they had proven themselves time and time again to the bitter cowboy.

Ty too had exercised caution where Bishop was concerned. He hadn't taken the man to the caves where the powder was made. Caleb looked at the broad back of his leader and friend, Major Tyler Kincaid. Caleb, along with their friend Jake Anderson, had followed Ty from Wyoming to North Carolina to fight for the South in a war that had ripped the country in two. They had survived it so far, miraculously escaping with nothing more than a wound to Ty's shoulder and the loss of a few horses—and more comrades in arms than they could count. Ty's wife, Cat, had followed him also, at first content to stay at his family plantation in North Carolina. But the realization that she was with child had brought her into the wilds to find her husband and bring him home, to Wyoming, and away from the dangers of the war.

Caleb smiled as he watched the couple ride side by side in front of him. What other woman besides Cat would have the audacity to follow her husband into battle? Jenny Duncan would. But Jenny and her husband, Chase, along with the rest of the friends that Caleb considered family, were safe in Wyoming.

How much longer would he have to wait before he could return to the safety of Wyoming?

The meadow ended and the trail led them into a deep stand of trees growing on a ridge above a rocky stream. They fell into single file, with Caleb taking a position behind Bishop, who rode behind Ty and Cat. Jake and young Willie fell in line a few riders back, with everyone guiding a keg-laden mule.

The braying of the mules had alerted every forest creature for miles around to their presence, leaving nothing but the creak of leather and the jingle of a bit as accompaniment to the merry gurgling of the stream below.

It was a beautiful day. A great day to be alive. Caleb smiled as he looked at Ty and Cat riding in front of him. They were going to have a child. *We're all so blessed. . . .*

The skin on the back of his neck prickled. Caleb

3

turned his head, dark eyes searching, suddenly aware
that he had been dreaming about peace in the middle
of a war. If only the mules wouldn't make so much
noise.

There was a hiss, a flash of light, the sudden impact
as the breath was knocked from his body and he went
flying through the air.

What was happening? He knew there was noise, but
his ears refused to hear it. They couldn't. He couldn't
see, either; something was on top of him.

And then there was the pain that brought a blanket of
darkness. . . .

"Caleb!"

His ears rang as the realization that someone was
calling his name sank into his brain. *Ty . . . Cat screaming and crying.*

He felt as if he were suffocating. Something, someone, was lying on top of him, and he could feel something jabbing into his back. His left leg throbbed with a
red-hot searing pain all the way up into his groin.

What happened? he wondered.

"Caleb?" Ty said.

"Ty?"

The weight was gone, and Caleb blinked against the
sunlight that danced through the swaying treetops.

"Oh, God," Ty said as he caught sight of Caleb's leg.

"Is it bad?" Caleb asked as he raised himself up to his
elbows. Bile rose in his throat, and he swallowed hard
to keep it down as he looked at the blood-soaked
ragged remains of his left boot.

4

"Let's get you out of here," Ty said. He ripped a belt from the body that lay beside him and quickly tied it around Caleb's leg as a makeshift tourniquet.

Tuttle—that's Tuttle, or what's left of him, Caleb realized as Ty pulled him up.

"Where are Cat and Jake?" Caleb asked as Ty threw an arm over his shoulder. The forest swam before him and he grabbed Ty's sleeve. He was in trouble. Deep trouble.

"Let's get you to cover," Ty said.

"Leave me. Find Cat and get out of here."

"Let's go," Ty insisted and half dragged, half carried him down the trail. They heard hoofbeats in front of them and behind, the sounds of soldiers, undoubtedly Union troops coming to claim their victory.

"Cat?" Ty asked. Her face emerged from the undergrowth, and she gasped when she looked at Caleb's leg.

"Take him," Ty said as he lowered Caleb to the ground.

Caleb's lower leg felt numb, yet the pain throbbed up his thigh and into his spine. He had to stay awake; he couldn't give in. Too much was at stake. Lives were at stake.

"What?" Cat asked.

"Take him. I have to cover the signs or they'll find him."

"No!" They said it together, Caleb and Cat. Caleb realized that Ty was going to offer himself up to protect the two of them. *You can't do this, Ty* . . .

"You will never survive in a Yankee prison. Not with an injury like this." Ty's steel-blue eyes bored into Caleb, then turned to Cat. "Drag him into the brush and keep quiet. No matter what you hear, keep quiet."

Don't do it, Ty. God, what has happened to us? Who did this?

"Now, Cat." Ty wasn't asking. He was commanding. His voice held the resolve and the responsibility of leadership. He was responsible for their lives. All of theirs.

Cat grabbed Caleb under the armpits and started dragging him up the ridge. Caleb tried to push with his right leg, to help her, but the pain was getting worse. It edged into the corners of his brain, dimming the light. He had to remain conscious.

Ty stuck his head under the brush to watch them. "When this is over, when Caleb recovers, I want you to go home."

"I'll get him there," she said.

Every root and rock was working against them as Cat dragged and Caleb tried to push. He concentrated on pushing with his leg. He had to make sure they were safe. If Cat was captured, there was no telling what Ty would do to try to save her.

"No, I mean home to Wyoming," Ty said. Cat stopped, and gratefully Caleb sucked at the air, hoping it would help to take the pain away. *Please, God, take the pain away* . . . "It's time, Cat," Ty said.

"No. I won't leave you."

Please don't cry, Cat. I won't be able to bear it if you cry . . .

"I love you," Ty whispered.

Caleb realized he shouldn't be here, an unwilling witness to his friends' passion and pain. It was too raw, too intense. If not for him and his wound, Ty and Cat could be gone from this place of death and destruction.

Cat pulled Caleb back and then hauled him up so that she supported him. Caleb's head fell back against her shoulder, and he found that he didn't have the strength to move it.

"I'm sorry, Cat."

"Shhh, it's not your fault." She whispered it again as they listened to the sounds of Ty's booted feet moving away.

Caleb was shaking and couldn't stop. He grabbed Cat's hand and held on for dear life as they listened to the yells and screams, the impact of steel, the sound of gunfire.

"Oh, God, please don't let him die."

He heard Cat praying and realized he was praying also, over and over again. The sounds faded and the forest quieted. Caleb concentrated on the light that barely penetrated the dense mountain laurel they were hiding under. He had to stay awake. He had to take care of Cat.

"Do you think it's all right now?" Her voice trembled.

He had to sit up. He had to be strong. He couldn't move. *Do something, Caleb. Anything.*

He cleared his throat, willing his voice to be strong even if his body wasn't. "I don't know. We need to look around first."

Cat eased out from beneath him and lowered him against the solid trunk of a hemlock. Her hair caught in the wandering branches of the mountain laurel and pulled loose from its rawhide thong. Caleb's hand trembled as he fought with the tangle that held her captive. The look Cat gave him barely hid her terror.

"Don't worry, Cat, I can't feel a thing," he lied.

She nodded and turned away, snaking on her belly down through the underbrush.

"Caleb?" Cat called from a short distance away.

How long had she been gone? Had he lost consciousness? He was trying to hold on. God, he was trying.

"Coming," he said finally, attempting to wriggle toward her.

Sweat poured down his face and down into the collar of his shirt as he half slid, half crawled down the ridge to the trail. Standing wasn't any easier, especially since it brought dizziness.

"Should I loosen the tourniquet?" she asked when he reached her.

God, don't touch it. Don't even look at it, his mind screamed. "No, I think that's all that's holding my foot on right now." He was trying to make a joke, but the fear in Cat's green-gold eyes showed him he had failed miserably.

They made their way to a tree that had fallen and he eased himself down against it. Thank God there was something solid he could hold on to.

Caleb pulled his gun from the holster and handed it to Cat. "We need more weapons, Cat. And a horse."

She nodded, and he watched as she swallowed her fear and looked up the trail in the direction that Ty had gone. They were both desperate to know the fate of their friends. The floor of the forest was littered with bodies, or parts of bodies. They had to know if Ty was one of them. And Jake. Where was Jake?

Caleb could guess the answer. Jake would have gone down in a blaze of glory, firing away, taking as many of the enemy with him as he could.

Cat began to retch. Caleb watched helplessly as she emptied her guts on the trail.

"Cat?"

"I'm okay," she said, defiantly wiping her mouth with the back of her hand. She had a lot of grit, but God help both of them if she found Ty dead. Caleb watched as she disappeared from his sight. He held on to the tree for dear life, knowing that his hold on consciousness was tenuous at best without Cat there to distract him from the pain. He had to hold on. Tears streamed from beneath dark lashes as he fought his battle. He had to hold on.

He blinked his eyes, fighting the haze that threatened to overtake him. Cat was standing before him, her face grim.

"Anything?" he managed to get out. She shook her head. No sign of Ty, which probably meant he'd been captured. He was still alive—he had to be. "Cat, what happened to Jake?"

"He's gone, Caleb. There's nothing left."

Oh, God—Jake. Caleb swallowed hard. "Willie too?"

She looked as if she were going to be sick again. "Willie too."

The wind whirled through the trees, stirring up dead leaves and swirling them down the trail.

"They won't hurt Ty, Cat. He's an officer," he assured her.

She was trying not to cry. She was fighting the tears, but her body shuddered and she fell against him. Caleb wrapped his arms around her and hung on for dear life. She needed him. They needed each other.

"What are we going to do?" she sobbed against his chest.

If only he knew. He wasn't going to last much longer. It would be dark soon, and it looked as if a storm was threatening to the west.

A crashing sound in the creek below them brought both their heads up.

"It's Scarlet," Cat exclaimed. Her horse was standing in the water with her reins dragging and the whites of her eyes showing.

"Bless her heart, she came back," Caleb laughed weakly as he watched Cat slide down the bank to catch the shiny chestnut mare. Something good had happened. He watched as Cat expertly ran her hands over the mare's legs and flanks.

"She's okay!" Cat announced.

"Thank you, God." Caleb breathed a sigh of relief. The storm must be quickly approaching. It was getting darker by the second.

"Caleb!"

Suddenly Cat was before him, with Scarlet. He must have lost consciousness for a moment, but he was still sitting against the tree. He hadn't loosened his grip.

Pull yourself up . . . Cat was talking to him. She wanted him to do something. He had to move. She wanted him to mount Scarlet. He laid his face against

10

the cool leather of the saddle as he held on to the pommel with both hands.

"Pull!" she yelled as she shoved him up from behind. He managed to make the stirrup with his right leg, but he couldn't get his left leg to go over.

"You've got to do it, Cat." She grabbed his knee and swung it over Scarlet's back just as darkness overtook him.

"Cat?" Caleb's mind swirled through oblivion as the disaster of the day hit him with a jolt of pain that shot up his leg and through his spine. Where was he? His dark eyes found the dim light of a small fire. A cave. Cat must have somehow carried him to this shelter. How?

"I'm here." He felt her move beside him. "How do you feel?"

He had to move, just to prove that he could. She had to know she could depend on him. She had to know she wasn't alone.

"I'm alive, I think. My leg hurts like hell." He managed to push himself up and leaned against the back of the cave, but something felt strange. His equilibrium was off. He felt . . . lopsided.

"Caleb . . ." Cat touched his arm. "It's gone."

"What?" What was gone? What was she saying?

Cat disappeared into the darkness and then reappeared with a stub of candle. Caleb fastened his eyes upon it as a beacon of hope in the never-ending despair that surrounded them. She moved the candle down his leg, and he made his hand follow, dreading

11

what he knew he was going to find, or not find. He flinched when his hand met the air where his foot had been.

"Oh, God," he said, covering his face with his hands.

"I'm sorry, Caleb. Your foot was shattered. There was nothing for me to do but take it off." The words tumbled out as she fought and lost the battle with her tears. She dropped the candle, and the darkness once again surrounded them, suffocating them.

"I can't believe you did it."

"I'm sorry. I'm so sorry."

She thought he was blaming her. Caleb reached for Cat and pulled her to his chest. "No. No. I can't believe you were able to do it, Cat. I don't blame you; it's not your fault. You did what you had to do. Shh. It's all right." He felt her arms circle his waist as they clung to each other in the darkness.

"Oh, Caleb, what are we going to do?"

"Go home."

Caleb felt her agreement as she nodded against his chest. "Do you think you can ride?" she asked.

"I guess I'll have to. I'm not much for walking right now." He tried to smile to make her feel better, but realized that she couldn't see it.

The call of nature suddenly became more urgent than his pain.

"See if you can find something for me to use as a crutch. And hurry."

"You need to take it slow."

"Some things won't wait, Cat."

"Oh."

He hated his weakness. What if she had to help him? He couldn't ask that of her, but the alternative was wetting himself and he refused to humiliate himself like that. He tried to stand while she went out. How could he stand with only one leg? He'd better figure it out; he had no choice in the matter now.

"I'm okay," he said when she came running to help him. She placed a branch under his arm and it supported him, for which he was immensely grateful. He rested his head against the rocky entrance to the cave and leaned heavily on the crutch as the relief of his body reacting normally after the crisis washed over him. He was alive. That was more than Jake could say. That was more than they knew for sure about Ty. His duty now was to make sure that Cat survived.

"Caleb?" She was worried about him. He had to be strong. She was carrying a child. Ty's child. He had to protect them.

"We might as well start now. I don't know if I have the strength to get up again." They needed to leave the battleground before the scavengers came. They'd been known to kill wounded men on the battlefield for the simple belongings to be found in their pockets. They had no way of knowing where the sympathies of the locals lay. This part of Virginia had been divided in two, just like the rest of the country. If he and Cat ran into Union sympathizers, they would be killed without mercy. Both of them.

"Do you want something to eat first?"

"No. I don't think I could keep anything down right now."

13

Cat went for Scarlet. "Do you think you can mount?"

"I'm going to have to, aren't I?" He managed to haul himself up; he didn't even know how. As he settled in the saddle, the world began to spin again. "You'd better ride behind me. I don't know how long I'll be able to stay upright."

He was conscious of movement. He fought to stay awake and kept his spine stiff so he wouldn't fall off the horse. He had to make sure they were safe. Cat kept her arms wrapped around his waist.

Caleb kept fighting, but his eyes grew heavy as the darkness swirled. His head fell forward and he jerked upright again.

"Cat, look."

It was Ty's horse, standing in a small clearing with his ears perked toward the trail, waiting for his master as he was trained to do. The horse seemed glad to see them, and Scarlet was happy for the company.

"He's been trained to wait," Caleb commented unnecessarily. Talking kept him in this world where he needed to be. "He just went on a little farther than he was supposed to."

"All the explosions must have spooked him."

"Maybe. He should be used to it by now." Cat stopped on the trail. Caleb realized that she was afraid of spooking the horse. "Go on. He's used to me. Just ride up to him and grab his reins."

"What do we do now?" Cat asked as she secured the horse.

"Tie me to the saddle."

"What?"

"You can't keep holding me up, and if I fall, I'm a goner for sure. And if I take you with me, you might lose the baby." Just talking made him weary. His head hung forward; it took too much energy to hold it up. "My foot is gone, and my leg is sure to follow if you don't get me home soon. It's a four-day ride from here if nothing goes against us. Tie me to the saddle and keep going."

"Talk to me, Caleb."

Where were they? They were still moving. He had been conscious of it, but the journey was lost in a blur of pain and intense heat.

"Talk to me about home."

Home. How he longed to be there. Back in the bunk-house with Zane cutting up and Jake growling at him. Chase mooning over Jenny and Ty frustrated with Cat. And Jamie.

Grace's home cooking, and riding for miles with the wind in his hair, and knowing there was a safe place to come home to and people to care for him.

"Home?" He wasn't home. He was somewhere else. Hell, perhaps.

"Wyoming. Home. What do you miss about home?" Cat was talking to him, but she sounded far away.

There was a river. They were splashing into a river.

"Is this the New?" he managed, grasping onto reality.

"Yes."

"Then we're close to home."

"I hope so."

The water felt so cool on his legs. On his leg. If only

15

he could just lie in it. If only he could let the cool rushing water of the New River cover his body, let the current float him away to a peaceful place.

"What's your favorite thing to eat?"

Leave me in peace, Cat. Let me fall into the river and let it carry me away . . .

"Eat?"

"That Grace would fix. What's your favorite thing?"

Grace. Grace would take care of me. Take me to Grace.

Grace was miles and miles away. She was a lifetime away.

"Apple pie." He had to say something. Cat was trying to help him.

"Yeah, me too."

Poor Cat. It should have been Ty with her, not him. He should have made Ty take her to safety.

"Her biscuits," he added, since he was thinking about it. Wishing . . .

The thought of eating was painful.

"Uh-huh," Cat agreed. "How about her blueberry cobbler?"

"Jenny's sugar cookies were good."

"You mean the ones that got baked instead of thrown around?"

He had to smile at that memory. The memories were good. *God, let me get lost in the memories again so I don't have to feel this pain.*

"And her ginger cookies," he managed to add because Cat was expecting it.

"Remember the ham we had last Christmas at home?"

He tried to draw a breath. He felt as if he had climbed the riverbank by himself instead of just hanging on to Scarlet.

"Yeah. It had . . . pineapple? That was the funniest-looking fruit I've ever seen."

"Grace had a hard time figuring out how to peel and slice it."

"Your father"—the darkness was coming again—"your father always found the most wonderful things." Caleb's eyes searched for something familiar in the wilderness and then settled on Cat. "He always knew how to make things . . . special for all of us." He felt so cold. He had to hold on. Just a little bit longer and they would be home. "That was the last Christmas we were all together . . ."

"Where am I?" There was a roof over his head. A high ceiling, part of it darkened with smoke from a stovepipe. A hand smoothed his hair away from his forehead. Cat.

"You're home." She looked calm, but something was wrong. Who were all these people?

Ty's brother Parker, and Zeb, his slave. Portia and Silas, the house slaves and a strange man. He tried to push himself up. What was he on, a table? The kitchen table? Parker's house. Parker's kitchen.

"What's happening? What are you doing?" Caleb asked.

Stricken faces looked at him, then at Cat.

"Caleb, the doctor is here and he needs to operate on your leg. It's infected, and he has to take some more of it off so you'll be able to use a wooden leg."

They were going to take more of his leg off. Or he would die . . .

"The problem is, there is no morphine because of the blockade. We were hoping you would stay unconscious . . ."

Terror seized his gut and twisted it around. No morphine. More pain. He licked his dry lips and he saw the doctor with a saw in his hand.

"Cat?" Maybe he was dreaming. Maybe it was a fever. Maybe he was back home in Wyoming and the past years had all just been a nightmare. Maybe he would wake up and they would all go to town and laugh and carry on and have a good time . . .

"Shh, Caleb. It will be all right. You just have to hold on," Cat said.

They were holding him down. Cat held his head. Hands held his body in place, and someone was talking to him.

God, I can't stand it. What's that sound? It's pieces of my flesh being flung away. Make it stop . . . make it stop . . . please, God, just make it stop. . . .

Chapter One

Wyoming, 1865

The foot pained him. It was amazing how something that was buried by a creek bank on the other side of the country could cause so much pain now. It twitched and it itched and at times it seemed as if it were on fire, and there was nothing he could do to relieve the sensations. He just needed to learn how to live with them.

Caleb pulled the sock up over his stump and pulled on the knee-high boot that was filled with a wooden form so it fit snugly over his calf. He had waited until the bunkhouse cleared out before he rose from his bed and dressed. It was easier to wait for the others to leave than to deal with their questions and offers of help. He knew that his friends meant well, that they genuinely cared for him, but it was just easier to deal with his problem alone.

Caleb tested the foot as he always did before he put any weight on it. He had a constant fear of taking a step and falling flat on his face. Falling didn't scare him as much as the looks of pity that would be present in his friends' eyes as they hauled him to his feet.

He really should stop feeling sorry for himself. There were others who had lost so much more than he had. Men had been blinded, horribly scarred, lost entire arms, legs, both. Lives had been shattered and destroyed, and he was still mourning for an ankle and a foot that had probably made a meal for some varmint nosing around a creek bank in Virginia.

Ty and Cat had lost their baby. Caleb still felt guilty about their loss even though he knew it wasn't his fault. But he couldn't help thinking that if Cat had not experienced the hardship of caring for him and getting him to a doctor, she might have carried her baby full term. She should have been caring for herself instead of him. Whenever he thought about their loss, it made his seem trivial. Caleb knew he could live with his handicap. He knew he could get over it and move on. He just wished that his friends would quit watching him and worrying about him.

He heard the sound of Jake's bootsteps as he paced back and forth in front of the bunkhouse. Jake always waited for him after the others departed. Jake's wife, Shannon, would already be over at Grace's cabin preparing breakfast for the men before they went out to put in a hard day's work on the ranch. They were getting ready for the spring roundup. The winter had been a mild one and the cattle were already acting rebellious.

It was going to be a job to drive them all together from one end of the range to the other. As long as he stayed in the saddle, Caleb knew he could handle it. But once he dismounted, as he would surely have to do many times during the day, it would become difficult for him to get around.

Once Caleb felt confident that the leg would hold him for another day, he strapped on his gun belt, placed his hat over his shaggy dark locks and picked up his coat. The brisk air and weak sunshine of early spring in Wyoming greeted him as he opened the door to the bunkhouse.

"Zane said we kept you all up last night," Jake said as Caleb slid his arms into his coat and swung his leg off the stoop.

Caleb's dark eyes twinkled and he flashed a gentle smile at Jake's comment. A year ago a comment like that would have infuriated Jake. But since Shannon had come into his life, he was much easier to get along with. He was happy. The pale blue eyes that used to seem frozen over with ice now had a warm glow. He was easier to talk to. Caleb had always considered Jake his friend even though most of the time Jake seemed unapproachable. It was his defense against the world, an instinct developed from the abuse he had suffered as a child. Jake had said more than once that Shannon had saved him. She had found him in the creek, hidden by the body of his dead horse. The tall Irish girl from the mountains of West Virginia had nursed Jake back to health, and the two of them had fallen in love and gotten married on Christmas Day. Jake and Shannon were now living in what had once been the storage shed attached to the bunkhouse, and occasionally the sounds of marital bliss and mutual satisfaction drifted through the stout planks of the shared wall.

"Trust me, Jake; we can't hear anything over the sound of Zeb snoring at night."

"That's what I thought," Jake laughed. "The first night we slept in there, Shannon was convinced that we had moved in next to a sawmill."

"Does she mind?" Caleb asked.

"The sawmill?"

"Not having her own place?"

"If she does, she hasn't said anything," Jake replied, looking intently at the handsome face of his friend. Caleb looked tired and worn, yet in spite of his own loss he still worried over how Shannon felt about their living arrangements. It was remarkable how Caleb could see inside people just by looking at them with his deep brown eyes. What was more remarkable was his talent for capturing the true essence of a person with paper and pencil. But his friend had not picked up charcoal or sketch pad since the day he lost his leg.

Jake wondered if perhaps Shannon would want a place to call their own. She knew that the people who lived on the Lynch ranch were more of a family to Jake than the mother and father who had raised him. She seemed pleased with the room attached to the bunkhouse that Jenny had fixed up for them while they had made the trip to Minnesota to see Jake's father. But maybe he should start thinking about finding them a place of their own.

"It feels like it's getting warmer every day," Caleb said as they made their way toward Grace's cabin and the warm meal that was surely waiting for them. It did feel as if spring had come to the rolling range. The breeze in the small valley that held the heart of the Lynch ranch had a mild feeling to it even though it had swept down from mountains still peaked with snow. In the series of corrals that had been built to protect them, this winter's foals tested their long legs in short dashes from their mother's sides while their sire, Storm Cloud, pranced and danced, anxious to stretch his own legs over the wide-open spaces that surrounded his tiny domain.

"It feels good," Jake agreed. "But I'm betting that we're in for some more snow." The two friends walked on in companionable silence to the porch of Grace's cabin. Justice, Cole Larrimore's mixed-breed dog, stood to greet them with tail wagging and accepted a quick pat on the top of his huge dark head. Laughter over the strong cries of a baby could be heard as Caleb haltingly climbed the four steps, placing his good leg on one and bringing the bad one to join it before he moved up to the next. Jake could be inside eating by now, but instead he patiently waited for Caleb to reach the top before he made his own trek up the steps.

"No seconds until everyone has had firsts," Shannon was saying with a twinkle in her green eyes. She emphasized her point by rapping Zane's hand with a wooden spoon.

"Ow!" the handsome young cowboy exclaimed as he flashed his dimpled grin and stuck his bruised knuckles in his mouth.

23

Jake laughed at his friend as he circled his wife's waist from behind and dropped a kiss on her neck. "Do you want me to shoot him for you?"

"She can take care of herself," Zane protested as he perused his hand.

Shannon laughed at his antics and filled plates for Jake and Caleb. They joined the ranch hands, Dan, Randy, Zeb and Cole, at the table.

"So what's the plan for today?" Jake asked Cole as he attacked his eggs. Cole was a former Texas Ranger who had shown up on the ranch four years earlier. In that time he had married the ranch cook, Grace, and recently fathered the baby girl who was kicking up a fuss in the adjacent room.

"Chase is up at the big house now getting orders from Jason," Cole replied mentioning the ranch's owner, who was like a father to each of them. "I think Jason wants to make sure that all the homesteaders who grazed their cattle with ours are going to help with the roundup."

"Is he afraid that someone will accuse him of stealing their cattle?" Caleb asked.

"I just think that he would rather play it safe than sorry," Cole said. "There's been a lot of talk going around about homesteaders fencing the range and such. A lot of the big ranchers are complaining about it."

"They should have done what Jason did and bought up the land instead of expecting the government to support them," Zane said.

"They should've, but they didn't. There were some harsh words exchanged at the last association meeting," Cole volunteered.

"Like what?" Jake asked.

"Insinuations mostly, of stealing and plotting, that type of thing," Cole explained.

"No wonder they can't get the schoolhouse built," Shannon said. "Sounds like the association members are spending all their time arguing."

"Jason was pretty frustrated when he came home last night," Cole said. "Especially since the new owner of the newspaper has aligned himself with the Cattlemen's association." His gray eyes lit up when Grace came out of their bedroom carrying their daughter, Jenny Catherine. Grace handed the baby to her father, who immediately smothered his daughter with gentle kisses as his wife twirled her warm brown hair into a bun, jabbing pins in it as she walked over to the stove.

"How did she sleep last night?" Shannon asked as Grace took the lid off a pot.

"Better," Grace said. "I'm hoping she'll make it through the night before too much longer." She pulled her apron off a peg and tied it on. "Like I said before, I'm way too old for this."

"Pish," Shannon said. "Little miss will keep you young."

"If she doesn't kill me first," Grace laughed. It had been quite a surprise for her when she realized she was pregnant in her late thirties after years of thinking she would never have a child.

Caleb leaned over Cole's arm to look at the baby, who was alternating between sucking on her fingers and blowing bubbles with her rosebud lips.

"It looks as if her eyes are going to be the same color

25

as yours," Caleb commented as he touched a finger to a delicate hand. The baby wrapped her tiny fingers around Caleb's and held on tightly.

"Jenny Catherine," Cole cooed to his daughter.

"That's quite a handful of a name for such a tiny baby," Caleb said.

"We're open to something shorter," Cole replied.

"Can't use Jenny or Cat," Caleb commented. The baby girl was named after Jason's daughter and granddaughter, who both lived on the ranch.

"How bout J.C.?" Zane said from his end of the table.

"Sounds like a man's name to me," Cole replied.

"Why don't you ask her?" Caleb suggested.

"J.C.," Cole said, and the baby stared off toward Caleb while sucking on her fingers.

"You've got to talk her into it," Shannon suggested from the stove.

"Jaaay Ceeeee," Cole said, exaggerating the letters.

She promptly took her fingers out of her mouth and stared up at her father.

"Jacey?" Cole said, looking down on his daughter in amazement.

The baby girl stretched out her hands toward her father's face.

"Jacey," Cole said again.

Grace leaned over his shoulder to look at her daughter. "Does she like it?" she asked as Cole drew in closer so the baby could touch his face.

"Jacey," Cole said and she stretched her rosebud lips into a smile. Grace cooed over her husband's shoulder as he deposited a kiss on the tiny forehead.

"Told you so," Zane bragged as he shoveled in his second helping of scrambled eggs.

"You do have a way with the ladies," Cole agreed.

"Chance, come here!" they heard Jenny yell from outside.

Shannon peered out the window over the sink as the sound of Justice barking filled the morning air. "You'd best take care of your dog before he gets himself in trouble, Cole," she said, a smile dancing at the corners of her mouth. Jake joined her at the window, and a smile spread across his features, too.

"What in the world?" Grace said as she went to the other window. "Cole!"

Cole handed Jacey to Caleb as the table cleared and everyone gathered to see what was causing the commotion. They could hear Jenny and Chase between the barks, but their voices were not loud enough to make out their words.

"What is it?" Caleb asked.

"Looks like Chance and Justice are fighting over a skunk," Zane replied.

"You'd better call your dog off before that skunk gets mad," Grace said.

"I'm not going out there," Cole retorted. "He's on his own in this battle."

"Little critter must have just woke up from his hibernation," Zeb observed. "Po' thing is likely starving."

"Looks a mite cranky, too," Jake added.

"You would know," Zane couldn't help commenting.

Jake didn't even bother to give him a nasty look.

* * *

"Chance, come to Mama now," Jenny Duncan said firmly as she held on to the collar of Fox's shirt.

"I want to see, too," Fox protested as he screwed his neck around to look up at the beautiful but worried face of his adoptive mother.

"You don't want to see that, darling, or smell it either," Jenny said as she held a hand out to her rebellious son Chance.

Chase, his father, had come down from his meeting with Jason at the same time that the skunk had waddled out from beneath the porch, catching the attention of his curious son, who had run up to the animal thinking it was a new exotic cat. Justice had leaped off the porch upon seeing the wild animal, and between his barking and Chance's calls of "Here, kitty, kitty," the skunk was becoming just a tiny bit agitated.

"Chance, come here right now," Chase said firmly as he too extended his hand.

"Look at the new kitty, Dad," Chance said, turning his bright blue eyes on his father.

"It's not a kitty, Chance. It's a skunk, and something you don't want to mess with," Chase impatiently explained to his three-year-old son, who was quickly becoming as stubborn as his mother.

"Why?" Chance asked as he waggled his fingers at the skunk, which was still standing its ground against Justice.

"Just come here. Now!" Chase was trying his best not to yell, but his exasperation at Chance won out over his good sense.

"I'm coming," Chance said with a stomp while pushing his lower lip into a pout.

"Watch out!" Jenny hissed as the skunk arched its tail.

Chase took a running dive for his son at the same time that Justice let out a yelp and a whimper. He came up holding a squirming Chance by his shirt collar.

"Ow, it burns," Chance squalled. Chase extended his son to arm's length as the smell overpowered his nostrils. Justice had his nose buried in the dirt and was scraping at his face with a paw. The skunk waddled toward the bunkhouse, confident that his morning stroll would continue uninterrupted.

"What am I supposed to do with him?" Chase asked Jenny, who had pulled her shirt up over her nose, exposing the slight rounding of her belly. Fox squeezed his fingers over his nose, pinching his nostrils shut as he looked up at his cousin. Chance dangled from his father's grip, kicking his legs as if that would make the smell go away.

"Give him a bath!" Jenny said, her voice muffled beneath her hand and the shirt.

"*You* give him a bath!" Chase protested, his dark eyes snapping with frustration.

Jenny patted her stomach. "I don't think the smell would be good for the baby," she said, her bright blue eyes twinkling with mischief. "Besides, you probably got a dose of it, too."

Chase gave his wife a look that would have made a normal man shudder in his boots. Jenny just tossed him a saucy wave as she climbed the steps to the cabin.

"I'd like to wring his neck," Chase said. "Yours, too," he added as he looked down his regal nose at Justice, whose face held the same pitiful expression as his partner in disaster.

"Go ahead. Wring away." Jenny waved her hand in dismissal as she hustled Fox into Grace's.

"Thanks a lot," Chase said to Chance.

"Make it go away, Daddy," Chance begged as he dangled in the air, sure in the knowledge that his father's strong grip would hold him tight.

The door of the cabin opened a crack and a half-dozen canning jars appeared, filled with tomatoes.

"This will take the stink away," Shannon yelled through the window.

Chase arched an eyebrow in disgust as he lowered Chance to the ground. "Help me get the jars, son. Looks like we're going to have a bath."

For once, his son didn't argue over the prospect of a bath as he scampered up the steps after Chase.

"You might as well come too," Chase said to Justice, and the dog fell in behind him with tail dragging as he led his son to the shower stall behind the bunkhouse.

"That was stinky!" Fox exclaimed as the adults around him dissolved into laughter over the mishap. His face was shining with moisture, and Grace took a moment to run her hand over his forehead.

"Yes, it was," Zeb said as he ruffled the boy's copper locks.

"Enjoy yourselves now," Jenny said as she straightened her shirt over her protruding stomach and smoothed back her long blond hair. "Chase will likely kill all of us when he's done with those two."

"Did you see the look on his face?" Zane exclaimed with his hazel eyes lit with glee. "He looked more put out than Chance or Justice."

The sounds of the group's laughter surrounded Caleb as he bent over Jacey and gently blew on her belly. She kicked her legs and pulled on his hair with her fist as she cooed in contentment.

Jenny grabbed Jake's arm as the group continued to laugh over the incident with the skunk.

"Look," she whispered, nodding her head toward Caleb. A smile lit his face, a genuine smile of happiness instead of the tired and patient smile that he had worn since his return from the war.

"Dang," Jake said as he looked at his friend.

"Hello, Jacey," Caleb said to the baby girl.

Chapter Two

The difference between dreams and reality was always a blur for Amanda Myers. Maybe it was because both had been so bad for so long. Now she lay safe in a soft wide bed on the second floor of the big house above the valley. But still she fought the dreams.

She dreamed she was all alone on the ranch, entrusted with the care of the two small boys. Surely she was capable of watching two little children, but she was afraid. Afraid of the silence, the shadows, the empty house.

And that was when she heard the voice.

Get out of the house now!

The boys didn't hear it. Why was she the only one who heard it?

She walked over to the door of the parlor and looked into the wide hall that ran from the front of the house to the back. It seemed to go on forever.

She heard the ticking of the tall case clock behind her and the fire crackling and popping in the hearth, except the sounds were like explosions in her dream-muddled brain.

There was a wide staircase off to one side—the same staircase that she climbed every night to go to bed. At the end of the hallway was a wide door with windows on either side.

She caught the reflection of light through one of the windows, and then out of nowhere a man suddenly appeared. The tall man with indecipherable features seemed to materialize out of the door itself.

Get the boys out of the house. Hide.

The words seemed to be coming from inside her head. Did this mean she had finally gone mad?

"Chance. Fox. Come here," she called.

"Is someone here?" Fox asked.

The air around her turned cold, and in her dream Amanda clutched the covers tightly.

HIDE!

She was losing her mind, but she was still responsible for the safety of the two boys.

"Let's go down to Grace's," she said.

"But no one is there," Chance protested.

In her dream she convinced them, just as she had on that night months ago.

They're coming . . .

They hurried out the back door and down the hill just as the sounds of horses pounding up the drive filled their ears. Justice went racing past them with teeth bared, and the sound of breaking glass added impetus to their flight.

Where could they go? Where would they be safe? Was she imagining all of it?

The fear on the boys' faces and Justice's reaction told her no. But where had the voice in her head come from?

Amanda led the boys to the shower stall. She grabbed the chair and took it inside. She placed both boys in her lap and then pulled her feet up so they wouldn't be seen by anyone passing by.

"I'm cold," one boy said.

"I want my dad," the other one said.

She knew how they felt. She wanted it all to go away. All of it. All of the past since the time she'd been taken from her home, since the nightmare began . . .

Amanda awoke with a start. The full light of day poured through her upstairs window along with the sound of Justice barking. Close by she could hear Agnes, the housekeeper, airing out the upstairs rooms, and the sound cleared away the cobwebs left by the disturbing dream. It was one she had been reliving all too frequently since the attack on the ranch before Christmas.

Amanda would have offered to help Agnes, but the energetic housekeeper was just too much for her. Amanda felt as if she were caught up in a whirlwind when Agnes was near. It was almost as if she couldn't catch her breath as the elderly woman went about her job, attacking the dirt with a fierce diligence.

Amanda went downstairs and into the study. The newspaper was there and she picked it up to read, then almost immediately folded it with a sigh and dropped it in a chair. Everything was too much for her.

The light was too bright, the outside too big, the noise too loud, life too hard. Everything had been much simpler when she'd been taking opium. She'd only had one thought in those days, one goal. Keep the opium coming. Stay in the fog. Do as she was told so they wouldn't take it away. For the reality of the life she had been forced into was worse than the dependency on the drug. Never mind that the days and nights of her life had turned into one long, horrible dream. Never mind that the world had forgotten all about her and no one came to save her. Never mind that the men who visited her all blended together into one faceless terror. Just keep the opium coming, because without it she couldn't survive.

Death would have been preferable. She had wished for it many times; death would have been a mercy. But Wade Bishop and his sister Roxanne were not merciful at all. They were very careful of the girls that were kept captive in the upstairs rooms of the whorehouse in New York. They made very sure their girls stayed just conscious enough to interest the paying customers. Amanda had quickly learned how to act, how to encourage a man to go with her so she could get her fix for the night and float away to a land where there were no men pulling on her and poking her and forcing her to do things she would never have done had it not been for the opium.

She still craved it. Sometimes she woke up in the

night and her body screamed for it. The doctors had warned her Uncle Cole that it would be like this. She had come off of it too fast. She should have been weaned gradually from the drug, they said. But the doctors didn't understand.

She still wanted to die. She was glad Uncle Cole had found her. She was happy that she wouldn't die alone and have her body stuffed in a bag, weighted down with rocks and tossed in the harbor like all the girls who died. But she still wanted to die. She'd been sure she would not survive the withdrawal process. A nun had sat by her side and prayed. The nun had bathed her skin and forced her to drink water and eat soup. But the entire time the nun had prayed for her soul, Amanda had wished for death. She would have prayed for it, but she had given up on her prayers being heard a long time ago.

That was why she was still alive. God had listened to the prayers of the nun and ignored hers, just as He had during all those years when she prayed that someone would find her and save her. God chose not to listen to her prayers, and so she was alive.

But she had stopped living a long time ago.

"Agnes?" called out Jason Lynch. Amanda turned from the window and looked for a place to hide. It was silly, of course, to hide from Jason; he had been nothing but kind to her, as had everyone on his ranch.

"Good morning, Amanda," Jason said with a smile. "Have you seen Agnes?"

"She's cleaning upstairs." Amanda was startled by the sound of her own voice. She used it so seldom these days, it seemed strange when it came out, almost as if it didn't belong to her.

"Thank you," Jason said, still smiling benevolently. Amanda knew he was being kind. The problems besetting the ranch had not been mentioned to her, but she was not oblivious to the people around her. She had felt the tension when Uncle Cole stopped to pay her a visit after having a conference with Jason and the dangerous-looking half-breed who was the father of the boys. She also knew from reading the newspaper that trouble would be coming their way. Once upon a time, before she had been taken off the streets of Laredo, she would have cared that the newspaper was biased toward the group of big ranchers instead of dealing fairly with the homesteaders who were pouring west. Once upon a time she had hoped to write for a newspaper. She had been well on her way to achieving that goal when a walk down a busy street in the middle of the day had become the start of a living hell.

Amanda wondered once again if she would have been better off if Uncle Cole had not found her. Perhaps she would be dead by now. It would have saved her uncle a lot of heartache if she were. She knew he was worried about her, just as she knew that Jenny, the one who'd first discovered her in New York, was frustrated with her. There had been times when she first came to the ranch that she had sensed that Jenny wanted to talk to her, but she was afraid of what Jenny would say so she kept as far away from her as she could. It was the Fear that had made that decision for her.

Life had been so much better when she was controlled by opium instead of by the Fear. Opium had been dependable. She knew what to expect when she took it, and she knew what it felt like when she needed it. Opium made life bearable. She could pretend it was all a horrid dream.

The Fear was different. It snuck up on her. Some days she would awaken and feel as if she could go down to the cabin and sit at the table with her Uncle Cole, his wife, Grace, and their new baby. She imagined herself smiling and chatting with the hands as they came into the warm cabin to gather around the table. But then she remembered that such pleasures weren't for her; she didn't deserve them. All she had was the Fear.

"Miss Amanda?" It was a breathless Agnes. Amanda had heard her hurried footsteps on the stairs. "I hate to bother you, but I was wondering if you could help me."

Amanda's gray eyes widened in surprise. What could she do to help the housekeeper? The woman had the house so organized that it practically cleaned itself.

"My daughter and her husband are down with the chicken pox, and someone has to take care of the baby."

Amanda was totally confused. Agnes wanted her to take care of a baby?

Jason stepped up behind the housekeeper. "There's an epidemic in town," he explained. "Agnes has already had chicken pox, so she can take care of her granddaughter."

Amanda nodded in agreement. That made perfect sense.

"So you'll take care of the house and Mister Jason

while I'm gone?" Agnes rushed forward and threw her arms around a startled Amanda. "Bless you, child."

"Go pack your bags, Agnes. I'll have Zeb drive you into town," Jason assured the older woman as she hustled off to her room.

Amanda looked after Agnes's back as she trotted down the hall, wondering what had just happened.

"You don't have to," Jason said.

"What?" Amanda blinked as she looked up at Jason.

"I'll be fine. I'll take my meals down at Grace's while Agnes is gone. I just knew she wouldn't leave unless she was sure everything was taken care of." Jason turned to go down the hall toward the door.

"I'll do it!" Amanda said, and immediately placed her hand over her mouth before another outburst spilled out.

Jason's look was a mixture of amusement and concern.

"No, really, I can cook, and the house is so spotless I can't imagine it will be too difficult to keep up with."

"Amanda, I appreciate the offer, but you don't have to do anything."

"It's the least I can do for you and Agnes. You've both been so kind to me." Amanda marveled as the words came flowing out of her mouth. She couldn't recall the last time she had contributed to a conversation beyond the obligatory yes, no or thank you.

"Would you like Agnes to show you anything before she leaves?" Jason seemed doubtful of her abilities.

"No, I'm sure I can find everything I need."

Jason gave her a reassuring nod and a smile as he walked out the door, but Amanda saw the doubt in his eyes. She watched through the window as he walked down the hill with his long stride.

"I've got to show him I'm not completely useless," she told herself as Jason disappeared out of view behind Grace's cabin.

"Why did the kitty make us stink, Dad?" Chance asked as he held his arms up for Chase to pull his shirt over his head.

"It wasn't a kitty, Chance, it was a skunk."

"What's a skunk?" His tiny face was screwed up and his bright blue eyes were held tightly shut against the atrocious smell.

Chase flipped the ruined shirt over the shower stall in exasperation and wondered if he had pelted his own father with as many questions as he had to answer in a day from his two sons. His head felt bleary and his nose was running like he was getting a cold. He didn't have time to get sick, and he certainly didn't have time to deal with his son's misadventures. Add to the equation a hundred questions and Chase was already feeling the effects of a bad day. And he hadn't even had breakfast yet. Losing his patience with his son wouldn't help the situation at all, but if Zane or anyone else sitting safe from the smell in Grace's cabin so much as smirked at him, he was going to let them have it.

"A skunk is . . . a kitty that stinks. You can tell it's a skunk because it has a big white stripe down its back."

"Oh." The pants came down next, and Chase realized

that Chance was still wearing his shoes. He lifted the child and pulled off his shoes and socks. One quick whiff of the socks landed them in the pile with the discarded shirt. Chase looked doubtfully at the shoes. They still looked practically brand-new. He and Jenny had taken the boys to town to get them and had come home exhausted after spending the day in Laramie with the two energetic, precocious boys.

"Does it live under the bunkhouse?" Chance asked and swiped at his nose.

"Hopefully, it's just hiding there until it can go to its home somewhere on the prairie."

"Are we going to give Justice a bath, too?"

Chase looked through the open door of the shower at Justice, who was alternating between rolling in the dirt and burying his nose in a hole to escape the smell.

"I guess we'd better," Chase said with a sigh and whistled the dog over to the shower stall. He stripped off his own clothes and opened one of the jars of tomatoes, sniffed it dubiously and then dumped the contents on the dog's back. Justice whined at the insult, but the smell was better than the previous one, so he endured the mess as it seeped into his fur.

"Help me scrub him down," Chase said and knelt beside the dog as he opened another jar.

"Mister Chase?" Zeb called out. Zeb had been a slave all his life, owned by Ty's family back in North Carolina. Though the big man had quickly adjusted to life at the ranch, he still clung to some of his old ways and had to be reminded on occasion that he was now a free man.

"Zeb?"

"Miss Jenny done sent me with some clothes for you to put on. She said for me to burn what you was wearin'.'"

"That's probably a good idea, Zeb."

"I got a brush for the dog and some old sacks to dry him with."

Justice licked Chase's face in gratitude as he scrubbed around his ears and neck. "I'm sure he'll appreciate that. Along with everyone else on the ranch," Chase said as he looked into the remorseful dark eyes of the dog. "Hold him still while we rinse him," Chase instructed his son as he pulled on the chain that would release the water from the large barrel overhead.

The water sluiced down, bringing goose bumps to their skin. "It's still a bit cold for outdoor showers," Chase said to Chance as his teeth began to chatter.

"I'm cold!" Chance exclaimed as Justice shook the water from his coat and sprayed them again.

"I'm turning him out, Zeb. You might want to catch him before he makes himself a mud bath."

"I got him," Zeb replied and snagged the dog as he jumped through the door.

"Our turn now." Chase opened another jar and with a mischievous grin dumped it out on Chance's head. "Start scrubbing." He did the same to himself, and Chance burst into laughter at the sight of the tomatoes sliding down the bare skin of his father's wide chest. Chase slathered the stuff over his body while keeping an eye on Chance to make sure he was doing the same.

"Get your back, too," he instructed.

"I can't reach it."

"Here, turn around." When Chance turned around,

Chase knelt and rubbed the juice over his son's skin. "What's that?" he asked.

"What?"

"That bump." Chase moved a tomato skin out of the way to see an angry red blister on the soft skin of Chance's back.

Chance looked over his shoulder. "I got one here too, and here, and here." He pointed to multiple locations on his chest and stomach.

"Dang," Chase said.

"You got one, too." Chance pointed to a blister on Chase's rock-hard stomach.

"Dang!"

"Is it bad?" Chance asked as he examined the bumps on his stomach.

"It's chicken pox!"

"Jenny, I think Fox is coming down with something," Grace said. The two women were at the sink, cleaning up the breakfast dishes. "He felt warm, and he looks flushed."

Jenny turned to look at Fox, who was picking at his breakfast. The men had all gone on to work, Jacey was down for a nap, and Shannon had gone into the cool room to find something for the midday meal. "You think so? They both felt hot yesterday, but I didn't notice anything today. Chase dressed them this morning before he went up to Jason's." Jenny placed a hand on Fox's forehead. "How to you feel, darling?"

"Itchy," Fox replied as he built a mountain with his eggs.

"Where does it itch?"

"Everywhere," Fox replied, replacing his r's with w's. Jenny pulled up the front of his shirt and was amazed to see a series of tiny red blisters running across the pale skin.

"Grace?"

"Chicken pox," Grace said with authority. "Have you had it?"

A memory of sharing her parents' bed with her twin brother Jamie filled Jenny's mind. The window had been covered with a quilt to keep the room dark, and they'd had cold compresses and soda baths. Then there was the comparing of scabs and daring each other not to scratch. Her hand went to an almost invisible scar beneath her ear.

"Yes."

"So have I. Jacey should be protected since I'm nursing her, but it might be a good idea if we keep her away from the boys."

"Of course." Jenny's head was already reeling as she tried to figure out how she was going to care for two sick little boys. "Will it hurt the baby?" she asked, placing a protective hand over her stomach.

"Not as long as you've already had chicken pox," Grace assured her. "We need to find out who has had it and who hasn't."

"Had what?" Shannon asked as she popped up through the cellar door.

"Chicken pox."

"Who's got it?"

"Fox. Probably Chance, too."

"I haven't had it, at least, not that I recall," Shannon said.

The door swung open. Chase stood bare-chested with his damp hair sweeping around his shoulders. He held Chance on his hip with a towel wrapped around him.

"We got a problem," he began.

"I know. The boys have chicken pox," Jenny interrupted.

"Dad's got it, too!" Chance announced.

"What's chicken pops?" Fox asked, dragging his hand across his stomach.

"Don't scratch!" Jenny said, moving the boy's hand. "Do you really have it?" she asked her husband.

Chase put Chance on the floor, revealing the blisters that had multiplied on the walk over from the shower. "We must have got it in town," he said, moving his hand to scratch.

"Don't scratch!" the women said in unison.

"I guess that being raised among the Kiowa, you were never exposed to it," Jenny said.

Chase looked down his regal nose in exasperation at the three women. "Well?" he said expectantly.

Jenny looked at Grace.

"Put them to bed," Grace instructed. "It's going to get a lost worse before it gets better."

"Just what I needed to hear," Chase grumbled.

"Use cool compresses with soda water," Grace advised. "Licorice tea to drink and put on the sores. Oatmeal works well also. And whatever you do, don't scratch!"

"We hafta go to bed?" Chance asked incredulously.

"Trust me, little man, you're not going to feel like doing anything else before this day is over," Grace said. "Now all of you get out of my cabin before you give it to everyone else."

"I'm betting that's already happened," Jenny said. She took the tin of soda from the shelf as she herded her complaining men through the door.

Chase ducked back in and grabbed his breakfast plate off the table. "I need to keep my strength up," he explained.

"Best to eat now while you still feel like it," Grace replied. She remembered well the chicken-pox epidemic that had swept through her family's plantation when she was still a girl. Some of the slaves had died from it, and though children usually handled it well, the illness usually caused a lot of problems in adults.

"I'll see if I can catch the men to warn them," Shannon said and skipped out the door behind Jenny.

Grace smiled knowingly as she watched Shannon scamper toward the barn. It was more likely that Shannon was hoping to get another good-bye kiss from Jake than anxious to warn the men. "If things keep going the way they are, we'll have three babies around by this time next year," she said to the sinkful of dishes.

"What's that about babies?" Jason asked as he came into the cabin.

"Just waiting for the inevitable with Shannon and Jake. Did you see Jenny and Chase?"

"Yes. As a matter of fact, the reason I came down here was to tell everyone that there's an epidemic in town.

Agnes went to stay with her daughter and son-in-law. Both of them have it."

"Any sign of illness in Agnes's grandchildren?"

"Not yet," Jason said. "I also wanted to let you know that Amanda has agreed to take care of the house while Agnes is gone."

Grace sat down in a chair, overcome with surprise at the notion. "Really? Amanda said she'd help out?"

"Yes, she did."

"Well, dang!" Grace said and the two of them burst into laughter at her use of the phrase so common among the men of the ranch. "Jason, have you ever had chicken pox?"

"I should be safe. I had it as a boy."

"That's good to hear. We're trying to figure out who's had it and who's likely to get it."

"This is not a good time for everyone to get sick," Jason commented.

"Is it ever?"

"No, but this is one of the worst. We're leaving for roundup day after tomorrow."

"We'll just all have to work harder, then," Grace sighed. It seemed like everyone had been working harder for the past several years to make up for the men who had gone to fight the war. But the war should be over soon and then everyone would come home. And at last they could all experience some peace. It couldn't happen soon enough to suit Grace.

Chapter Three

"I look like the dartboard at the tavern!" Shannon wailed as she gazed into the mirror that hung over the bureau in the storage room. She had awakened before dawn feeling feverish and had stumbled from the bed she shared with Jake to find herself covered with red blisters.

"You look like you have chicken pox," Jake said as he wrapped his arms around her waist from behind.

"I'm covered with spots! Don't even look at me," she cried as she pushed him away.

Jake held up his hands in mock surrender and backed off, not wanting to rile the flaming temper of his redheaded wife. "At least it's a good time to be sick," he said, hoping to give comfort. He pulled on his clothes as he spoke.

"Why is that?" Shannon blew her nose, which had turned a bright shade of red.

"I'm leaving on roundup today, remember? Don't know how long I'll be gone."

"Just stay gone until the spots disappear," Shannon wailed as she flopped back on the bed and pulled the covers over her head.

"Should I send out a scout to make sure?" Jake pulled the blanket down. "Or maybe you could run up a flag or have Chase send some smoke signals?"

"He'd kill you for saying that," Shannon mumbled as she wrestled the blankets back over her head.

"Not in the shape he's in. Not today."

"I thought Jenny said the boys were getting better."

"The boys are, but Chase isn't. It always hits harder with adults."

"Thanks a lot," Shannon cried.

Jake deposited a kiss on the blanket in the general direction of her forehead. "Take care of yourself. I'll see you in a few days."

"That's the thanks I get," Shannon grumbled when she knew he was safely away from the room. "After all the care I gave you when you didn't even know your name." She kicked the covers away and went back to the mirror. "Thank you, Lord, for taking him away." She picked up the brush. "I look a fright."

Caleb leaned over Zane's bed and listened to the sound of his labored breathing. The spots didn't look so bad in the dim light, but Zane's skin was glistening and he sounded as if his nose was stuffy. Several attempts at waking him had ended in nothing more than a mumbled curse.

"You're not going anywhere today," Caleb said and looked over to where Zeb sat wearily on the edge of his top bunk with his head in his hands. "You either, Zeb."

"I got to, Mister Caleb. Mister Jason said I was to go on the roundup."

"Zeb, it's just Caleb now. And Jason will understand. You won't be any good to anyone on the roundup, sick as you are. You'll just make more work for us."

"I itch all over," Zeb moaned as he flopped back on his bed.

"I'll tell Jenny," Caleb assured him. "Why don't you move down to a bottom bunk so she can take care of you?"

"I'll do that, Mist . . . Caleb, as soon as I is able."

Caleb stepped out into the quietness of the predawn morning. He noticed the soft illumination of lamplight in several rooms up at the big house and wondered why Amanda was up at this early hour. He knew Agnes had gone to town to stay with her daughter and smiled at the thought that perhaps Amanda had made breakfast for Jason. The thought of seeing Cole's elusive niece in the pink glow of dawn warmed his senses in a way that he had not felt in a while.

"Now, where did that come from?" Caleb asked himself as he walked with his swinging gait toward Grace's cabin.

"Where did what come from?" Jake asked as he led his and Caleb's horses from the barn. "Where is everyone?"

"Dan and Randy are eating. Zane and Zeb aren't going anywhere."

"Pox?"

"Yes."

"Dang, Shannon's got it too."

"What a great time for a roundup."

"Better than hanging around here, that's for sure," Jake said, and the two of them dissolved into laughter.

"What's so funny?" Cole asked from the darkness of the porch.

"Zane, Zeb and Shannon all have the pox," Caleb reported.

"That's funny?"

"Nope," Jake said. "We're just glad that we don't have to deal with it."

"You boys do yourselves a favor and don't gloat too much. Jenny and Grace will ring both your necks, since they'll be stuck here taking care of things without a healthy man on the place."

"It anyone can do it, those two can," Caleb said as they went in to eat.

"What is this stuff?" Chase asked as he made a face at the cup Jenny held beneath his chin.

"Dandelion tea."

"Why do I have to drink it?"

"It will take the fever away."

"The boys got to drink licorice tea."

"You drank it, too, and it didn't work."

"Let me try it again."

"You did."

"I didn't try enough."

Jenny rolled her eyes in exasperation at her cranky husband and jiggled the cup between his lips.

"You're the one that told me about this stuff. Now drink," she commanded.

Chase made a horrid face as the tea hit his tongue but bravely took a gulp and dropped back on the pillows. Jenny wiped the sweat off his face with a cool cloth and then trailed it down his wide chest and over his rock-hard stomach. Chase's fever was worse than his sores. Luckily, most of the pox were on his torso, with only a few stray bumps on his face and hands. She hoped there would be no more scars added to his collection. Jenny's fingers caressed a puckered mark on his shoulder. There was a matching scar on his back where a bullet had passed through. He might have lost his arm from the wound in his shoulder if not for the amazing talents of Dr. Marcus Brown. Chase had escaped death twice so far, at least that she knew of. She shuddered to think about how many risks he might take when she wasn't around.

"What are you thinking?" Chase asked. His voice was hoarse and his breathing ragged as his system fought against the fever that raged in his body.

"That I might just keep you here for a while."

"Can't, I've got to go on roundup tomorrow."

"You missed a day. They're leaving this morning."

"This morning?" Chase kicked at the blankets. "I've got to go," he gasped as he sat up.

Jenny proved her point by pushing him back down with her index finger. "You can't even stand up, so what makes you think you're going to get on a horse and chase a bunch of cows around?"

"It's my job."

"No job for you today."

"Jenny," Chase gasped. "I've got to."

Jenny placed her hands on her hips and looked at him with disgust. "What is this, some sort of I'm-a-better-man-than-you contest?"

"Jenny," Chase moaned as he sat up.

"Go ahead, then. Ride on out of here. If you can get yourself dressed and on a horse, that is." She stepped back.

"Where are my pants?"

"In the wardrobe."

Chase's face took on a stubborn expression when he realized that she wasn't going to help him.

Jenny turned away and went to busy herself folding up her mother's wedding-ring quilt, which had been keeping her warm at night while she slept in one of the wingback chairs before the fireplace. She dropped the quilt into one of the chairs and then pressed her hands into the small of her back and stretched. The babe inside her kicked, and Jenny patted her stomach.

"Don't you be giving me any grief, little one. I've got enough to deal with out here without you acting up."

"What?" Chase was still sitting on the side of the bed with his head in his hands, gathering his strength to get dressed.

"Nothing," Jenny said sweetly and poked her head into the boys' room. They both were sleeping soundly, and she was relieved to see that there was no sign of a recurrence of their fevers, which had broken the afternoon before.

A loud crash sounded behind her. She didn't even

flinch when she turned to see Chase lying face down on the floor between the wardrobe and the bed.

"I love you," she said to his prostrate form as she stepped out into the faint light of dawn to find someone to help her get him back into bed.

By the next evening the bunkhouse had been made into a hospital for those that had come down with symptoms. Jenny made Chase move to the bunkhouse, which was no easy feat considering how weak he was. She put the boys in with her in Shannon's room since Shannon was now in the bunkhouse. It made it easier for Jenny to have all the patients in one place. Chase was getting better but was grouchy at being confined. Shannon and Zeb were holding their own and were lucid enough to help take care of themselves, even though they were feverish.

Zane, on the other hand, was worrying everyone. He had blisters upon blisters. Huge masses of them. They covered every square inch of his body. Jenny was amazed to find them in his hair and between his toes. He even had blisters in his mouth, which made it nearly impossible to get anything down him. His fever was so high that he was incoherent and rambling.

"I'm really worried about him, Chase. His breathing is labored, and he hasn't passed any water since yesterday morning."

"If he doesn't have anything going in, then there's nothing to come out," Chase observed as he weakly sat down on a cot.

"We've got to get some water down him. He's sweating so much that I'm afraid he'll die of thirst."

"We need to get the doctor out here to look at him."

"We tried. Grace went yesterday to get him, but he can't come. He's swamped with patients in town. Grace said eleven people have died, all of them adults."

"So did the doctor give her any medicine?"

"He said that if we could find some quinine to use it."

"But with the war still going on, it's impossible to get any," Chase concluded for her.

"Have you tried any of that nasty tea you made me drink?"

"I've tried everything, including lots of prayer."

Chase looked down at Zane, who was practically unrecognizable with all the angry red blisters on his face. "I guess he'll either get over it or he won't." He stood and stretched his aching muscles. "I'm going to take a shower," he declared.

"Good," Jenny replied, wrinkling her nose. "It's starting to smell a bit gamy in here."

"I'd be happy to take a bath if someone would let me," Shannon said from her bed.

"Not till your fever breaks," Jenny said.

"Pish!"

Jenny laughed at Shannon's rebellion and went out into the cold mountain air to check on the boys. She had allowed them to play in the barn for a while in a fort built of hay bales. She had been doing what she could for the stock when she had a chance, but with her advancing pregnancy and the burden of caring for all the sick, it came down to nothing more than feeding and watering, with a promise to spend more time with the horses at a later date. Storm Cloud seemed especially offended at the lack of attention, and the gray stud spent a lot of time in his corral stomping about and shaking his head. He was in need of a good run, but there was no one to take him out at present. He'd just have to get over it, Jenny mused as she watched the stallion go through his antics. It was close to dusk, but the gathering clouds on the western horizon blocked the usual peaceful beauty of the sun's passage. Not that she had time to notice it lately with so much work and the way her back ached from the constant bending. Jenny pressed her hands just above her waist, arching against them to give relief to her tired muscles. "You and I are in need of a rest, little one," she told the babe inside her tummy.

Jenny wondered when the men would get back. She hoped it would be before the weather turned bad again. Jason had assured Chase that with the help of the homesteaders, they should get the roundup done quickly. She could see the dark form of Justice up on the ridge by Jamie's grave, his eyes turned north as he waited for Cole to come home. His joyful bark sounded the alarm, and he jumped to his feet with tail wagging.

"Grace!" Jenny yelled. "They're coming!"

"It's about time," Grace called from the porch swing where she had just given Jacey her evening meal. She quickly wrapped the baby up in her blanket and took her into the cabin so she could warm supper for the hungry men.

Jenny ran to the series of pens beyond Storm Cloud's corral to open the gates so the men could herd the cattle in quickly. She took up a position so she could close the gates when the pens were full. It wasn't long before she heard the familiar "yip yip" of the men urging the cattle on as they came around from behind the ridge and toward the pens.

The men's faces seemed jolly beneath the bandanas they wore over their mouths and noses to keep the dust out. They whooped and hollered and stung the backsides of the more reluctant cattle with their coiled ropes as they herded them toward the pens. Justice joined in the melee from his post on the ridge and nipped at the heels of those cattle that dared to stray from the path.

Jenny jumped onto a gate and rode it shut after the pen was filled with cattle. Quickly she slipped the noose over the post to hold the gate shut.

"Should you be doing that in your delicate condition?" Jason yelled at her.

"I've probably put in a harder day than you have," Jenny sassed back.

"If you had to listen to Zane whine, then you're right about that," Jake added.

"He hasn't done much whining," Jenny yelled as she jumped onto the next gate. "But I'd still rather be out cowboying."

"You'd be better than some," Cole growled and tossed his head toward Dan and Randy on the other side of the herd.

"Caleb!" Jason hollered and waved his arm toward

the narrow passage that ran between Storm Cloud's corral and the cattle pens. "Watch that cow!"

One of the older and wiser cows had decided at the last minute that she would be much happier back out on the range. She had avoided getting into a pen and had taken off toward freedom by dashing down the chute with her calf bawling along behind her.

Caleb saw the cow make her break and spurred his horse after her. Storm Cloud decided at the same moment that the noise of the bawling cattle was too much of an affront and reared in protest. The cattle across from his corral responded by kicking at their fence boards, which in turn further upset the stallion. The young gray stud reared again and twisted to buck. His hooves resounded against the wood of his enclosure, and he gave it another kick. The escaping cow was startled by his outburst and stopped dead in her tracks, causing her calf to plow into her backside. Storm Cloud kicked again and the cow tried to turn in her tracks but the space wasn't wide enough. She rose up and twisted around, getting her leg caught on the fence board. She bellowed in fear and protest as Storm Cloud kicked again. The calf cried piteously.

Caleb realized what was happening at about the same time his horse reached the chute between the corral and the cattle pen. He pulled his horse up quickly, causing the animal to sit back on his haunches. Storm Cloud saw it all as a threat and came after the animal with his ears laid back and teeth bared. Caleb's horse, which was young and inexperienced, tried to dodge Storm Cloud while backing away from the cow and calf. The cow finally loosed herself and bolted toward Caleb at the same time that Storm Cloud rushed the fence.

Caleb struggled to regain control of his horse as the animal attempted to get its legs underneath it. The cow hit them square in the horse's chest and they both went over, crashing against the boards of Storm Cloud's corral.

Caleb grunted when he hit the ground. He felt his right leg snap and prepared himself for the roll of his horse. He just prayed that he could kick his left leg free before the horse found its feet again. Ribs cracked as the horse rolled and came up against the rearing stallion. Caleb managed to roll out of the way, but not before a hoof struck him on the side of the head as his horse beat a hasty retreat from the battlefield.

"Caleb!" Jake yelled.

Why did they all seem so far away? Caleb heard the pounding of feet and heard Jenny's voice as she tried to soothe the stallion. He was aware that hands pulled him out of the corral and rolled him over on his back.

"Look at his leg," someone said, Dan or Randy, he wasn't sure.

"I see it. Watch what you're doing." That had to be Jake. The rest faded to black as the bawling of the cattle filled his ears and one last thought filtered through his brain.

"God, please don't take my other leg."

Chapter Four

Jenny finally managed to get a hand on Storm Cloud's halter and led the protesting stallion back into his stall. She turned him in with a slap on his rump and rushed back out to see about Caleb.

"Is he all right?" Jenny asked the circle of stricken faces.

"Someone needs to fetch the doctor," Jason said as he knelt next to the still form.

Jenny took one look at the leg bent out at an awkward angle, and her stomach rolled.

"It's busted," Jake said. "Busted bad."

"Probably cracked some ribs," Cole added.

"Doctor!" Jason ordered. "Now! And don't come back without him." Dan and Randy rushed to their horses and took off.

Grace and Chase came running up to the corral. "What happened?"

"Caleb's hurt."

Grace slid between the boards and rushed to where Caleb lay. "We can't just leave him here."

"We need to get something to carry him on," Cole observed. "We'll mess his leg up worse if we pick him up like that."

"Find a board and a blanket," Jason commanded. "We'll take him to the bunkhouse." Cole and Jake went in search of a board, and Grace took off to get a blanket.

"No," Jenny said. She smoothed back the wisps of hair that had escaped from her braid as she calmly looked up the hill at the big house. "Let's take him to the house."

Jason looked at his granddaughter, who seemed completely calm amid the storm that had engulfed them.

"Jenny?" Jason asked doubtfully.

"Trust me," she said and flashed her grandfather a familiar grin.

Amanda checked the stove to make sure the crust on the blackberry pie didn't get too dark around the edges. It was her first attempt at baking since . . . before . . . and she wasn't sure how hot this stove was. Before . . . when she had lived at home with her mother, she knew exactly how long it took for a pie crust to brown or a cake to cook all the way through. She had done most of the cooking for them, since her mother kept odd hours as a midwife. Now she would have to get used to a different stove in a different house in a different part of the country.

Amanda knew her mother was dead. Uncle Cole had told her and shown her the letter. He even said that all of their belongings were being stored down in Laredo by an old friend of the family, but she had no desire to see the items. She preferred to remember them where she'd last seen them, to pretend that her mother was still waiting there for her to come home. She'd decided not to cry, or even to mention her mother's death; she was afraid that once she started, she would never be able to stop.

It was all because of the Fear. The Fear made her do things. Or maybe it was the Fear that kept her from doing things. The Fear was a wall that she couldn't get over, under or around. It kept her surrounded in a tiny, cold room where no one could come in and no one could get out. And the strange thing was that as long as the Fear was there, she felt safe. It was a handy barrier that kept her from contact with the outside world.

It was an excuse.

At least she was expanding her world a bit. Jason had gone on roundup and left her all alone in the big mansion. Grace had asked her to come down and stay with her and the baby, but Amanda had declined. She liked being alone and knowing she could walk the halls and not have to talk to anyone. She wandered from room to room, going into all of them except for Jason's and Agnes's small room off the kitchen out of respect for their privacy. She was surprised when she found Cat's room. She barely remembered meeting the fiery daughter of her benefactor when she had been rescued in New York. But Cat actually lived here and would be coming home soon. Amanda knew that Jason was anxious for his daughter and her husband, Ty, to return from North Carolina. He was worried about them, as he should be. They had been lucky so far, extremely lucky, while others had not been so fortunate. She thought of the one called Caleb, who had lost his leg.

There were war headlines in the paper on the kitchen table, one that Grace had brought back from town on her last trip. Amanda had taken care of Jacey the day she went, although it had been a trial to get the baby girl to take a bottle when she was used to being nursed and rocked by her mother. All Amanda could do was rock her and sing until the baby fell into an exhausted sleep, still sniffling tears as she laid her moist cheek against Amanda's breast.

What would it be like to be a mother and have someone depend totally on you? What a great responsibility it would be. And worry. Had worry over Amanda's fate been the cause of her mother's death?

Trying to distract herself, Amanda sat down to read the paper while she waited for the pie to bake. Federal troops had entered Richmond, and Lincoln had come right behind them. The Confederate Army was in retreat. How much longer before they would have to surrender?

Amanda turned the page. Inside there was an editorial about the homesteaders. Never mind that the Homestead Act of 1862 had given these people the right to settle the land and improve it; the cattlemen wanted them out. They would not tolerate these newcomers stealing cows and fencing the range. Things had been fine around these parts for years opined the writer with everybody working together and taking care of each other. There was no room for these new people.

Amanda feared that with the war sure to end soon, there would be more homesteaders heading to Wyoming.

The light was starting to dim, so she lit a lamp. She checked the pie again and was satisfied with the look of it, so she pulled it from the oven and placed it to cool on the windowsill.

Amanda gazed out the window at the rolling prairie. It looked as if it stretched on forever into the darkness of the coming night. Wasn't there enough room here for everyone?

Her peaceful musing was interrupted by the slam of a door.

"Amanda?" Jason called out to her.

She stepped into the hall.

"Go turn down the bed in the room across from yours. Caleb is hurt."

Without thinking, Amanda rushed up the stairs to do his bidding. She heard the sound of steps on the back porch and wondered how badly he'd been hurt. Was he dying?

Caleb was the quiet one. The one with the dark hair who had lost his leg in the war. They had exchanged a few words, but only a few. She had helped him with Justice the night the house had been broken into. She remembered his struggles to rise to his feet with the dog in his arms.

She really wasn't afraid of Caleb, she realized as she pulled the covers down on the bed and lit the lamp.

The sounds on the stairs suggested that several people were coming. Several men. Jenny swept into the room at the same time that Amanda moved to the corner next to the window with the lamp in her hand.

She recognized her Uncle Cole of course, and then there was the blond one with the dangerous eyes. Jake was his name and Shannon was his wife. His wife was the one who sang so pretty and played the guitar. The other man was the one who scared her so much, even though he had been the one who saved her. She remembered his fight with Bishop the night she had been rescued. He was wearing nothing but his pants and a pair of boots now, and his damp hair swept across his shoulders. His back and chest were covered with scabs. It was strange to think of him with chicken pox.

The sight of Caleb's twisted leg sickened her and she placed her hand over her mouth so she wouldn't lose her dinner.

"Help me get his boots off," Jenny said. Cole held the left leg and Jake yanked off the boot, taking Caleb's prosthesis with it. The amputated leg ended at mid-calf and was covered with a sock.

The thigh bone of the other leg was broken. The group looked down at it for a moment, then Chase and Cole took a firm grasp and nodded to Jake, who pulled the boot off as quickly as possible.

Caleb groaned.

"You'd better go take care of the boys," Jenny said to Chase. "Grace will have her hands full with Jacey."

"I'll manage," Chase said and dropped a kiss on her cheek. "You just take care of Caleb, and yourself." He placed a hand over her stomach and then left after giving Caleb another glance.

"I hope that Dan can talk the doctor into coming," Jenny said. "He was too busy to come when Grace asked him."

"It's been that bad?" Jason asked.

"Zane's in pretty bad shape," Jenny said. "I'm scared to leave him for too long."

"How's Shan—" Jake began.

"She's fine, and probably fuming that you're not there yet. Zeb's doing fine also. I'm sure they're wondering what's happened."

"I'll go check on her and Zane," Jake said. His conflict over leaving his friend to check on his wife showed on his face.

"Chase knows what to do if Zane needs anything," Jenny said.

"You don't think that Caleb will . . . lose that leg . . . do you?" Jake's sunburnt face was pale in the dim light of the lamp.

"Not if I have anything to say about it." Jenny looked at Amanda, who had taken a few steps toward the bed. "Why don't you set that lamp down and help us get his clothes off so the doctor can have a good look at him when he shows up?"

Amanda set the lamp down on the bedside table. Cole and Jason stepped back to let the women take over.

"Would you unbutton his shirt?" Jenny suggested as she pulled a suspender down Caleb's arm.

Amanda reached tentative fingers toward the top button of Caleb's shirt. She squeezed her eyes shut as memories of another man in another room demanding the same thing filled her head.

This was different. This man wasn't here to abuse her. This man needed her help. Her fingers flew to her eyes and rubbed them, hoping to erase the memory. But it was no use. She couldn't help him. Jenny could do it. Grace could do it. Let the doctor do it.

"Amanda," Jenny said. The men had left, and Jenny was watching her from the other side of the bed. "We really need your help. Grace and I have more than we can handle, with everyone sick from the chicken pox."

"I thought you said they were better."

"I just said that so Jake wouldn't worry," Jenny lied and kept her sapphire-blue eyes focused on Amanda. "Will you help us? Will you help Caleb?"

Amanda was trapped, and she knew it. What could she say without sounding ungrateful?

Amanda looked down at the handsome face and the dark shaggy hair that swirled around Caleb's ears. His jaw was covered with dark stubble from his days on the range, and a streak of dirt was smudged under his chin. A trickle of blood had come out from under his hair and dried in a line dashing down to his eyebrow. Impossibly long dark lashes rested against his sunburnt cheeks. He had been kind to her. He was hurt.

"I'll do what I can," she said. She only hoped it would be enough.

Chapter Five

Amanda had trouble with the buttons. She managed to get the shirt undone just fine, but the buttons on his pants . . . her fingers fumbled, and her hands were shaking so much that she couldn't get them to perform the simplest task. It wasn't as if he were going to hurt her. He was unconscious.

Amanda pressed her fingers to her eyes again as flashes of memories or dreams—she didn't know which—filled her mind. Nameless faces, sweaty bodies and the stench of alcohol-laden breath assaulted her senses. Pain that was consumed by a dense fog flashed into her mind.

She pressed her hands hard against her forehead because she was afraid that she would push on her eyes so hard that she would blind herself.

She shouldn't have been given this responsibility. She

couldn't be trusted. What if she hurt him? What if he died?

He needs your help.

Amanda jerked her hands away and looked into the darkened corners of the room. It was the voice again. She recognized it from the night of the attack. It was the same voice that had told her to get the boys out of the house.

She was insane. They wouldn't want a madwoman taking care of their friend. How would she even know she was doing the right thing? She would go now and tell Jason and Jenny she couldn't do, she shouldn't do it. They would just have to find someone else.

Amanda rushed around the side of the bed and stubbed her toe against the bed frame. She grabbed the post to keep from falling, and the mattress shook as she stumbled against it.

"What?" Caleb, suddenly jarred awake, blinked as he tried to identify his surroundings. "Where am I?" he asked.

Amanda kept a steady grip on the post as she turned to look at him. "You're in Jason's house, in one of the upstairs rooms."

"Amanda?" he asked.

"Yes." She stepped into the glow of the lamp. "They asked me to take care of you until the doctor comes."

Caleb tried to push himself up to a sitting position and grimaced as pain shot through his body. He placed a hand across his ribs and looked down at his leg, which lay at an awkward angle.

69

"Damn," he moaned. "Damn it all." He punched his fist into the mattress.

"It should be all right." Amanda went to his side. "Once they set it."

"How am I supposed to walk on a busted leg? It's not like I've got another one!" Caleb exploded. Realizing that his stump was exposed to her view, he stuffed it under the quilt. He looked up to see that Amanda had backed into the darkened corner of the room. Her pale face reflected the light of the lamp.

Caleb covered his face with his hands as he realized that he had frightened her. "I'm sorry, Amanda. I didn't mean to scare you."

Amanda fought to restore her breathing to its normal pace. Caleb wouldn't hurt her. She took a step toward the bed.

How did she know that Caleb wouldn't hurt her? She stopped in her tracks again as he looked down at his leg and winced. He had to be in pain. The leg needed to be set, and she was trembling like an idiot. The least she could do was make him comfortable until the doctor arrived.

"We need to get your clothes off before the doctor comes," she said, amazed that her voice did not betray the trembling that consumed her. "Can you move enough to do that?"

Caleb looked down the length of his body, taking inventory. As if he hadn't been humiliated enough when Amanda had seen his stump, he was now supposed to undress in front of her. Or worse, she was going to help him undress. Obviously, that was what she had been doing before he'd woken up; his shirt and, dang, his pants were unbuttoned. Couldn't she just leave him alone to wallow in his misery? They could *cut* his clothes off, for all he cared.

But they had asked her to take care of him. And she had generously agreed. How would she react if he told her not to?

"I think I can get my shirt off," Caleb volunteered, although he could feel the heat of a flush crawling up his neck.

Caleb eased his shirt over his shoulders and caught his breath as he leaned forward to take it off. "Dang," he gasped. "I must have busted some ribs."

"Wha . . . what happened?"

"My horse and I got caught in the middle of a fight between a cow and Jenny's stud. I hope my horse is all right. Did they say anything about Banner?" he asked as he pitched his shirt down to the foot of the bed.

"They didn't mention him," Amanda said.

Caleb raised the hem of the long-sleeved undershirt he wore to look at his ribs. One side of his ridged abdomen was already turning black and blue. "Dang, that hurts," he said.

"How's your breathing?" Amanda asked.

"It only hurts when I do it," Caleb said wryly, and was pleased to catch a glimpse of a smile flashing across Amanda's face.

Maybe he had imagined it. He carefully pulled the undershirt over his head and flung it on top of his shirt. He suddenly felt extremely vulnerable as the cool air of the room washed across his bare chest. He flipped the quilt, which had only been covering his left leg, over his waist.

"Why don't you get one of the guys to help me with my pants?"

"They all went down to Grace's to get something to eat," Amanda explained.

"Oh."

"Are you hungry?"

"Starved. Or I was when I rode in." Caleb placed a hand over his stomach. "Now I don't know if I could eat or not."

"I made a blackberry pie," Amanda suggested. "You could try it and see."

"That sounds great," Caleb said and tried to smile.

Amanda nervously nodded in agreement and dashed from the room, happy that she could do something to make him feel better.

Caleb let out a sigh of relief after Amanda left. The last thing he wanted was a woman to see how helpless he was. He raised himself up to scoot his pants down, hoping he could get the task done before she returned. It was hard to raise himself, however, since all he had to use for leverage was his stump. The other leg was useless. He broke into a sweat, and waves of nausea washed over him.

There was no way he was going to eat anything, he thought as he swallowed back the bile that rose in his throat. He managed to get his pants down to his thighs but cringed at the prospect of getting them over the break in his leg. He could see his thigh bone pushing against his skin, even though he was wearing long drawers beneath his pants. He had to get them off or die trying, and the way he felt at the moment, death was preferable.

Caleb bit his lip to keep the moan of pain from escaping as he pushed the pants down to his knees. The room swam, and lights danced before his eyes. He couldn't reach any farther without his ribs screaming in protest, but he would be damned before he'd let Amanda come in and catch him with his pants bunched around his knees as if he were incapable of taking care of himself. He took a breath, leaned forward and gave another push. The left leg slid out, but the right pant leg caught on his foot, twisting the leg. Pain shot up his thigh, up his spine and into his head before it burst before his eyes with a great white light. Caleb was unconscious again before his head hit the pillow.

"Are you sure that was a wise move?" Chase asked as he shifted Fox to his other shoulder. The boys had fallen asleep at Grace's and since Chase was feeling better, Jenny had decided the family should move back to their own cabin to sleep.

As they trudged across the small valley, Jenny looked up at the light shining from the second-story window of the big house. Caleb had been placed in the same room that she had stayed in when she first came to the ranch.

"Sometimes people need help finding answers," Jenny said.

"Answers to what?"

"Their problems." Jenny tugged on Chance's hand. "Come on, little man, get a move on."

"Carry me, Mama," Chance begged.

"I can't, darling. The baby's too big, and you're too big, and Mama's back hurts."

"Fox got carried," Chance grumbled.

"Fox didn't wake up. You did."

"Jenny, are you playing at matchmaking?" Chase asked after Chance sighed and trudged on.

"It wouldn't be the first time someone fell in love over a broken leg," Jenny said, reminding him of their own first meeting.

"And you think these two should fall in love?"

"I think they should do *something* instead of just existing. That's all Caleb's been doing since he got back. He's just going through the motions, and Amanda is nothing more than a vapor. Half the time I'm afraid she'll disappear in a puff of smoke."

"She's terrified of me," Chase stated.

"I wonder why," Jenny tossed over her shoulder as she helped Chance up the steps. She looked at the regal face of her husband and wondered where he would be and what he would be if their paths had not crossed. He should have been a leader of many men; it was in his bearing. He looked every part the warrior, even with a child in his arms. Amanda had seen his fight to the death with Wade Bishop, had seen him drop the man from the window without remorse because he was a threat to Jenny. Yet Chase also held compassion in his soul. Even after being separated from his people for so long, he still wondered about them and worried about them. The attack and subsequent killing of 150 Kiowa and the destruction of their lodges at Adobe Walls the previous November had saddened him, even though his people had rejected him.

"What do you mean, you wonder why?" He followed Jenny into the boys' room. Jenny pulled Chance's shirt over his head, took off his shoes and socks and dropped his pants.

"Potty?" she asked. Chance nodded yes and stumbled sleepily toward the door that led out back.

"This guy is out," Chase said and deposited Fox on the bed.

"Which means I'll be washing sheets tomorrow." Jenny arched her back and stretched.

Chance came back into the room a few moments later. Chase ruffled his son's dark hair. "Did you make it to the outhouse or did you just stand on the stoop?"

Jenny smiled at the conversation as she tucked Fox into bed. Her great warrior husband was talking about potty habits with his son. *Thank you, God, for sending him my way.*

"I didn't want to get my feet dirty," Chance mumbled as he fell into bed. His parents pulled the covers over the two boys and placed kisses on their soft cheeks.

Chase placed an arm around Jenny's waist as she straightened after kissing the boys. "You need a rest yourself," he whispered in her ear. Even after four years of marriage and the responsibility of a family, all he had to do was touch her and her spirit soared, no matter how tired she was.

"I know, but I can't, not yet. Not until Zane is better." They walked into the main room of the cabin. Jenny looked longingly at the big bed she shared with Chase.

How many nights had it been since she'd crawled into it and slept? She longed to lose herself in its paradise with her husband.

"You need to take care of yourself and the baby." Chase's mouth moved against her forehead.

"We'll be fine," she assured him, even though her heart wasn't in her words.

"Jenny," Chase said firmly. He placed a finger under her chin to tilt her face up. "You've got big circles under your eyes. You're worn out from taking care of everyone else. You need to take care of yourself."

"And who'll take care of Zane?" Jenny asked. "Shannon's fever just broke, and Grace has her hands full with Jacey and cooking for everyone. Someone needs to watch him. He's got it bad, Chase; he hasn't even been conscious since he got sick."

"You're right. Someone needs to watch him and take care of him. I just wish it didn't have to be you right now." Chase had long ago realized that when Jenny took a notion to do something, there was no talking her out of it.

"He's been alone too long as it is," Jenny said as she turned away to leave.

"Jenny—" Chase stopped her. "As soon as he's better, you're going to rest." His face held the haughty set that she knew so well, that of a king looking down on his subjects. But it also held all the love he felt for her.

"I will," she promised. "I'll even let you take me out to the lake."

The lake was Chase's favorite place on the ranch. It was the place he had gone to when seeking solitude and companionship with God, and it was the place he'd taken Jenny when she had finally discovered that she loved him. He had known it all along and dreamed of the day when he could take her there. Jason had left the area as wild as the day he'd discovered it, appreciating the natural beauty of the spot as much as Chase did.

"It's a date," Chase said and dropped a kiss on her lips. Jenny leaned in and wrapped her arms around his waist. Chase hugged her to his chest and rubbed her back.

If I could just stay here for a while, Jenny mused as her cramped muscles yearned for the feel of his hands. She didn't want his caresses to stop.

But she had to go. Zane needed her. If they were lucky, the doctor would come, but if he didn't, then someone would have to set Caleb's leg. She prayed Doc would show up, because she was afraid for Zane, too. He wasn't getting any better.

"I've got to go," Jenny said and walked out the door.

Was he asleep? Amanda set the plate down on the bedside table and cautiously leaned in to listen to the sound of Caleb's breathing. He was breathing. That was a relief. For a moment, when she had seen his face so pale against the pillow, she had been afraid for him.

How had he managed to get his pants off? Amanda wondered as she picked them up from where they hung halfway to the floor. They were stuck on something beneath the covers, and Amanda tugged.

Caleb groaned in pain, though still unconscious. She lifted the blanket and saw that the pants were still wrapped around his right foot. And she had jerked on them.

She was such an idiot. It was just as she had thought: She couldn't take care of him. She hadn't even helped him get his pants off. Instead she had run off on a foolish mission, hoping to impress him with a piece of pie.

Carefully she slid Caleb's pants from beneath his foot and started to fold them. She realized then how dirty they were from his days on the roundup and placed them on top of his shirt, making a mental note to include them in the wash.

Caleb worked just as hard as the other men, in spite of his handicap. She had watched many times from the window as the cowboys worked around the barn and rode in and out of the small valley. She had noticed that Caleb was able to keep up with them, especially on horseback. She could tell by the stubborn set of his chin, even while he was sleeping, that he wouldn't give in. Yet his face also held a childlike innocence. It must be the eyelashes. She had never seen such eyelashes on a man, and she had seen a lot of men, she mused as she gently arranged the covers.

Amanda stood up straight as the thought flashed through her mind. Since when had she become so casual about what had happened to her? It was the first time she had ever recalled anything about her experience without being overcome by a feeling of terror.

Could it be because she wasn't thinking about herself anymore?

If his clothes were this dirty, then his body had to be dirty, too. Cleaning him up would surely make him feel better, she decided, and gathered up his clothes to put with the laundry. She'd take care of them herself. No sense in adding to Grace's load when she already had so much to do. Amanda left to fetch some soap and water for Caleb.

How could something so simple give one such a feeling of peace? Amanda wrung out the washcloth and dabbed again at the blood that stained Caleb's forehead. She traced the trail up into the dark curls of his hair and found the abrasion from the horse's hoof. A lump had formed there and the skin was broken, but the wound didn't look serious. He wouldn't require stitches, which was a good thing. The dirt that streaked his face had come off easily enough even though the washcloth had dragged across the stubble of his beard. She caught her breath when it snagged. The last thing she wanted to do was cause him more pain. A look at the dark eyelashes assured her that he was still sleeping.

Another dip into the basin and the wringing of the water broke the peaceful silence that held nothing more than the soft sound of Caleb's breathing and the restless bawling of the cows in the pens below. Amanda wiped the cloth up under his neck and around his ears. Should she lift his head up to get the back of his neck or should she wait for another time? She decided to wait and moved the cloth down across his chest.

He was strong. He had to be. His pectoral muscles stood out in sharp relief under the smooth skin of his chest. She wiped the cloth across his chest and then picked up his arm and ran the cloth down the length and underneath. She gently laid his arm on the cover and noticed his fingers. They were slim and refined in spite of the calluses that hardened the palm. He was an artist, she had heard someone say.

Amanda leaned across Caleb's chest and picked up his left arm. She was so engrossed in her work that she did not notice the flickering of the dark lashes against his cheek. The cloth dipped into the hollow on the inside of his elbow and then swept over the curve of his bicep and over his shoulder before caressing the triceps on its journey back down to the hand. She gently returned the arm to its resting place after taking time to wash the long, lean fingers. Then she moved the bedcovers down past his waist.

The washcloth swirled over the ridges of his abdomen. He might not be as tall as the other men, but he had to be as strong. There wasn't a part of his body that she had seen so far that seemed weak. Even the thigh that supported his wooden leg bulged with muscle, she mused as she looked down toward the foot of the bed. Her glance was interrupted however by the sight of another bulge.

Amanda gasped and turned to find a set of dark eyes beneath impossibly long lashes glowing up at her. She stood up quickly and dropped the cloth into the basin with a slosh as Caleb reached for the covers and pulled them up over his chest.

"I'm sorry," he said hoarsely.

Amanda felt the slow burn of her skin as a blush crept up her neck and into her cheeks. She threw her hands over her face and with a sob ran from the room.

"Amanda! Wait!" Caleb called after her. He sat up and

doubled over as the pain in his ribs caught him off guard. "Dang," he said and then looked at the basin of water sitting on the table next to a piece of blackberry pie. A curse split his lips, and he dropped back on the pillow. "Why don't they just shoot me?" he wondered out loud to the ceiling. "They put horses out of their misery, why can't they do it for me?"

Chapter Six

"It's broke, all right," Dr. Green said. The elderly doctor had always been one to state the obvious. "Busted some ribs, too," he declared as he finished his examination of Caleb. His manner was brusque, but his touch was gentle as he and Jenny wrapped the bandages tightly around Caleb's abdomen.

"How's that feel, son?" he asked as he finished the job.

"Hurts," Caleb replied. "Can't breathe."

"You'll be glad of that in a minute or two. We still got to set that leg." The doctor nodded to Cole and Jake, who were waiting to help. "You two hold him down and I'll see if I can jerk it into place."

Caleb cringed at the words. Last time someone had held him down, the doctor had a saw in his hands.

"Here, bite on this." Dr. Green handed him a polished piece of oak that held the imprint of many sets of teeth.

Caleb shook his head in disgust and turned away.

"Suit yourself, just don't go and bite your tongue off," the doctor said as he dropped the piece into his bag. "Everyone ready?"

Cole and Jake grabbed on to Caleb's shoulders as Jenny placed her hands on either side of his waist.

Caleb took a breath and wondered how many more indignities he would face before the day was over. The doctor picked up his foot and gave his leg a quick jerk. Red-hot pain shot up his leg and through his spine, and Caleb gritted his teeth and growled.

"Did you get it?" Jake asked.

"Looks like it," the doctor said. "Hand me those splints."

The pain faded from a white-hot flash to a dull throb as the doctor splinted and bandaged Caleb's leg.

"Lucky for you it was a clean break. I didn't feel any chips in there, so you ought to heal without any trouble."

"I will?" Caleb asked, almost afraid of the answer.

"You'll be hopping around in no time," the doctor replied. "Or about six weeks, whichever comes first." He gave Caleb what passed for a smile. "Just stay off of it until I tell you different." He gathered his things and looked at Jenny. "Next patient. While I'm here I might as well make the rounds."

"We appreciate it, Doc," Jenny said as she led him out of the room.

"Not like I had a choice in the matter," Dr. Brown snorted. "Those two cowboys of yours practically held a gun to my head to get me out here."

"See, I knew you'd be all right," Jake said to Caleb as

the sound of the doctor's gruff complaining faded from earshot.

"Yeah, I'll be hopping around in no time," Caleb said miserably. "How's my horse?"

"He's fine. Zeb brushed him down and fed him. He's in his stall now acting like nothing happened."

"He's not the one who's busted up, either," Caleb groaned.

"It could have happened to any of us, Caleb," Cole said consolingly.

"It's probably a good thing it did happen to me," Caleb said. "It's not like I was going to be much help anyway."

"Dang it, Caleb—" Jake began, but Cole placed a quieting hand on his arm.

"We'll let you get some sleep," Cole said. "Do you want me to send Amanda up with some supper?"

Caleb's answering snarl raised an eyebrow on both men, and they left the room in an awkward silence.

The last thing Amanda would want was to come into his room, Caleb mused as he lay back against the pillows. It wouldn't have surprised him to hear that she had run screaming from the house after her brief confrontation with his manly parts.

Was there some way he could have prevented his reaction to her? he wondered. It had been a long time since he had been with a woman. He had not lain with one since before the war, and it wasn't likely that any woman would ever lie with him again unless he had plenty of coin in his pocket.

It wasn't as if he had a lot of experience with women, either. Sure, he had gone to Maybelle's plenty of times with Zane and Jake, and he had kissed some of the nice girls that came to the dances, but that was about the extent of it. It wasn't as if he were naturally gifted in that department like Zane was, but none of the girls had ever turned away from him in disgust. At least not until now. Until Amanda had run sobbing from the room.

When she first began washing him, he'd thought he was dreaming. And then he'd hoped that everything that had happened to him in the past year had been a bad dream and he was finally waking up. If only her hands hadn't felt so soft and gentle and just plain good. He could still feel the sweep of her dark hair across his chest as she had leaned over him to wash his arm. And the way her fingers had worked the washcloth down each of his fingers as if it were all part of a slow and steady seduction. At least that was how his body had responded to it. And when the cloth had dipped around his hips and over his waist . . .

Don't think about it. Don't think that way at all. Caleb clenched his fists in frustration. He didn't know which hurt worse, the pain in his leg or the pain in his groin. After the look of terror Amanda had given him, he felt that he was no better than any of the men that had put down their coin to use her.

To make matters worse, he was hungry and was starting to feel the need to relieve himself.

Why didn't they just shoot him?

* * *

"How long has he been running this fever?" Dr. Brown asked as he examined Zane.

"Several days," Jenny replied. She wrung out the washcloth that she had placed on Zane's forehead before she had gone up to the big house.

"I don't like it," the doctor said as he dropped his stethoscope back into his bag. "Fever should have broke by now. What have you been giving him?"

"Dandelion tea, licorice tea, oatmeal baths and a red pepper poultice for the sores," Jenny answered.

The doctor peeled Zane's eyelid back and looked into the hazel eye. "Ice would be good if you could find some. I've ordered quinine, but it's hard to tell if and when it will get here," he said. "If this fever continues, he's liable to have a seizure of some sort, and that could lead to brain damage."

"Brain damage?" Jenny said in disbelief.

"Get the fever down," the doctor instructed. "And try to keep those sores clean." He looked around the bunkhouse. "Anyone else sick?"

"Everyone's better now except for Zane."

"Then consider yourself lucky. Death toll in town is up to twenty."

"How're Agnes's family?"

"They came through it just fine, but it will be a while before she'll get back out here."

"Tell her we'll be okay," Jenny assured him.

"And how are *you* managing?"

"Me? I'm fine," Jenny said, surprised by the doctor's question.

"You don't look fine. You look worn out. You should go to bed and let some of the others take care of things around here."

"If I do that, there's no one to take care of Zane," Jenny replied. "I can't lie in my bed doing nothing when he's this sick."

"Suit yourself," the doctor said. "I'm going to get something to eat and then find myself a bed right here. I'm too old, and it's too cold for me to be running around the country in the middle of the night. At least out here I might be able to get a decent night's sleep without half the town banging on my door."

"How are you doing, son?" Jason asked as he stood in the doorway of Caleb's room. He was amazed to find Caleb sitting on the edge of the bed, and he quickly stepped into the room to check on him.

"You wouldn't happen to have a chamber pot handy, would you?" Caleb asked sheepishly. His face was pale yet covered with a sheen of sweat. Obviously, his struggle to sit up had not been easy.

Jason quickly went to the washstand and got the pot that sat on the shelf beneath it. "Pretty foolish of us to forget about the most basic of needs, wasn't it?"

"I guess it's not really something that you plan in advance," Caleb answered. He set the pot on the floor and wondered what he should do next.

"Do you need some help?" Jason asked.

Caleb hated to admit it, but he did. It was either that or flood the bed, and he was positive he would rather die first. Jason managed to pull him up enough to support his weight, and Caleb relieved himself with a sigh, even though his face was flushed with embarrassment.

"I'll make sure that doesn't happen again," Jason said as he eased Caleb back on the bed.

"Thank you, sir," Caleb replied, wanting to distance himself after the intimacy of the moment. "But maybe it would be best for everyone if I just moved to the bunkhouse."

"Jenny's got her hands full down there with Zane."

"I don't want to be a burden."

"You're not," Jason said firmly. "Don't even think that way. We all take care of each other here. And that includes everyone."

"Even Amanda?"

"Even Amanda." Jason eyed the plate that held the blackberry pie. "She's one heck of a cook, too. I just had a piece of this downstairs and it was delicious."

"I'm just not so sure that she wants to help . . . me," Caleb said.

"Do you have a problem with her taking care of you?"

Caleb looked down at his one set of toes tenting the sheets and swallowed uncomfortably. How could he tell his employer and benefactor that he had probably scared the poor girl to death with his uncontrollable . . . urges? "I just don't want her to feel . . . er . . . trapped . . . in any way."

"She agreed to do it. She's been coming out of her shell the past few days, and it seems like she's making an effort to be a part of things. How would she feel if she thought she wasn't wanted?"

Oh, she was wanted. He had proved that earlier when she had touched him. Just remembering it caused another embarrassing reaction. Caleb adjusted the blankets to hide what was happening.

"I just want to make sure that she hasn't taken on something she's not ready for."

Jason laid a comforting hand on Caleb's shoulder. "I'll make sure, on the condition that you quit worrying about being a burden and let all of us help you."

Caleb nodded in agreement. He wasn't in a position to argue.

"How's Zane doing?"

"Not good. His fever is out of control. If it goes on much longer, I don't know if he'll survive."

Suddenly Caleb's broken leg didn't seem so bad anymore. At least he was certain he wouldn't die from it. Embarrassment and frustration might be another matter, however, depending on how long he was stuck in bed.

Around Amanda.

"Say a prayer for him," Jason added. "I'll go down and tell Amanda you need something to eat."

No, don't, Caleb wanted to say. He just nodded in agreement as Jason left the room. He was, after all, pretty hungry.

Chapter Seven

Amanda gathered her shawl around her shoulders and folded her arms across her chest as she leaned against a post on the porch that stretched the width of the front of the house. The painted floorboards still held the scars from the horses' hooves when the men who attacked the ranch before Christmas had ridden right into the house on their path of destruction. Jason had said the hands would fix the floor after the roundup. He had spent the winter months making repairs to the inside of the house. Now the only reminder of that horrible night was the scuff marks on the porch.

The evidence of violence and destruction were easily removed in a house by the sweep of a broom or the swipe of a paintbrush. If only it were that easy with people. If only she could erase the memories and the fears.

What exactly are you afraid of?

At least she was getting used to the voice. It no longer

sent white-hot terror shooting through her body as it had the first time she'd heard it. It didn't make her wonder about her sanity as it once had. It was just something that was there, so she listened to it. What *was* she afraid of? It was not as if Caleb would hurt her.

How did she know that? What made Caleb different from all the other men who had come to her room and used her? Some of them had been nice, or tried to be. But when they realized she wasn't really there, that she had nothing to offer them besides compliance, they quickly got bored with her. Some of them had sweet-talked her and made promises to come back for her, but she had soon learned that the only thing she could count on was the sweet escape offered by the opium.

So what made Caleb different from any other man who had come to her in the same condition he had shown earlier? How did she know that he would not hurt her?

She just knew.

Uncle Cole talked about learning to trust his instincts while he was a Texas Ranger. Some men could be trusted, some could not. Most could be bought, but there were a few who would rather die than give up their principles.

How lucky she was to have landed in a place peopled by the latter.

Caleb wouldn't hurt her.

So why was she standing here on the porch close to freezing when he probably needed her help upstairs? What was she afraid of?

A few snowflakes drifted down and landed on the

dark flat stones that created a walkway to the front porch. Amanda looked up into the never-ending blackness of the sky as more flakes followed, mystically appearing out of the darkness of space. A late spring snow had appeared out of nowhere to once again blanket the land and hide the scars that covered the earth. Wasn't it funny how snow could make the ugliest scenery beautiful as it hid all the flaws that were usually visible to the eye? It made you forget what was underneath.

If only she could forget.

"Guess we made it back from roundup just in time," Jason said as he stepped up beside her.

Amanda was surprised. She had been so engrossed in her thoughts that she hadn't heard him come out.

"It's pretty," she commented as the flakes sifted onto the ground, turning the drab brown to white.

"Yes, it is. But knowing that I'll be sleeping in a warm bed tonight instead of on the cold, hard ground makes it prettier," Jason said as he leaned against the porch rail. It was unusual to hear Amanda contributing to a conversation, and he hoped to prolong it as much as possible.

"I imagine it does," Amanda returned. She stuck her hand out and let the flakes hit the warmth of her skin and then instantly melt. How many winters had she spent behind a window that had been nailed shut, longing to feel the touch of the snow or the cool caress of a breeze? And how many months had she spent in her room since coming to Wyoming, keeping herself a prisoner of her own fears?

"How's Caleb doing?" she asked. "Did the doctor set his leg?"

"He'll be fine," Jason replied. "He's frustrated, however. He was making progress getting used to his new leg, and then this had to happen."

"He's very proud," Amanda commented. She pulled her hand back into the confines of her shawl.

"Always has been. I remember the first time I saw him. He was nothing but a scrawny boy then with a mop of shaggy hair. He was drawing pictures of people on the street and selling them for a penny. I offered him enough money for a bath and a meal, and he said he didn't have enough paper to draw that many pictures for me. He didn't want any charity, just wanted to make a living."

"Where was his family?"

"His mother died when he was born, and his father the winter before I met him. He had made his way from the mountains of Georgia, working from town to town, drawing pictures to support himself."

"I hear he's a good artist," Amanda said.

"He's a great artist. It's a shame he's given it up."

"He has?"

"He hasn't drawn a thing since he got back from the war."

Amanda chewed on her lip as she considered what Jason had said about Caleb. "Maybe he just needs time to heal on the inside," she finally said, breaking the stillness of the snow.

Jason looked down at the dark head beside him and

marveled at Jenny's wisdom in putting Caleb under Amanda's care. Maybe it was just what the two of them needed to get back into life. Maybe what they needed was each other.

He only hoped that they both had the courage to admit it.

"I promised Caleb I'd find him something to eat. It's been a long time since breakfast."

Amanda quickly straightened up. "He's probably starved. I'll see what I can find."

Jason looked on with a smile as Amanda hurried into the house, then turned back to watch the snow drift down to earth. It was a peaceful scene, one that would normally fill him with contentment. If only Cat and Ty were home and the war was over and the problems between the homesteaders and the ranchers were solved. If only the school was built and a teacher found and Zane was better and back to his usual wisecracking self. If only Caleb had not lost his leg and Cat had not lost her baby and Jamie had not died.

Jason quickly chastised himself. He had so much to be thankful for. Everyone at the ranch did. But when you cared for people, you also worried about them. Jason felt a responsibility to everyone under his care on the ranch, and even to those who needed someone to stand up for them outside of his domain. He had been the victim of his own father's corruption and he had spent his life making sure that no one else suffered the same. It was a heavy burden to bear, but one he carried willingly.

Amanda was right. The snow was pretty, he decided as he went into the warmth of the house.

* * *

Jenny wrung out the cloth and wet it again before she placed it on Zane's forehead. The sores on his face and scalp had burst, leaving raw lesions on his skin. The risk of infection was great, and he had so many blisters she was afraid she couldn't treat all of them.

Zane was rambling again. He spoke hoarsely in disjointed phrases carrying on rambling conversations that only he knew the meaning of. Occasionally one of the names of the people who lived on the ranch was mentioned, but mostly he spoke nonsense. Jenny wondered what torments filled the mind of the usually happy-go-lucky cowboy.

Nothing was working to bring down his fever. She had tried every remedy that any of them could think of. Chase had suggested some remedies used by the Kiowa, but he was in no condition to go out looking for the plants and herbs needed, even if it were possible that they could be found at this time of year. Zeb had suggested things his mother had used, but Jenny had no idea how to find those ingredients either. She mostly had to rely on common sense and prayer, and she felt as if she were running short of both.

If only they could get their hands on some quinine. But even if the shipment did arrive in a timely manner, the chances were that Zane was pretty far down on the list of patients to receive it. It would go to the children first, then the mothers and fathers. She could only hope there would be some left for a lone cowboy.

If only he were not so weak. Jenny had tried to force some soup down his throat, but he was unable to swallow and it just trickled out the side of his mouth.

He was dying before her eyes, and there was nothing she could do about it.

Zane weakly tossed his head, fighting the fever. The cloth fell sideways and Jenny straightened it, taking time to push the sweat-dampened hair away before she placed the cool compress against his forehead. She was surprised to see hazel eyes staring up at the ceiling. Jenny leaned in closer to make sure her eyes were not deceiving her in the dim light of the lamp.

"Zane?" she asked, fearful of what his sudden awakening might mean.

"Jamie says it's snowing." The words were as clear as if he'd said, "Please pass the potatoes." Jenny blinked at the import of the statement. Was Zane now so close to death that Jamie had come to take him over to the other side? The hazel eyes fluttered closed again, and Zane resumed his restless rambling.

Jenny shook her head, wondering if she had dozed off and dreamed the entire incident. She rose from her chair and stretched her arms over her head. How long had it been since she'd had a decent night's sleep? No wonder she was hallucinating; she was close to dead on her feet.

Jenny pushed back the blanket that curtained Zane's bed from the rest of the bunkhouse. Dan and Randy, exhausted from the roundup and their dash to town to bring back the doctor, slept dead to the world. They needed their rest. The new day would bring more work, and they were down another man with Caleb's injury.

Jenny frowned at the thought that Chase would be out there doing his part instead of taking more time to recover from his illness.

She realized that she really couldn't get mad at Chase when he had just asked her to rest, too. When this was over with; she would grab her handsome husband and the two of them would hide in the big bed in their cabin for a week. If only she could get someone to take care of the boys and the stock and do all of their chores. She decided she would just settle for a peaceful Sunday afternoon at the lake.

Jenny moved on quiet feet to Zeb's bed and heard the even breathing that signaled a peaceful sleep. The big man's fever had broken at about the same time as Shannon's, and the two of them were well on their way to recovery although they were both still weak. Shannon had moved back into the room she shared with Jake.

Jenny went on to the door. The fire was getting low in the potbellied stove that warmed the room and it was growing chilly. It was late in the spring for such a cold snap but not unusual. She stepped out onto the porch and was surprised to find the small valley covered with white.

Jamie said it's snowing. . . .

The place would be a mess by this time tomorrow, she mused as she picked up some kindling for the fire. Chase and Zeb would probably get sick again from the cold and the wet.

Suddenly she stood straight up as the realization of what Zane had said hit her. "Jamie said it's snowing!"

Jenny whirled into the bunkhouse with her arms full of kindling.

"Zeb." She kicked the side of his bed as she dropped the wood into the bin next to the stove. "Wake up."

"Miz Jenny?" Zeb asked. "What's wrong?"

"It's snowing, Zeb."

Zeb rubbed his eyes in the dim light of the lantern, wondering why Jenny had to wake him up to tell him about the weather.

"I need your help."

"Yes, ma'am," Zeb said and threw back his covers.

"The doctor said we have to get Zane's fever down."

"Yes, ma'am." Zeb pulled on his pants over his long underwear and hooked his suspenders over his shoulders.

"He said ice would help, but we don't have any."

"You want me to go to town and get some?"

"No, Zeb. We've got snow." Jenny flipped back the blanket that covered Zane's feverish body. "Help me get him outside."

"What you gonna do, Miz Jenny?" Zeb asked as he easily picked the unconscious cowboy up in his arms.

"We're going to lay him in the snow."

"Dang," Zeb said, and his wide smile lit up the darkness of the bunkhouse. He followed Jenny down the steps. She spread a blanket on the ground and Zeb placed the feverish cowboy on it.

"We need to bring his body temperature down," she explained.

"If this don't work, nothing will," Zeb observed.

"I know. Let's pray it does." Jenny wrapped the blanket around Zane and then packed snow on his chest.

Zeb knelt to join her, and they soon had his whole body except his head covered with snow.

"What do we do now?" Zeb asked.

"Wait and see," Jenny said, shivering.

Zeb saw her trembling and quickly went into the bunkhouse. He returned with coats, gloves and blankets for both of them, and they settled down on either side of Zane. The heat from his body quickly melted the snow, and they kept packing on new snow to keep him covered. His restless ramblings soon ceased, and Jenny checked his breathing to make sure he was still with them.

The snow had stopped as suddenly as it had come, leaving the ground covered with a good two inches. The heavy clouds that had dumped the snow quickly moved on, carried by the stiff wind that careened over the mountains. The light of the moon broke through, bringing bright rays that bounced off the surface of the snow and cast an eerie glow over the small valley.

"Is it working?" Zeb asked, his breath clouding the air as he spoke.

"I don't know," Jenny sighed wearily. What else could she do?

"Dang," Zeb suddenly whispered.

"What?" Jenny turned to see what had caught the big man's attention.

"Fox in the chicken coop," Zeb whispered and pointed toward the back of Grace's cabin. Jenny watched as a bright red fox trotted through the snow between the cabin and a series of small sheds.

"I best get my gun," Zeb said, stealthily rising to his feet.

"No. Wait." Jenny stopped him by grabbing his arm.

The fox stopped and raised its sharp snout into the breeze, testing the smells it carried around the small valley. Grace and Cole must have kept Justice inside because of the weather, Jenny mused, or else the big dog would be raising a ruckus about now. The fox resumed its mission, passing by the henhouse and making its way between the bunkhouse and cabin.

"Must have a belly full of rabbit," Zeb whispered as the fox came closer. Jenny rocked back on her heels as the fox kept coming.

"Come on," she whispered to Zeb. He looked at her in confusion but stood at her urging and the two of them moved back from where Zane lay in the snow.

The fox kept coming, showing no fear of the two who stood silently watching its progress. It stopped suddenly and sat to look at them, its mouth open in what could be called a smile.

"That fox has got the crazy fever," Zeb hissed into Jenny's ear.

Jenny sensed the tensing of Zeb's body and knew the man was preparing to protect her.

"Wait," she whispered. "Just wait."

The fox watched the exchange with bright eyes and tongue lolling, and then, satisfied that the humans posed no threat, went on with its mission. It trotted up to where Zane lay in the snow and bent to sniff around his body. The animal went full circle, sniffing the snow, sniffing the blanket where it showed through, and then ending with Zane's head, which Jenny had protected with the tail of the blanket. The fox circled a few times, and then lay down in the snow next to Zane's head, curling the black tip of its tail over his nose.

"Dang," Zeb whispered. "What's it doing?"

"Watching over him," Jenny whispered back. "It's watching over Zane."

"Really?"

She nodded. What else could it be? Chase and Ty both swore that Jamie had appeared to them as a red fox and they credited Jamie with saving Chase's life. Jamie had seen a red fox in the vision he'd experienced in a ceremony at Gray Horse's encampment many years ago. And now Jamie had told her how to save Zane, much in the same way that he had told Amanda to get the boys out of the house during the attack last fall.

Her brother was now their guardian angel.

"Dang. What are we supposed to do?" Zeb asked, but Jenny ignored him.

She took a step toward Zane.

"Jamie?"

The fox lifted its head and looked into her eyes.

"Jamie."

"Dang," Zeb breathed behind her.

Zane moaned restlessly. He was shivering!

The fox shook the snow from its coat and turned.

"Jamie, wait!" Jenny called.

The fox took off at a run. Jenny ran after the animal a few steps and then watched as it raced up the ridge and disappeared over the side.

"Miz Jenny, Zane's 'bout to freeze hisself," Zeb called out.

Cindy Holby

Jenny turned, as if waking from a dream, and looked in amazement at Zane, who was shivering violently.

Zeb scooped him up in his arms. "Shouldn't we be gettin' him inside and dry?"

"Yes. We should." Jenny followed after Zeb, who quickly carried Zane into the cabin. She stopped when she reached the door and turned to look up toward the ridge where the lone grave lay covered in snow.

"Thank you," she said and then looked toward the heavens. "Thank you so much."

Chapter Eight

The first pink light of dawn trickled through the window and then warmly caressed Jenny's face as she snoozed in the chair. Slowly and regretfully, her eyes blinked against the brightness of morning as she came to awareness in the soft peace of the bunkhouse. Her mind swam as she fought against the constant fatigue to orient herself to her surroundings.

She was exhausted.

The steady sound of men snoring assured her that the other inhabitants were still sleeping soundly—not surprising after the amount of work they had put in over the past few days. Jenny leaned over to check on her patient and was greeted by a pair of hazel eyes set in a pale and scabbed face.

"Howdy." Zane's voice was cracked and weak.

"It's been a while." Jenny smiled in response. "As a

matter of fact, we thought you might not make it," she whispered.

"Scared you?" he asked softly.

"Yes."

Zane's dimple showed as he slowly smiled and licked his lips.

"Thirsty?"

Zane nodded, and Jenny poured a cup of water from the pitcher on the table next to his bunk.

"What happened?" Zane asked after his thirst had been satisfied.

"You got the chicken pox," Jenny replied.

"I did?"

"Yes. As a matter of fact, I'd say that you got more than your fair share."

Zane held up his arms and then placed his hands on his face. "Dang, I'm covered with them." He lifted the blanket and looked down his chest, then followed with his hands, taking careful inventory of his body parts.

"Nothing fell off that I know of," Jenny assured him with a wry grin.

Zane rolled his eyes.

"So how do you feel?" Jenny asked.

"Like I've been run over in a stampede. How do I look?"

"Like you've been run over in a stampede."

"Thanks a lot. What'd I miss?"

"Nothing much, just the roundup, and Caleb breaking his leg."

"Which one?"

"The good one."

"Dang."

"That pretty much sums it up."

Zane twisted his head to look around the bunk-house. "So where is he?"

"Up at the big house with Amanda. I had my hands full taking care of everyone else that was lying about."

"Did we lose anyone?" Zane asked.

"Nope, everyone pulled through."

"Guess we were lucky," he said with a grateful sigh.

"You were lucky," Jenny assured him. "Do you remember anything about the past few days?"

Zane's face screwed up in concentration and he shook his head. "It seems like I remember dreaming about something . . ."

"What?" Jenny asked in anticipation.

"I don't know, I just remember dreaming." Zane's hand scrubbed the side of his face.

"Don't scratch, you'll get scars." Jenny batted his hand away.

"Best tie me up then, 'cause I itch all over."

"A good soak in an oatmeal bath will help that. Shannon's fixed a poultice to put on your skin that will help you heal."

"Oatmeal and poultices. Sounds wonderful."

"Better than the alternative," Jenny said as she stood and quietly stretched.

"What's that?"

"Looking like rotten meat."

Zane made a face. "Guess I won't be making any trips to town in the near future."

"I'm sure the ladies at Maybelle's will survive in your absence." Jenny pressed her hands into the small of her back. "Do you need anything?"

"Probably, but I'm too bleary to think about it right now."

"I'll have Shannon check on you," Jenny said. "Since you seem to be fine, I'm going to bed."

"Jenny?" Zane stopped her. "Thanks for taking care of me."

"We were all worried about you, Zane."

"It's nice to know that."

Jenny looked around the bunkhouse as if she was forgetting something.

"I remember what I dreamed," Zane said as she turned to go.

She tilted her head to look at him.

"I dreamed about a fox."

"I know." Jenny flashed her famous grin. "Me, too," she said and left the bunkhouse.

Zane watched her go, wondering exactly what it was that he had just missed in the conversation. He scratched halfheartedly at the stubble on his chin and wondered how bad he looked. It was probably best that he didn't know, and he was fairly certain that his buddies would be sure to tell him in great detail. At least he would have the luxury of lying about while the rest of them were working. With that thought to cheer him, he fell back asleep, letting his body do what was necessary to heal.

* * *

"I didn't know it had snowed," Shannon said as she came out of her room. "Zane must be better. You're smiling," she added as she fell in beside Jenny.

"He is," Jenny assured her. "Fever's gone, and he's already worried about going to Maybelle's."

"That one is full of himself," Shannon laughed. "He needs to be turned down a time or two."

"What he really needs is to fall in love," Jenny said, adding her laugh to Shannon's. "The problem is that the girls at Maybelle's aren't the type he needs."

"Only according to you and me," Shannon said saucily. "And speaking of falling in love, Jake thinks you're playing matchmaker with Caleb and Amanda."

Jenny glanced up the ridge at the big house where a lone light shone in the kitchen window.

"Tell Jake to keep his mouth shut and let nature take its course," Jenny replied.

"If all men were like Jake, nature would never get anything accomplished," Shannon commented.

"Sometimes they just don't get it," Jenny said. "But then again, it took me a while to get it too, but once I did, there was no turning back." Jenny looked toward the spot at the back of the bunkhouse where she had cornered Chase on a hot summer day almost five years earlier and seduced him into kissing her. She could easily imagine Shannon doing the same with Jake. "Can you watch over Zane today?"

"I will. Go get some rest, and tell Chase I'll watch the boys, too."

"You'll have your hands full."

"It will be good practice."

Jenny cast a sideways look at Shannon, who blushed.

"For someday," she added at Jenny's questioning look.

"All things come in time," Jenny said reassuringly.

"And the trying is fun," Shannon replied. The two women dissolved into a fit of giggles as they reached Grace's cabin. The smell of bacon frying assaulted their senses, and smoke from the chimney filled the crisp morning air.

"What's got you two so tickled?" Grace asked as the two young women burst through the cabin door in high spirits.

"Zane is better," Jenny declared.

"And Jake is home," Shannon added mischievously, which led to another fit of giggles.

Grace had to join in the contagious laughter as she saw the blond and red heads bent together in easy companionship.

It was just good to hear laughter filling the cabin again. Grace found herself hoping that the war would be over soon and Cat and Ty would return and they could all get back to a normal life. Or as normal as it could be for those who lived and worked on the Lynch ranch.

Shannon fell into the routine of fixing breakfast for the hands with Grace. Jenny, however, couldn't stop giggling.

"Why don't you just go to your cabin and get some rest?" Grace urged. "You're so tired that you'd laugh at anything."

Jenny stretched her arm out on the well-worn wooden table and laid her head against it.

"I don't think I can make it that far," she said, her voice muffled by the heavy blond braid that had fallen over her face. "What I really want is to take a bath. But right now it's just too much trouble."

"Why don't you go up to the big house and take one? It's not as much of a chore up there, and I'm sure Amanda won't mind."

"Maybe the tub is already being used," Shannon said with a devious air as she kneaded out the biscuit dough. "Bathing your patient is part of nursing, isn't it?"

"Shush!" Jenny dissolved into another fit of giggles.

"What are you two talking about?" Grace asked, jumping when the fat from the bacon popped and hit her arm.

"Nothing," Shannon said, waving her floured hands at the blister that was quickly appearing on Grace's arm.

"I'm going to take a bath," Jenny declared. "Then I'm going to sleep for a week. Don't wake me unless the world comes to an end, or one of the boys—"

"Go!" Grace commanded. "We'll take care of things. Get some rest."

Jenny staggered from the cabin and wrapped her arm around a post to steady herself. She looked longingly at her own cabin across the valley and then up the hill toward the big house. If she went home now, she would just get caught up in the usual morning chores, dressing the boys and straightening up the mess that was sure to have occurred in the short time she had been gone. Chase could deal with all that.

And she surely would sleep better if she smelled better. Her mind made up, she started up the hill toward the big house.

The house was comfortably quiet in the stillness of early morning. A creak from upstairs let Jenny know that Jason was up and about as she came in through the back entrance. The light from the kitchen gave a welcoming glow, so Jenny pulled off her boots, which were wet from the quickly melting snow, and padded down the hall towards the light. She was surprised to hear Amanda humming as she worked, her tune accented by the clink of a plate and the clack of a metal utensil against a pot or pan. Jenny stood in the doorway and watched as Amanda busily went about the business of preparing breakfast and then artfully arranged it on a tray to be carried up to Caleb. The most surprising thing, however, was that she had her hair tied up with a purple ribbon. It was strange to see Amanda, who had for months made herself as unnoticeable as possible, suddenly take an interest in her appearance. Weary as Jenny was, it brought a smile to her face. She wondered if she should comment on the way Amanda looked.

She didn't get a chance. Amanda picked up the tray and turned to find Jenny standing in the door. She was so startled that she let out a screech and dropped the tray, spilling Caleb's breakfast all over the floor.

"I'm so sorry," Jenny cried as she knelt to help with the mess. "I guess I should have said something."

Amanda covered her face with trembling hands as Jenny cursed herself silently for her stupidity. Why should she think that everything was fine just because Amanda had a bow in her hair?

"It's my fault," Amanda said as she wiped her hands on her sleeves and picked up the pieces. "I just wasn't thinking."

"Poor Caleb," Jenny said quickly to keep the conversation going. "I hope he's not too hungry."

"Jason's helping him with . . . er . . ."

"I'll help you fix him another breakfast," Jenny interrupted as she saw the color rise to Amanda's cheeks. She cursed herself again for overlooking the fact that Caleb would have to answer the call of nature. There was nothing like making an awkward situation even more awkward. She had probably made a mess of things instead of being a successful matchmaker.

Chase would never let her forget it, either. And Lord help her if Zane ever found out about what she was up to.

"I can do it," Amanda declared as she quickly mopped up the bits and pieces with a linen napkin.

Jenny leaned back on her heels, surprised at the passion in Amanda's voice. She suddenly realized that Amanda had used some of the odds and ends of the nice china, which had been seriously depleted after the attack on the house before Christmas. She had gone to a lot of effort to make Caleb's breakfast. She had wanted it to be nice.

"It won't take any time at all," Amanda continued as she stood up with the tray. "Would you like something? I can set an extra plate for you with Jason."

Jenny wondered if the world had suddenly turned

upside down since the strange experiences of the night before. A week ago Amanda would have crawled into the nearest hole to hide after dropping the tray. Now she was offering to fix breakfast for her instead. Maybe she had been right about sending Caleb here, after all.

The Duncan grin spread across her face. "That would be wonderful. I am so tired that I didn't realize how hungry I was."

"So Zane is better?" Amanda asked as she went back to the chore of slicing bacon.

"Yes, his fever broke last night, after Zeb and I packed him in snow."

"Really? It seems like I've read somewhere about that being done before. It makes a lot of sense. A fever makes you hot, so you need to cool down. Snow would do it faster than anything else."

Jenny looked longingly at the coffee pot for a moment but realized it would probably keep her awake in spite of her bone-numbing weariness. She poured herself a glass of milk from a crockery pitcher and sat down at the table.

"Do you like to read a lot?" she asked.

"I always had my nose buried in a book bef. . . ."

Jenny watched a shudder go down Amanda's spine as she straightened quickly at the counter. "You sound just like my brother," Jenny quickly said. "He'd read a book while we were riding to school in the mornings."

"That's pretty much the way it was for me, too. I always got swept away by the stories and the characters."

"Jamie used to read to us all the time. He could make a story come alive."

"He must have been very special."

"He was." *He is. Very special.*

"I wish I could have known him."

Jenny's sapphire-blue eyes widened in surprise. Amanda was actually reaching out to her with compassion.

"You would have loved him. Everyone who met him did."

"Jason said that Fox looks just like him."

"He does," Jenny said with a proud smile. "Acts like him, too."

"Are you two talking about my perfect grandsons?" Jason asked as he came into the kitchen.

"Yes, we are," Jenny said as he brushed a kiss on her cheek.

"How's Zane?" Jason poured himself a cup of coffee and added some milk.

"Worrying about the women."

"Good," Jason laughed. "Looks like everything's going to get back to normal."

"I didn't have a chance to ask how the roundup went. Was there any trouble?"

"Depends on how you look at it. We didn't have any. A lot of the local homesteaders showed up and helped, then took their cattle and went home. But there was some trouble west of here. Mike Johnson showed up in the middle of the night looking for Doc because someone was shot. I didn't get the details."

"I'm sure it will be in the latest edition of the newspaper," Amanda said.

Jason arched an eyebrow at Jenny, who quickly buried her grin in her glass of milk.

"A one sided version of it anyway," Amanda continued.

"Amanda can see through the rhetoric and the politics that make up our local newspaper," Jason explained.

Jenny couldn't remember the last time she had read a newspaper.

"It's owned by the local Cattlemen's Association, so of course it's going to tell their side and no one else's." Amanda set a platter of eggs and bacon down between Jenny and Jason. "Excuse me while I take Caleb his tray," she said as she left.

Jason squeezed Jenny's hand as her mouth dropped open in shock at Amanda's behavior. "You're pretty smart, you know," he said.

"I am?" Jenny asked in amazement.

"You got her thinking about something besides herself."

"I wouldn't have believed it if I hadn't seen it myself."

"So when are you going to start thinking about yourself?"

"I am," Jenny said. "That's why I'm here. A good meal, a hot bath and then a very long nap. I came up here to take the bath. Less hauling involved."

Jason patted her hand in his loving way. "Take care of yourself and my granddaughter."

"Do you know something I don't?" Jenny laughed.

"Just a feeling. Just like I had when I met you and Jamie."

Jenny's eyes glowed as he squeezed her hand. It was good to know she was loved by this man who had come so late into her life. It was good to know that she still had some family left, after all the tragedies that had befallen the ones she loved.

A mighty yawn from Jenny interrupted the peace of the moment.

"Best get on with that bath before you fall asleep at the table," Jason laughed as Jenny's jaws popped in another yawn.

Jenny nodded in agreement and slowly moved toward the room off the kitchen that conveniently held a pump and a small stove for quickly heating water, an idea that Cat had come up with after one of her many trips east to visit her aunt. Jenny blessed her half-aunt for her ingenuity as she prepared the bath and gratefully sank into the tub.

Chapter Nine

He needed leverage. Caleb looked around the bedroom, hoping that an answer to his dilemma would suddenly occur. Usually he just braced himself with his good leg while he pulled on the boot, but today. . . .

He didn't have a leg to stand upon.

The irony of the situation struck him as he sat on the side of the bed and held the boot containing his wooden foot in his hands. Someday he might laugh at this very moment. Someday when he was old and gray and had grandchildren gathered about his knees begging him to tell them stories of what he did in the war.

Fat chance of that ever happening.

Why did he even care?

Because Amanda would be bringing up his breakfast and he didn't want her to think of him as anything less than a man. He smiled ruefully. Actually, his body had proven its maleness quickly enough when she touched him. No problem there at all. He was still feeling the effects of his surprising reaction this morning after spending a restless night chasing dreams and wrestling sheets.

Caleb looked longingly at the window. The mountains in the distance were covered with snow, and even though he could not see the small valley below the house, he knew that it was white with snow also. The reflection of the morning sun bouncing off the surface was bright and gave the air beyond the panes of glass a dazzling glow. Soon everyone would be up and the branding would begin. Later they would all gather in Grace's cabin, teasing and joking with each other, anxious to put the day's work behind them.

Caleb knew he could have done the job. On horseback he was as good as any of them. He could rope the calves by their hind legs and drag them out for branding. He had always been good at roping. If not for this busted leg, he could prove to them that he could still do a good day's work. That he was still an asset. That he was needed.

The sooner he got back on his feet . . . his foot . . . the sooner he could prove it to all of them.

Caleb looked down at his right leg, held rigid and straight by the splint. He crooked the knee of his left leg, positioned the boot over the stocking-covered stump and pulled with all his might. His calf slid in and he stomped the boot against the floor, settling the stump into its hollow.

Now if only he had a pair of crutches, he could get about. But unfortunately, he'd have to make do without them. Caleb grabbed the post of the bed and pulled himself to his feet.

Which was as far as he got. He had forgotten that his broken leg was stiff and straight. Putting pressure on it was not a good idea. For the time being, he was stuck just standing there.

"What are you doing?" Amanda asked as she swept into the room carrying a tray. She stopped in her tracks, and her face flushed a deep red.

Caleb looked down and saw that the pants Jason had lent him had slid indecently low, exposing a thatch of dark hair and pale white skin. He quickly jerked them up and looked past her in embarrassment.

"Jason lent these to me," he explained as a matching red flush crept up from behind the bandages around his ribs, over his bare chest and into his cheeks. Jason had handed him the old pair of pants this morning after ripping open the seam on the side to allow for the splint.

"I'll bring your clothes up as soon as they dry," Amanda said as she set the tray on a table. "Are you sure you should be standing?" Caleb looked around the room, wondering if there was a hole he could crawl in. "It seemed like a good idea at the time," he said with a shrug. "You shouldn't have washed my clothes."

"I had some washing to do anyway." She seemed nervous as she smoothed her hair back behind her ear and looked around the room. "Would you like to eat by the window?"

A slow smile lit Caleb's face. "Yes, I would." The window would give him a view of the outside world. It would give him something else to look at besides the bedroom walls. He was about to go crazy being locked inside, and it hadn't even been a full day yet. Good thing he had managed to escape the war with just losing his leg. He would have died if he'd been sent to prison, and not just from his wound.

He was surprised to see a warm smile come over her face. She was shy about giving it, letting it tentatively lift her cheek before it moved across her mouth. Caleb had never noticed that one of her eye teeth was crooked, turned just slightly to the side and out. Of course, he had never really seen her smile before, either.

She quickly moved the one chair in the room to face the view of the valley below and then pulled a small round table up beside it. Caleb watched from his position by the bed until she seemed satisfied with the arrangement and turned to him.

He had to get from the bed to the chair. Maybe this wasn't such a good idea, after all. He would never be able to do it without her help. Caleb tugged at the waistband of his pants again. The way his luck had been going lately, they'd probably drop to the floor with the first hop, revealing everything he possessed and sending Amanda screaming from the room.

"It's just a few steps," she said before he had a chance to protest and stay where he was. Amanda offered her shoulder as she stepped up beside him.

He gingerly placed his right arm around her shoulder as her left arm timidly crept around his waist.

Caleb gritted his teeth when her hand landed on the ridge of muscles along his side. What he wouldn't give for a quick dunking in a mountain stream. He stole a quick glance down to make sure nothing was showing that shouldn't be as she pressed up against him.

"Can you support yourself on your leg?" Amanda asked as she looked up at him.

Her chin was on a level with his shoulder. She was so thin that he was sure they would both go tumbling to the floor if he let go of the bed post, but he had to try. He could walk on his bad leg. He had done it thousands of times, but he'd always known that he had the other one to depend on. Caleb flexed his thigh and calf and commanded the wooden foot to move, and it did. He kept the other leg straight as Amanda took his weight and he propelled himself forward.

She was stronger than she looked. The fresh scent of recently washed hair wafted up into his nostrils as they moved the few steps to the chair.

She was wearing a hair bow. A purple bow that deepened the color of her eyes from a clear gray to more of an amethyst, as if the darker colors of dawn had all run together. The color struck him like a blow to the stomach as she raised her head after the awkward twisting and turning to get him in position to lower himself into the chair. She looked up just as he sat down, and their eyes met in passing. One heartbeat passed, one second of a day that had barely begun, and her eyes showed him the terrors that haunted her soul.

Was this what it meant when his friends said he could see inside people? Was this the reason why he could capture the essence of a person with pencil and paper? It was no wonder he could not bring himself to pick up his sketch pad again. There was too much pain in the world. He did not want to expose other people's vulnerability.

Caleb wrapped his arms over his chest as a chill ran up his spine. Goose bumps appeared on his back and shoulders and then quickly faded as Amanda handed him a quilt from the bed. She had seen he was cold before he even realized it himself.

"Thanks," he said gratefully as he pulled the quilt over his bare shoulders. The scents from the tray tantalized his stomach, just as her touch had quickened his body. Caleb took a bite of eggs and flashed Amanda a smile of approval.

Her shy smile came back at him from over the pillow she was fluffing as she straightened the bed coverings.

"Oh, Zane is better," she said. "Jenny said his fever broke last night."

Caleb's hand froze. Some friend he was. Zane had been at death's door with a fever, and he was too busy feeling sorry for himself to ask how he was. There would be twice as much work for everyone, with the two of them laid up. Not that he would have been much help, but he could have done the roping, at least.

"Good," he said, realizing that Amanda was waiting for some sort of response. He cautiously looked her way, wondering what she thought of his callousness. "I'm glad. He looked pretty sick the morning we left."

"He was. Jenny said they packed him in snow last night to get his fever down."

"They did? I guess it worked."

"Yes, it did." The tiny spurt of conversation faded as

Caleb went back to the business of eating and Amanda puttered around the room, straightening things that really didn't need straightening. The silence grew between them, accented by each clink of the fork on the plate. Caleb concentrated on chewing silently, certain that each movement of his mouth echoed as loudly as the pigs grunting at the trough.

"Looks like they're getting to work down there," he finally said when he could not stand the silence any longer. Amanda went to the window and watched as the men strode from the cabin toward the barn.

"There's Uncle Cole," she said as they observed Justice romping in the snow beside his long, lanky owner.

"Looks like Zeb's up and about, too."

"What will they be doing?"

"Branding and cutting mostly. It will be a hard day, and the snow will make it harder. The pasture behind the pens will look like a mud hole before the day is done."

"Doesn't sound like much fun for the cows," she said dryly.

Caleb looked up in surprise at her remark. Where had she been hiding her sense of humor? It sounded like something Jake would say, and Caleb had an image of all of them laughing around Grace's table, Amanda included. She was leaning over his breakfast table to look out the window, and her hair brushed across his arm.

He reached out his hand and brushed the soft, dark hair away, fearful that it would drag across his plate and get egg in the long tresses. The strands felt like silk in his hand as they flowed between his fingers.

"Oh, I'm sorry," she said as she gathered her hair away from him and flipped it over her shoulder. "I didn't mean to ruin your breakfast."

"No," Caleb protested. "I'm done. I was just afraid you'd mess up your hair."

She didn't believe him—he could see it on her face. She bent with her gray eyes hidden beneath dark lashes and picked up his dishes.

"I'll bring up your clothes as soon as they're dry," she said over her shoulder as she placed the dishes on the tray and quickly escaped the room.

He shouldn't have touched her. Caleb pulled the quilt around his bare chest as he watched the men mount up and take off toward the pens.

"Woohoo, Caleb!" Jake yelled and threw up his hand toward the house. Caleb waved back, but he knew they couldn't see him.

He shouldn't have touched her hair.

What was she afraid of? Amanda was shaking as she lowered the tray to the kitchen table. Nothing had happened. Nothing beyond the fact that her insides had turned to jelly at the sight of Caleb standing by the bed with his pants sliding down his hips. That sculpted chest and stomach had conjured up disturbing images in her vivid imagination.

Amanda dipped her hands in a pitcher of water and pressed them against her hot cheeks.

The gentle way Caleb's hand had touched her hair had been her undoing.

What was happening? Was her memory confusing

the room upstairs with the room that had been her prison in the whorehouse?

She couldn't recall ever feeling this way before. But opium had confused a lot of the things she had felt, until she couldn't tell the difference between what was reality and what was a horrible nightmare.

She suddenly noticed that water was seeping from under the door of the bathing room.

"Jenny?" Amanda called out.

Nothing.

Amanda knocked timidly on the door. "Jenny?" she asked again. She pressed her ear against the door. She didn't hear a sound. There should have at least been the sloshing of water if Jenny had heard her.

Amanda turned the knob and peered around the door. Sunlight poured through the window and enhanced the golden sheen of Jenny's hair as her head rested against the rim of the tub with her braid scraping against the floor. Her feet rested on top of a stool, where apparently a bucket had sat, waiting to be added to the water. She must have accidentally kicked it over when she stretched her legs out, because the water was now spreading across the floor and under the door.

"Jenny?" Amanda called again. Jenny was as still as death. Amanda went to the tub and touched Jenny's arm.

Jenny sighed and twitched. Her hand, which had been lying on the rim, flopped into the water as she moved around a bit. The water sloshed over her breasts and the small melon shape of her belly.

She had a horrible scar on her breast. What ever could have caused it? Amanda wondered as she looked at the raised ridges over Jenny's heart. It almost looked like a burn. Between Jenny's breasts lay a silver, heart-shaped locket. Its delicacy contrasted sharply with the ugliness of the scar. Or perhaps the scar made the locket seem more delicate and beautiful. Amanda knew somehow that Chase had given it to her.

"Jenny, wake up before you catch your death," Amanda said louder.

Jenny mumbled something unintelligible. She was dead to the world. Amanda tested the water and found it cooling, but luckily there was a bucket of water heating on the stove. She added it to the bath to keep Jenny from getting cold and left to get help.

Amanda tossed her shawl over her shoulders as she raced down the hill toward Grace's cabin. The snow was quickly melting, and the grass was slick beneath the soles of her leather shoes. Slowing down would probably be just as dangerous as running, so she prayed she could stay on her feet and not end up a patient like Caleb. She wondered if he was watching her mad dash down the hill from his window but didn't dare turn to look for fear of losing her balance. She was breathless from her run when she reached the steps of Grace's cabin and burst through the door.

"What's wrong?" Grace asked as Amanda came through the door. Grace's face held a look of terror as she held Jacey against her shoulder. Shannon also seemed worried when she looked up from her work.

"Nothing bad," Amanda assured her. "I'm sorry if I scared you; it's just that Jenny has fallen asleep in the tub and I can't get her to wake up."

Shannon and Grace looked at each other and then laughed. "Thank goodness," Grace exclaimed. "The way you came charging in here, I thought the house was on fire."

"Or poor Caleb had fallen down and broken something else, bless his poor soul," Shannon added.

"Best get Chase," Grace instructed. "Just go around the barns and you should find him."

Amanda took a moment to coo at Jacey before she took off again. Grace arched her eyebrows in surprise as she took off.

"First words I've ever heard come tumbling out of her mouth," Shannon said as the door slammed shut behind Amanda's back.

"Jason said she's been a big help. I guess she just needed to be needed."

"Don't we all," Shannon agreed.

Amanda skirted around the barns and saw the pens. A beautiful gray stallion with a dark face, mane and tail pranced around a huge corral. The horse shied when he saw her and bucked, snorting his contempt at her as she flew by. Amanda barely spared the animal a glance as she spied the men sitting atop their horses beyond the pens.

A wagon was parked off to the side, its back filled with the day's supplies and its bench filled with boys. Chance and Fox were sitting and watching the branding safely out of harm's way.

"Where's your father?" Amanda asked the boys.

"He's over there, and Mama's sleeping," Chance said, pointing to his father, who sat astride a tall buckskin.

"We're not 'sposed to wake her," Fox added.

"I don't think you could even if you wanted to," Amanda said. She climbed onto the wagon and waved her arms madly in Chase's direction.

His dark eyes spotted her immediately, and his horse parted the cattle as he came directly through the herd.

"What's wrong?" he asked, taking a swig from his canteen.

"Jenny's fallen asleep in the tub and I can't get her out."

A flash of white showed against the bronzed skin of his high cheekbones as he smiled.

"Doesn't surprise me a bit," he said. "Hop on." Chase sidled his horse up to the wagon.

What are you afraid of?

Amanda couldn't remember the last time she had been on horseback. Chase was waiting, and beyond she saw Uncle Cole watching her. She could do this. Chase would not hurt her. No one here would hurt her. She swung her leg over the back of the saddle and grabbed hold of Chase's jacket.

He clicked his tongue and the buckskin took off with a leap, causing Amanda to grab harder. She had to put her arms around his waist.

"Sorry," Chase tossed over his shoulder. "I haven't ridden him for a few days and he's feeling his oats."

The horse tossed his head as Chase pulled him in hand and they settled into a soft canter.

"She's not going to drown, is she?" Chase asked as they moved past the barns.

"No, she looked pretty comfortable."

Chase laughed at the thought.

"How's Caleb doing?"

"He's fine, but he'd rather be out here with you."

"I know the feeling," Chase replied.

The strong legs of the buckskin carried them up the hill, flinging mud behind him as he settled into the climb. Chase pulled him to a stop by the back porch and swung his leg over the front to dismount. Before Amanda had a chance to draw a breath, he had swung her down beside him and popped the buckskin on the flank to send him back down the hill.

Chase's long strides rang through the hall as he went toward the kitchen. Amanda followed after him, knowing there would be a mess around the tub to clean up.

The scene she came upon was intimate. She almost felt like a voyeur as she stood in the doorway and watched Chase kneel by the tub.

"Hey, sleepyhead," he whispered. He pulled off his glove and ran a hand down Jenny's cheek. "You're going to freeze if you stay in here much longer."

Amanda couldn't make out the words, but she heard Jenny's voice, thick with sleep as she responded.

"Have you got a blanket I could use?" Chase asked. Amanda went to the shelves that lined the wall behind the door and handed Chase a thick woven blanket. Chase flipped it over his shoulder, then lifted Jenny out of the tub. His body shielded her nudity from Amanda as he wrapped the blanket around her, tucking it in tight under her arms and around her head. He scooped her up in his arms, and Jenny settled against his chest with a sigh, her eyes still tightly closed.

Chase winked at Amanda as he walked past with his precious burden. "Sorry about the mess," he whispered.

"Don't worry about it," she replied.

Amanda picked up a towel to mop up the water but then turned and followed Chase through the hall. She watched from the window as he carried Jenny down the hill to their cabin.

What would it be like to have someone love you like that? What would it be like to know that you would always be protected and cared for? Her heart yearned to know the feeling of safety and contentment that Jenny must feel in Chase's arms.

What made her think that anyone would ever want her after she had been used by so many men?

With a heavy sigh, Amanda returned to the bathing room and mopped up the water that had puddled on the floor. Before she could finish, she was interrupted by the sound of someone pounding on the door.

Amanda peered cautiously around the door frame toward the front door. Who could it be? She was alone in the house, except for Caleb. She was tempted not to answer. *What are you afraid of?* Amanda pushed her hair behind her ear and went to the door.

It was the sheriff, or she guessed it was because of the badge he was wearing. "Is the doc here?" he asked as he tipped his hat.

"No, he left early this morning with a man named Johnson," Amanda replied.

129

"Thank you," he said and handed her a newspaper. "I thought Jason might want to see this." He was back on his horse and galloping down the drive before she had the door shut. Amanda unfolded the newspaper and looked at the headline that filled the page.

President Abraham Lincoln was dead.

Chapter Ten

Amanda carried Caleb's breakfast in on a tray as she had been doing ever since his accident. This morning, however, the tray also held a vase with one blood-red rose. Caleb was sitting up in bed, waiting for her with a welcoming smile on his handsome face. The sheet was folded down to his waist, revealing the smooth skin of his chest and abdomen. The whiteness of the linen contrasted with the warm browns of his hair, his eyes and the oak headboard behind him. A breeze billowed in through the curtains, causing the dazzling white panels to dance mischievously across the bed, teasing her with a sudden vision before his face disappeared again behind the muslin. The red of the rose was vibrant against the starkness of the other colors as she moved closer to him.

Caleb reached out and took the tray as she sat down on the edge of the bed. His smile broadened as he placed the tray on the opposite side of the bed and *picked up the rose. His other hand moved up her arm and behind her neck, pulling her close as the hand holding the rose brushed the soft blossom across her cheek. Their lips touched gently, briefly, before the salty taste of blood spoiled the kiss. Amanda pulled back in horror and saw the petals of the rose falling onto the white sheet covering Caleb's lap, dry and dead. Caleb looked in disgust at the stem, which was covered with thorns, piercing his fingers and causing huge droplets of blood to drip onto the dry petals.*

"It's ruined," he said. "Ruined."

Amanda sat up in the darkness of her room with a gasp. The dream had felt so real that she touched her lips, certain there would be blood on them. Nothing was there, of course. In the past, kissing was the thing she had most tried to avoid. The rest could be tolerated if she closed her eyes and let the opium carry her away, but the kissing . . .

A vision of heavy hands holding her head immobile while a thick tongue poked at her mouth gagged her; the blankets weighed heavily on her body. Amanda kicked them away and stumbled to her window. She lifted the sash and sucked in great gulps of the brisk night air until she was shivering in the darkness.

Ruined. Amanda slid to the floor and leaned her head back against the sill as she wrapped her arms around her knees. She was ruined. No man would want her, and she certainly didn't want to be with a man. So why was she dreaming of Caleb? Why did the sight of his bare skin cause her insides to quiver and quake with wanting?

Because Wade Bishop had made her into a whore. But she had never taken any pleasure in it before. At first it had been painful, but eventually she had gotten used to it. Death would have been preferable but that choice had been taken from her, so she did as she was told and tolerated the men. Then she would be given her reward and she wouldn't have to feel or care anymore.

So what was she feeling now? The sensations were unfamiliar, and because she did not know them, she feared them.

She didn't want to think about the past anymore. Amanda rose on bare feet to go down to the library to find something to read. Reading sometimes gave her an escape from the Fear, and she hoped it would help her forget these new feelings, too.

A sound drifted to her in the hall. Restless tossing and half-spoken words came through the door of Caleb's room, which had been left slightly ajar. Amanda moved softly to the door, her toes curling up against the cold of the polished wooden floorboards as she stood and willed the sounds of her breathing and her heart pumping to subside so she could listen.

"Jake . . . Willie . . . watch out." The words were disjointed, punctuated by the rustling of the sheets.

Amanda pushed the door open, praying the hinges would not creak; nothing sounded except for the gentle movement of air. Her eyes had grown accustomed to the darkness, and she could see his face, contorted with a dream as he tossed against his pillow.

"No. *No!*" he said, still dreaming, the words ripping into the dark peace of the night.

"Caleb?" she called out from the door.

A slight gasp sounded; then he sat halfway up and leaned hard on his left elbow as his right hand covered his eyes.

"Amanda?" he asked. His voice was hoarse.

"You were dreaming," she said.

"Did I wake you?"

"No. I was dreaming, too."

The creak of the mattress sounded as Caleb settled back onto his pillows. "Good or bad?" he asked.

Amanda stood in the doorway, thinking about the dream. "A little of both, I think." The first part had been good and sweet; the first part had been wonderful. "How about you?"

"The war. I dream about the war."

Amanda nodded in the darkness and then realized that Caleb probably couldn't see her reaction. She took a step into the room. "It must have been horrible."

Caleb's head turned toward the window. "It was." She could just make out his eyes when he turned back to her. "But no worse than what you went through," he said softly.

Amanda's heart skipped a beat. How could he compare the two? He had fought in a war. All she had done was become compliant. She swallowed hard. "I never had to watch people die. I never had to kill anyone." She had wanted to, at first. She had wanted to kill them all.

"I see their faces sometimes," he said.

"The faces of your friends?"

"Of my enemies." He turned to the window again. "Of the men I killed."

"They would have killed you if given a chance."

"Yes, they would have." The dark eyes turned back to her. "But I still see their faces."

"You did what you had to do to survive."

"Just like everyone else who was there," he said. "Just like you did."

She hated his knowing what she had been through. She had never mentioned it, but she was aware that everyone on the ranch knew. How could they not? They all knew what kind of man Wade Bishop was. They all knew where she had been found and what condition she had been in. Uncle Cole had been there. Jenny and Chase had seen her, along with Cat and Ty, whom she couldn't even remember meeting. They had surely discussed it many times among themselves. *Be careful of Amanda. She's fragile. She's been a whore and an opium addict.*

Ruined. Caleb knew what she was. She was ruined. And he thought she had done what she had done in order to survive. He didn't know she had done it because she had no choice. She would have chosen to die if she'd been given a chance. She wasn't even allowed that luxury.

"I didn't want to survive, Caleb." There. She had said it. She didn't want to live. Why should she? What did she have to live for? It wasn't as if she had a future or anything to offer the rest of the world. So why was she still alive? There were plenty of opportunities now for her to end her life. All she had to do was pick up a gun. "I wanted to die." Why was it so much easier to say what she was feeling in the dark?

"I'm glad you didn't."

Time seemed to stop as she took in his words. He was glad she was alive. Someone would have cared for him if she had not been here, so it wasn't because she was fixing him meals and plumping his pillows. He was glad that it was she, Amanda, caring for him. She had a purpose beyond taking up space in an unused upstairs bedroom. How many years had she just been taking up space? She drew in a deep breath of air as if doing it for the first time in her life. She was alive.

She had life. She had something left to give.

She cleared her throat before she spoke. "Do you need anything while I'm up?"

"No, I'm fine."

"Well, good night."

"Good night."

She went back to her room, her task of searching for a book forgotten. She had left the window up, and the cold air chilled her as she sank into the softness of the mattress and pulled the covers up over her body. She liked the feeling of the chill on her face and the warmth under the quilts. She snuggled under their thickness, listening to the sounds of the earth coming awake through the open window. It was going to be a beautiful day. She could just feel it.

The morning, when it came, was beautiful. The earth felt as if it had been saving itself for this very moment to burst into the glory of spring after winter's last-minute snowfall. The lone cottonwood tree that grew at the front of the house was covered with tiny buds, and a pair of meadowlarks flitted to and fro, busy building a nest.

Amanda quickly dressed as she heard Jason helping Caleb with his morning ablutions. Jason would be looking for his breakfast, but he would just have to wait. There was something important she needed to do.

Once more her feet flew down the hill to Grace's cabin. Like the day before, she had a specific purpose for her mad dash.

"Good morning," Amanda called out as she burst through the door again.

"Hold still," Shannon said to Zane, who was doing his best to dodge her attempts to put a thick white paste on his face.

"Are you kidding? The cure is worse than the disease," he protested.

"Well, ye don't want to have scars, do ye?" Shannon asked in exasperation, her frustration bringing out her Irish brogue.

Zane's face screwed up as he thought about the consequences. "No," he said finally.

"Then hush and take your medicine," Shannon said as she picked up another dollop of paste and spread it under his neck. "And then take this and put it on all the places that I'd rather not see."

"How do you know you don't want to see them? Could be they're better than what you're looking at now."

Shannon shoved a gob of paste into his mouth, which brought on a fit of gagging and coughing from Zane and a giggle from Amanda.

"What brings you down our way this morning?" Grace asked.

"Caleb needs his sketch book," she replied. "Do you know where I can find it?"

Grace went to a cabinet in a corner of the room. She returned with a sketch book and a narrow wooden box that held an assortment of pencils and pieces of charcoal.

"Thank goodness," Grace said as she handed the things to Amanda.

"Also, did Caleb have crutches, before?"

"He did, but they were lost in the fire after the ranch was attacked," Grace said. "Shannon and I are going in to town today; we'll stop by Doc's and see if he has a set."

"Do you need me to watch Jacey?"

"No, I'm going to take her along. It's such a pretty day, I thought she might enjoy an outing."

Amanda nodded in agreement. It was a pretty day.

"How's Jenny doing?"

"She's still resting up. The past few weeks have taken a lot out of her. Chase came by with the boys for breakfast and said she was having trouble getting up this morning. She'll probably be starving when she wakes up."

"Can I fix lunch for the men?"

Grace pointed to a pot of stew bubbling on the stove. "It's ready; all you have to do is dish it out when they show up. We made extra biscuits with breakfast, if you want to warm them up. Zane's supposed to be in charge of lunch, but I'm sure he'd appreciate your help."

"Tell Caleb I'll be up to see him in a bit," Zane added through the paste around his mouth. "As soon as this stuff soaks in."

"I'll tell him," Amanda said. "I'd best get back so I can make his breakfast."

Amanda clutched the sketch book and box to her chest and left the cabin in the same whirlwind that had carried her in.

"Is that the same girl who was hiding in her room at Christmas time?" Zane asked after she left.

"Kind of hard to believe, isn't it?" Grace laughed. "I'm just so grateful that Caleb wants his sketch book back. I didn't think he was ever going to pick it up again."

"It's not like he's got anything else to do," Zane said. "How long before this stuff soaks in?"

"Give it time," Shannon said.

"I feel like I fell in the lard bucket."

"You look like it, too," Grace said as she surveyed his scabby face.

"I'm glad that everyone here has an opinion about my looks. Hard to believe that just last week everyone was praying for my recovery."

"We're glad you're better, Zane, and you know it. It's just that when you were feverish, you weren't complaining so much."

"Dang it, Grace. I got a right to complain about something. Just look at me."

Grace dropped a kiss on top of his head. "You're right. But if you let Shannon take care of you, you'll be back to your old self in no time."

139

"All right," Zane grumbled. "But tomorrow I'm going to work. And I don't mean cooking and cleaning."

"Suit yourself."

Amanda passed Jason on her way up the hill. "What about your breakfast?" she asked breathlessly.

"I ate something; don't worry about me," he replied.

She felt a pang of guilt at neglecting him, but her excitement at presenting Caleb with his sketch book overrode it.

Surely he would be thrilled to have it back. Everyone had said he hadn't drawn since he'd returned from the war and now he had the time and the opportunity to do so. She couldn't wait to see the look on his face when she gave it to him.

The temptation to peek inside was too great for her natural curiosity, so she opened the book while waiting for his breakfast to cook.

The detail was amazing. Some of the faces she recognized, some she did not, but as she flipped the pages the people became familiar to her. Even though she did not remember her, she could see enough resemblance to Jason in one young woman to know it was Cat. There was a drawing of Grace with her sleeves rolled up and her arms covered with a dusting of flour, but her poise and natural elegance were still evident, even as she worked the dough. Jake and Zane were easy, although there was something different about Jake now, as if he were more at peace with the world. In some of the early drawings he looked downright scary. There were portraits of another cowboy that she didn't recognize, but she deduced it was Ty since there were drawings of him with Cat.

She recognized Chase and was amazed at how long his hair had been then, almost reaching to his waist. The first time she had met him it had been short, but now he was letting it grow again. The man with him in many of the drawings had to be Jamie, although there were no scars on his face. His eyes were the same as Jenny's and his smile also, but his nose and chin were both broader than hers. Amanda was sure that his son Fox would look just like him when he grew up. There were drawings of Jenny, too, and pictures of all three of them together.

She saw a drawing of her Uncle Cole sitting on the porch of the cabin with his legs stretched out on the rail and Justice lying beneath him, both of them staring off into the distance. Everyone she knew on the ranch was there except for the cowboys Dan and Randy and Zeb, who had all come after Caleb left for the war.

Of course there were none of Caleb, but a drawing of a man on horseback, done from the rear, captured her attention. The horse and rider were poised on top of a hill, surveying the countryside in the distance. It could have been any of the men, but something about the breadth of the shoulders and the narrowness of the waist made Amanda think of Caleb. Chase was bigger than this figure, Jake seemed leaner and Zane stockier. It was Caleb, she was sure of it—a vague self-portrait done before he left for the war.

What thoughts had gone through his mind as he prepared himself for the days ahead? Had he been frightened of what was to come? What had led him to go back to a country that he had left behind after he had been orphaned? Had he gone out of friendship or because of politics?

The smell of burning fat brought her back to the present, and she jumped up to turn the sausage, which had gotten a bit too crisp on one side. It wouldn't do for breakfast, so she set it aside to feed to Justice later on and started all over again. At this rate, by the time she got breakfast prepared, it would be time for lunch. She paid attention to her task this time and soon had the tray ready for delivery. She stuffed the sketch book and box into the waistband of her skirt at her back so she could surprise Caleb with it.

"Sorry I'm so late," she said as she entered the room. Caleb was sitting in the chair looking out the window. And he had shaved. She noticed the clean line of his jaw as she moved around to the front of the chair. He was wearing a shirt, and Jason's pants, ripped open to fit his splint, were held firmly in place by a belt.

"No need to rush," Caleb said. "It's not like I'm going anywhere." He pointed at his splinted leg, which now rested on a footstool from the study.

Amanda chastised herself for not realizing earlier that he would have been much more comfortable with his leg propped up. She really wasn't much of a nurse when it came right down to it, and on top of that failing, she was late with his breakfast. She hoped the sketch book would make up for her inadequacies as a caregiver.

She set the tray down on the table and then backed away so he wouldn't see his surprise.

"This is nice," Caleb commented. "Bacon and eggs one day, hotcakes and sausage the next. I could get used to this."

"I know you're just being nice," Amanda replied as she made up his bed. "You'd much rather be down at Grace's with your friends."

"It does get a bit lonely sitting up here all day when I know they're down there having all the fun."

"Work is fun?" Amanda asked. Caleb turned to see if she was teasing, which she was.

"I think you know what I mean," he said as he flashed her a grin.

"Zane said he'd be up in a bit, just as soon as the salve soaks in."

"Salve?"

"Something that Shannon was smearing on his face. He's marked up pretty bad from the pox."

"Poor Zane. He's always relied on his looks and charm to get him through the day."

"So now he's down to just charm?"

"You tell me, how bad is it?"

"He might have a few scars, but I don't think his looks will suffer much."

"Depends on who's doing the telling. If I know him, he'll be acting like his nose fell off or something. I'm sure he won't have any trouble getting the whores at Maybelle's to feel . . . sorry . . . for . . ." Caleb stopped as he realized what he had said.

Amanda froze where she stood, the towel she was folding suddenly stiff between her hands as she fought to get the Fear under control.

"I'm sorry," Caleb said. "Amanda?"

She was gone, the towel falling forgotten to hang haphazardly off the side of the bed. There was a soft slap on the wooden floor as she fled. She had dropped something, but Caleb couldn't see what lay on the other side of the bed.

A curse left his lips, sounding all the more violent in the heavy silence of the house. Where had she gone? Was she in her room? Had she gone downstairs? Was she at this very moment running down the drive to get as far away from him and his stupidity as she could get?

Why didn't they just shoot him?

Chapter Eleven

He was an idiot. A mindless idiot. Caleb slumped in frustration in his chair. If only he could move. He looked down at his useless legs, and frustration boiled up inside him. He needed to lash out at something, anything. The table holding his breakfast was convenient, and he swiped his hand at the tray, sending the remnants of his meal flying into a corner. Half-eaten pancakes stuck to the floor, along with a crisp piece of sausage. Coffee splattered against the wall and dripped down into a dark brown puddle.

He cursed again when he realized that he had just made a mess that Amanda would have to clean up. He should be horsewhipped before they shot him.

So what was he going to do about the situation? He couldn't just leave this mess.

Knowing he was probably going to regret it later on, Caleb braced his arms on the sides of the chair and pushed himself to a standing position, balancing himself on his wooden foot while using the back of the chair as a crutch. He tentatively placed the foot of his broken leg on the floor and exerted pressure on it to see if it would support some of his weight.

It would, but not without bringing tears to his eyes and beads of sweat to his face. He'd just have to deal with the pain. There was no way in hell that he was going to let Amanda clean up after him. She had done enough.

The small table that had held his tray was sturdy, so he pushed it out ahead of him in case he lost his balance. He moved a step, and then grimaced in pain as his leg protested against the abuse.

Ignore the pain. He had all day, all night and the day after that to get over it. Sweat dripped into his eyes, and he took another step. He swiped at the sweat with his sleeve, gritting his teeth as the throbbing shot from his thigh down into his toes and then back again. At least these toes were feeling something, which was more than he could say for the ones that were missing. Of course, he was used to the pain that came from the end of his shin bone from supporting his weight against a piece of carved-out wood. The skin flap was callused, and he padded it by wearing socks over his stump, but there would always be pain. He could handle it.

Another few steps and he would be there. Caleb braced his arms against the corner and leaned into it, taking in gulps of air, which was difficult with his ribs wrapped so tightly.

How was he supposed to get down to the floor to

clean up the mess? He had a wooden ankle that wouldn't bend and a knee that was held straight against a set of splints. He'd just have to get down there and worry about getting up after he was done.

Caleb turned himself into the corner and used the wall as a brace to slowly slide to the floor. He turned the tray right side up, picked up the plate, which was in three pieces, and used one piece to scoop up the remains of his breakfast.

He didn't know what to do about the coffee. He debated taking off his shirt and then remembered the towel that Amanda had been folding before he had stuck his foot in his mouth.

He scooted toward the bed on his backside. At least he wasn't crawling, he thought, although he should be. He should be crawling to Amanda right now and begging her forgiveness for being what Shannon would call a dolt.

He pulled himself up with his arms and managed to reach across the bed and grab the towel, although the pain it caused made him realize that he had better take it easy before he did serious damage to himself.

Mopping up the coffee wasn't too difficult, although the wall was stained and would have to be scrubbed. For now he just hoped no one would notice the spill. Caleb decided he'd point it out to Jason and volunteer to paint the wall when he was on his feet again.

If that day ever came.

Caleb sat with his back pressed against the corner, too tired to decide what to do next. With his luck, he'd still be sitting in the same place tonight.

"Dang," he muttered to the floor. He threw his head back against the wall and gave it a good knock just because he thought he deserved it.

Maybe he should think about getting up.

There was something lying on the floor. He could see just a corner of what looked like a book on the other side of the bed. Caleb twisted his head sideways and down. He saw a small wooden box and what looked like . . .

His sketch book.

Caleb sat up suddenly. Amanda had somehow gotten his sketch book. But why? Why did she have it? Did she expect him to draw her a picture? How could he, when all he saw in his mind was scenes from the war? Nameless faces and destroyed places that would never be the same again. They were ever present in his mind; he didn't need to put them on paper.

He hadn't put pencil to paper since the day he'd lost his leg. All of the drawings that he had done of his friends during the war had been lost then, fed to a fire to keep him and Cat alive as she struggled to get him home.

Lost sketches were nothing compared to a lost baby.

Dang. His sketch book.

Footsteps in the hallway alerted him that someone was coming, but unfortunately he still hadn't come up with a way to get off the floor. Might as well face the music . . .

"Dang, Caleb."

It was Zane. A feeling of relief washed over Caleb as

he looked up and saw his friend. "What are you doing on the floor?"

"Eating my breakfast. What does it look like I'm doing?"

Zane stood in the doorway and looked around the room. "Making a mess?" He bent to pick up the pencils and charcoal that had spilled from the box; carefully packed the things back in and then pitched the box and sketch book onto the bed.

"Do you need a hand?" he asked with a bemused expression on his face.

"Yes," Caleb sighed and stuck his arm out toward Zane.

When Zane hauled him up, he teetered precariously for a moment before settling onto his wooden foot. Zane hooked his foot around the chair leg and slid it over, turning Caleb until the chair hit the back of his legs and he landed on it with a plop.

"Thanks," Caleb said, unsure if he should be grateful.

"So what were you doing on the floor?"

"What difference does it make?"

"I don't know, people are just acting strange around here and I'm trying to figure it out." Zane sat down on the edge of the bed. Caleb took a moment to look at the scabs on Zane's face. "You look like someone tried to peel your skin off."

Zane rubbed his face. "Thanks for noticing."

"So, who's acting strange?"

"Well, Amanda, for one thing,"

"Amanda?"

"Yes. This morning she was all happy and laughing, and then a few minutes ago she blew into Grace's and told me to get the hell out."

"She didn't say that."

"No, but it felt like she said it. I was supposed to be in charge of lunch since Grace and Shannon took off for town, but Amanda told me to get out and she'd take care of it, so here I am. Then I come in here and find you sitting on the floor looking at what's left of your breakfast." Zane looked at the broken pieces of china. "You had a fight with her, didn't you?"

"No."

Zane crossed his arms and raised his eyebrows.

"I said something stupid," Caleb confessed.

"You said something stupid? I thought I was the only one who did that."

"No, you're not."

"So what did you say?"

"I mentioned Maybelle's and the whores."

"What's so bad about that?"

"Think about it, Zane."

"You mean because Amanda was a prostitute?"

Caleb shot a look at Zane that would have scared another man.

"Well, she was," Zane said in protest.

"No, she wasn't. She was a prisoner and forced to do things she didn't want to do. The girls at Maybelle's do it because they want to."

Zane thought about Caleb's words for a minute. "I guess you're right about that. Most of them act as if they like it." He pondered the matter a bit more. "You know, I really can't imagine a little girl telling her mama that she wanted to be a whore when she grew up, can you?"

"No, but the girls at Maybelle's can leave whenever they want. There aren't any locks on the doors or bars on the window, and they aren't fed opium every day so they'll do as they're told."

"I guess you've got a point. I'll have to ask Missy about it next time I see her." Zane scratched his chin.

Caleb shook his head. Zane was so predictable. "I hear you were pretty sick," he said as he looked at the scabs.

Zane shrugged. "I guess so. I don't remember anything much about it except that I dreamed there was a fox sitting next to my head, and when I opened my eyes I could see snow falling on my face, which at the time felt pretty good."

"Everyone was worried about you."

"I know," Zane said. "It's nice to have people worry about me instead of fussing at me."

"Quit giving them so much to fuss about."

Zane laughed. "So tell me, just how exactly did you break your leg?"

"I got caught between Jenny's wild stud and a mad cow."

"Ouch!"

"It wasn't pretty."

"And Jenny sent you up here to heal."

"Yes."

Zane laughed again.

"What's so funny?"

"I think Jenny's got some plans for you and Amanda."

"What?"

"Amanda has come out of her shell since she's been taking care of you." Zane explained.

"What are you saying, Zane?" Caleb asked between gritted teeth.

Zane held up his hands in mock defense. "I didn't say a thing. Nope, you didn't hear a word from me."

"Zane," Caleb ground out in frustration. Zane fell back on the bed and laughed for a minute before he sat up again with Caleb's sketch book in his hand.

"Grace sure did get excited when Amanda said you wanted your sketch book."

Caleb looked out the window with a scowl marring his handsome features. "I didn't ask for it," he said softly. A muscle in his jaw twitched, the only sign of the emotion that was raging inside him.

Zane looked at his friend for a moment before he dropped the book on the bed. "Well, at least it's here when you're ready for it." Zane stood and looked out the window. In the valley below the men of the ranch were coming in to eat. Chase and Zeb each carried a little boy on his shoulders, and Zane could hear their wild screams of joy as the two men pretended to charge each other. "Looks like lunch time," Zane said, laying a hand on Caleb's shoulder. "I'll send some stew up with Amanda." He stretched and yawned. "I've got to do the dishes," he announced proudly. "Then I'm going to take a long nap."

"Don't bother sending anything up for me," Caleb said. "I'm not really hungry." The truth was, he didn't want to cause Amanda any more trouble. Best if she stayed as far away from him and his insensitive words as she could get.

"Suit yourself." Zane picked up the tray. "I'll take care of this for you," he said with a sly wink.

"Zane," Caleb said. "Thanks."

"Hey, you'd do the same for me."

He would. It was a safe feeling to know that they could all depend on each other.

Caleb watched from the window as Zane went down the hill. He could easily imagine the camaraderie going on in Grace's cabin over lunch. He wondered if Amanda would join in with the easy banter or if she would remain silent and in the shadows as was her way.

She had not remained silent the night before. Caleb's mind drifted back to the conversation, which seemed almost as dreamlike as his nightmares. He had awakened to see her standing wraithlike in the doorway, no more visible than a shadow and a glimpse of ethereal white gown. Had he been dreaming? He had. But the dreams that came after her visit were more disturbing than the ones of the war that had come before. Quick visions of Amanda's quiet face, the feel of her gentle touch and a longing that did not disappear with the advent of morning. His mind was filled with thoughts that were better off left to the darkness of night.

He really needed to get out of the house and away from Amanda. He wasn't doing her any good at all.

And what exactly were the plans that Jenny had for them?

Chapter Twelve

The war was over. Grace walked into the big house and handed Jason the newspaper, along with a telegram from Cat. The war was over and she was coming home.

"She said to look for her and Ty next week. They're taking the first train they can get on," Jason said as he beamed over the telegram.

"The entire town has gone crazy," Grace reported. "You can hardly walk down the street without getting kissed or shot."

Gunshots sounded from the valley below, accompanied by some loudly screamed yee-haws.

"Shannon went down to tell the boys," Grace informed him.

Amanda stuck her head into Jason's study. "Is something wrong?"

"No," Jason replied with a broad smile. "Something's

right for a change. The war is over." He looked at Grace. "I think this calls for a celebration."

"I had a feeling you would say that," Grace replied. "I got provisions for a party."

Jason dropped a peck on Grace's cheek and looked over at Amanda. "Do you want to tell Caleb or should I?"

"I'll tell him," Amanda volunteered.

"There's a set of crutches in the wagon!" Grace called out after her.

The first shot jolted Caleb awake from the restless sleep he had fallen into as the boredom of the afternoon set in. His broken leg throbbed angrily from the morning's abuse, and the start the gunshot gave him didn't help the situation. His hand went to his thigh, where the pain was centered.

Another yee-haw quickly sounded. Caleb looked through the open window and saw Dan and Randy standing in the valley shooting off their guns. The noise was riling Storm Cloud, who snorted and bucked in his corral. "Go ahead and have your fun, you big stud," Caleb said to the horse. Jenny ran by, and Chase met her in the middle of the yard, followed by the boys. He bent her backward into a big kiss. Caleb could see the surprise on her face as Chase spoke to her, and then she threw her arms around his neck and he swung her around in a big circle. Chance and Fox jumped up and down as the antics continued.

"The war is over," Amanda announced from the door.

"I figured as much," Caleb said. Wouldn't it be great to be down there celebrating with his friends?

The war was over. The soldiers could go home. Which side had won? Did it even matter? The conflict had been so long, and so much had happened that he couldn't even remember his reasons for going off to fight. Too many men had been lost. Too many lives had been ruined. But he and his friends had survived.

"Jason's throwing a party to celebrate." Amanda came up slowly, cautiously, behind his chair and placed her hand on the back of it. "I'm sorry I left you alone so long this afternoon."

Caleb touched the hand that graced the back of his chair. The fingers were slim and soft. He remembered how arousing her touch had been on his body when she washed him. "I'm sorry for what I said, Amanda."

The silence in the room was deafening, all the more so for the noise outside. Caleb looked at Amanda's reflection in the windowpane. Her face was impassive, her eyes downcast as she searched for words to answer him. The fingers beneath his hand could have belonged to a dead woman, they were so still. She had not answered him. Maybe there was no answer. Caleb let his hand drop from hers. Maybe she should just smack him in the back of the head and tell him to go . . .

"You didn't say anything inappropriate, Caleb." She dropped her hand from his chair. "Those things are a fact of life."

"Not of your life." He watched her reflection in the glass. "Not anymore."

"I know. I try to forget it happened, but sometimes the memories just come back too hard and too fast."

"Especially when someone says something stupid and uncalled for."

"You were talking about Zane, that's all." Amanda's eyes rose and saw Caleb's watching her in the window. She turned and walked toward the bed. "I've got to learn how to cope. I can't hide in my room for the rest of my life." She picked up the crutches that she had left by the bed. "Grace brought these back from town. Do you think you can manage the stairs?"

"Anything to get out of this room," Caleb said with a relieved smile. He was beginning to feel that he would spend the rest of his life in this room. It had only been a week, but they had been the loneliest days of his life.

Amanda handed him the crutches and he used them to stand, his mind reminding his body that it was the other leg he had to favor now. "Being able to use my knee would help," he said as he teetered precariously while trying to hold his broken leg out of harm's way.

"Maybe we could change the splints?" Amanda offered. "Of course, there might be a reason why the doctor wants you to keep it straight," she added.

"There is. He wants me to be miserable." Caleb leaned heavily on the crutches. The pain on his stump was horrible, but he would not give up the chance to be mobile again.

Amanda laughed at his words.

"You should do that more often." His dark eyes glowed as he looked at her.

"What?" Amanda asked, wondering what she had done.

157

"Laugh."

Her fingers brushed against her lips as she realized that she had indeed laughed. A smile peeked from behind her hand and then traveled to her eyes, brightening the gray depths with a sense of wonder.

"See?" Caleb said, smiling back. He fought the urge to touch her. His hand ached to feel the softness of her cheek, so he kept it tightly gripped on the crutch under his arm. Touching her would lead to nothing but pain for her, and for him. Still, the yearning was there, calling to him in a voice that was hard to resist. Part of him wanted to think that if he touched her at just the right moment, the pain that hid in the depths of her soul would go away.

A door slammed, followed by a loud "yee-haw."

"Caleb!" yelled Jake and Zane, attacking the stairs like a herd of horses. They swept into the room and grabbed him from either side, settling him between them by making a seat out of their arms.

"Hope you're up to traveling," Jake said as he pushed the crutches toward Amanda.

"Depends on where we're going."

"Downstairs for a party," Zane said, his dimple flashing amidst the scabs on his face. The smell of his breath suggested that a bottle of something had already been uncorked. The last party they'd held at the ranch had been a doozy, followed by a collective hangover. One look at his friends' faces showed Caleb that they were in for the same tonight.

Jake and Zane carted him from the room, with Amanda following. Caleb considered himself lucky when they dropped him in a chair in the parlor. They had, after all, only banged his broken leg on the wall one time. Jake and Zane took off again with a wink and a promise to return with some supplies for the party.

Chance and Fox rushed in next, their blue eyes wide with excitement. "Caleb, the war is over," they both announced breathlessly. Caleb ruffled their hair with his hands as they dashed off, caught up in the joy that had suddenly come over the inhabitants of the ranch.

Caleb smiled and watched the boys go. To them, war was nothing more than a word and a game they played with a set of painted soldiers that Jason kept in a box in his study. To the rest of the country, peace meant the end of a painful era. Caleb prayed it would be an end to the death and destruction that had torn the country apart. The war was over. It was time to get back to the business of living. He looked up at Amanda, who was still holding his crutches and watching, the comings and goings. Just watching, as he had been doing ever since he came home.

"The boys don't quite know what to do with themselves, do they?" he said to Amanda as she leaned the crutches against his chair. *Just as I don't know.* He left that thought unspoken. What was he going to do with himself for the rest of his life?

"I know how they feel sometimes," she replied, her hand lingering on his chair. Caleb once again fought the urge to touch her. But he felt as if she might be reaching out to him in her quiet way. Some of the things she said led him to believe that maybe she wanted to . . .

Amanda left the room. He wished he had touched her.

* * *

"Wish I could ride him," Jenny said wistfully as she sat on the fence that enclosed Storm Cloud's corral. How long had it been since she'd taken off across the prairie without a care in the world?

"Don't even think about it," Chase warned her. "There is no way you're getting on this brute in your condition."

Jenny made a face at Chase as he settled into the saddle. Storm Cloud tossed his head in protest, but the hand on his reins was steady and in full control.

"What this guy needs is a good run," Chase said as he patted the stallion's proudly arched neck.

"Don't we all," she sighed.

Chase looked down at Jenny in that superior way he had. If she weren't so madly in love with him, she'd be infuriated, she decided as she stuck her tongue out at him. Chance, Fox and Justice watched the exchange from their places next to the gate.

Chase urged the stallion into a trot around the corral and then put him through a series of turns and stops.

"Open the gate, boys," he said when he was satisfied. Chance and Fox jumped on the gate and lifted the loop, riding on the bars as it swung open. Storm Cloud took off for freedom with a hop, only to be quickly settled by a sharp command from Chase. The stallion moved out into a full run as Chase sent him down the trail that led to the plains.

Jenny watched with her hand shielding her eyes from the midday sun as horse and rider topped a ridge. Suddenly Storm Cloud reared, his forelegs pawing at the sky. Chase fought to control the horse as he turned skittishly in a circle, fighting against his rider's desire to go forward.

"What in the world?" Jenny murmured as a strange clamor filled her ears. Justice watched with head cocked to the side. Suddenly the hackles on his back rose and he took off toward Chase at a full run.

Another dog topped the ridge. This one seemed smaller than Justice and had a patch of white on its chest. The two dogs met in the valley with all the ferocity of two trains churning toward each other at top speed. Fur flew and ferocious growls sounded as they rolled and tore at each other, stirring up a massive cloud of dust.

"Boys, go get Cole," Jenny instructed as she watched the dogfight. The boys took off to do as they were bade. Chase had finally settled Storm Cloud down, although the stallion still tossed his head anxiously against the bit.

"What's going on?" Cole asked as he came running from the cabin. Grace and Shannon appeared behind him, while Jake, Zane and Zeb came out from the barn. Jenny pointed at the dogs, but then stopped to look in amazement as a white wave rolled over the ridge. Storm Cloud reared and bucked as the wave surrounded him.

"That horse is going to toss him, Miz Jenny," Zeb said. The wave flowed down the hill with two riders coming along behind. At about the same time, a covered wagon approached by way of the road. One of the riders stayed on the ridge with Chase, while the other kept coming, parting the wave like Moses had parted the Red Sea.

"Are those sheep?" Zane asked, aghast.

"Sure does smell like it," Jake said. Shannon and Grace grabbed the boys and pulled them on to the porch, while the men joined Jenny on the fence. The area between the houses and the barns filled up with a flock of bawling sheep as the dogs continued rolling and snarling in the dirt.

"We're home!" Cat announced as she rode up to the fence.

"We were wondering what the holdup was," Chase said as he and Ty looked down from their mounts at the melee in the valley below. "We figured you'd be showing up sometime last week."

"We ran into a bit of trouble," Ty said.

"You don't say?" Chase replied, as if a flock of sheep showing up on a cattle ranch were a common occurrence. "Cat have anything to do with it?"

"In a roundabout way." Ty pointed to the wagon. "Those two might have a different story."

"And they are?" Chase asked.

"Pharaoh and his daughter Cleopatra. Recently come west from Macon, Georgia, and former owners of these sheep."

"Former?"

"Former."

"I reckon you only want to tell it once."

Ty nodded wearily and looked about the valley. "It's good to be home, Chase."

"It's good to have you back," Chase replied as he studied his friend. The war had aged Ty. There were lines around his mouth and his steel-blue eyes seemed harder, closed off, lonely. "So what are we going to do with the sheep?" Chase asked.

Ty shook his head and laughed. "I have a few ideas in mind."

"Roast lamb sounds good," Chase said with an evil glint in his dark eyes. He rubbed Storm Cloud's neck. "I don't think this guy will go for herding sheep, so we're heading out for a run." The horse and rider took off as one. "Have fun!" Chase yelled over his shoulder.

Caleb stood at the window leaning on his crutches. What was a herd of sheep doing in the valley? If not for the pain in his leg, he would think he was dreaming. He looked down at his toes, which were a sickly shade of green with some yellow overtones. He had suffered for the abuse he'd given the leg several days earlier. It was covered with a bruise that ran the entire length and hurt so much that he had only now been able to rise from the bed again. The fact that he had come down with a fever had not helped, either. It hadn't been a bad one, just enough to keep him miserable for a week. Miserable because he was lonely for the companionship of his friends. They all came to visit, but they were also busy since they were a man short.

Amanda had been indispensable. She showed up three times a day with his meals, cleaned his room, gave him privacy so he could bathe himself. Caleb returned the favor by staying quiet. He didn't dare say much to her beyond thank you because he didn't want to risk hurting her again.

But now there was a flock of sheep milling around in

the small valley below. And what looked like a dogfight. Jason was already sprinting down the hill, and Caleb could make out the top of Amanda's head on the step as she looked down to see what was going on.

Chase was talking to a rider on the ridge by Jamie's grave. Something about the set of the newcomer's hat. . . .

It was Ty. Caleb would recognize his seat on a horse anywhere. How many times had he followed him into battle, keeping his eyes on Ty's back to protect him from harm as they slashed their way across lines of Union soldiers? He hadn't seen Ty since the day they'd been attacked.

The war was over now and at last they were all home. A great feeling of relief washed over Caleb. He blinked hard and realized that a tear had formed. He squeezed his eyes shut, willing it to go away. It was just because he'd been sick and he felt weak and useless.

A loud squeal from below brought his attention back to the present. *Cat.* Jason stood in the middle of the flock, with Cat hanging from his neck and kissing every square inch of his face.

A covered wagon had pulled up right past Jenny's cabin, and an elderly colored man and a lighter-skinned young woman dismounted. They must own the sheep, but what were Cat and Ty doing with them, unless . . .

A picture of Cat presenting him with a bright red knitted muffler before they went off to battle filled his mind. She had also knitted during the entire trip home from North Carolina. Was she determined to keep a supply of wool handy? Caleb mused as he shook his head at the insanity of it all. Catherine Lynch Kincaid was the only woman he knew who would have the audacity to bring a flock of sheep into cattle country.

He needed to get downstairs. Caleb braced himself on his crutches and, gritting his teeth, started out of the bedroom.

He teetered at the top of the stairs as he heard voices outside. Amanda was talking to Ty. The back door creaked open, and boot steps sounded on the wooden floor. Caleb was wondering how he could get down the stairs when his broken leg was unable to bend at all because of the splint.

"Dang, Caleb, messing up one leg wasn't enough for you?" Ty said as he appeared at the bottom of the stairs.

"I figured I didn't do a good enough job with the first one," Caleb said. "Thought I might keep at it until I don't have any limbs left."

Ty shook his head at his friend's foolishness as he ran up the stairs. The men flung their arms around each other and began the ritualistic pounding of each other's backs that spoke volumes when words failed them.

"I never got a chance to thank you for saving my life," Caleb said.

"You got Cat home safely. That was enough for me."

"It was more the other way around," Caleb protested.

"You know she would have chased after me if you hadn't been there," Ty protested in return. "It's all over now and we're all home and safe. I'm just really sorry you had to suffer for my stupidity."

"I'm a grown man, Ty. I knew what I was getting into when I made the decision to enlist."

"Then you were way ahead of me," Ty said, his steel-blue eyes clouding with memories.

"Ty . . . let's go downstairs."

And Ty picked him up bodily and started down.

The dogs had been separated and the sheep had been herded to the south pasture with the help of Zeb, whose dark eyes lit up at the sight of Cleo and her father, Pharaoh.

"Their owner was an old lady who loved ancient history," Ty explained about the pair that evening as everyone gathered in the big house. "According to Pharaoh, she named all her slaves after great figures in ancient history. There was Hector, Achilles, Paris, Alexander, Hannibal, Caesar, Marc. Of course, none of the slaves had any idea whom they were named after. She died a few months back, and since she didn't have any family, she freed her slaves and left everything to them. According to Pharaoh, all she had was a broken-down house full of books, a dried-up well and a flock of sheep. Pharaoh took the flock as his share and started west."

"We caught up with them about a hundred miles east of here," Cat added. "Pharaoh was about to be hanged."

"For bringing sheep into cattle country?" Cole asked with a sinister smile on his face.

"Cat bought the herd off Pharaoh for a dollar and then dared the cowboys to hang her," Ty added.

The group burst out laughing

"I knew you wouldn't let that happen," Cat said to her

husband. She settled back into her place under her father's arm on the sofa. "They took one look at Ty with his rifle, and the whole group skedaddled like their tails were on fire."

More laughter followed. Caleb watched the smiling faces of his friends as he sat in one of the chairs by the fire. Chase and Jenny sat in the window seat, Jenny letting Cat have her father all to herself. Grace sat in the chair opposite Caleb's, with Jacey sleeping in her lap. Cole stood protectively behind them.

Jake, Shannon and Zane were all three squeezed onto the love seat, while Ty joined Jason and Cat on the sofa and the boys sat on the floor, totally enraptured by the stories being told.

Which left Amanda sharing the footstool with Caleb's leg. She was wearing the purple ribbon again, and her dark hair shone with light reflected from the cheery fire that had been built to drive away the chill of the spring evening. She had been quietly observant during the evening—Caleb knew, because he had been observing her. He couldn't keep his eyes off her, and he smiled when he saw her laughing with the others.

Amanda was making strides forward. Cole had noticed it also, and his quick glance at Jenny behind the sofa showed her own satisfied smile as her sapphire-blue eyes circled the room and danced with happiness that finally everyone was together again.

Chase dropped an arm over Jenny's shoulders and she leaned into him. Shannon was sitting on Jake's lap to make room for Zane, and her head rested intimately on her husband's shoulder. Jake had confided to Caleb in one of his visits that Shannon wanted a baby and was wearing him out in the pursuit of it.

And of course Ty and Cat wanted one to replace the babe they'd lost, but Ty had confessed to Caleb earlier that they'd had no luck.

Cole leaned forward and whispered in Grace's ear. Caleb felt himself surrounded by the intimacy of all the couples in the room. They seemed to all complete each other. Jenny had tamed Chase's savageness; Ty's steady ways were a perfect complement to Cat's impetuousness. And Jake was happy in a way that no one ever would have dreamed now that he'd found Shannon.

Caleb wondered if love would ever come to him. His hand twitched as he once again wondered what it would be like to run his hand down the length of Amanda's shiny hair.

He didn't dare touch her. It would have to be enough that she was here and part of the group. But it would be so nice to be able to touch her.

Chapter Thirteen

A day at the lake. How long had it been since they'd had the opportunity to sneak off and just be together? Jenny looked at the handsome profile of her husband as they rode side by side and realized that he must be thinking the same thing, because he reached over and took her hand and raised it to his lips for a gentle kiss.

She was riding one of the gentler mares. Chase was on his steady buckskin, with a picnic basket and Jenny's quilt tied to the back of his saddle. The boys had protested at being left behind, but Zeb had volunteered to take them out to visit the sheep, which was a new adventure for them. Jenny was certain that Zeb had other motives for visiting the sheep than distracting her boys for a day, but she didn't complain. The dark-eyed Cleopatra would have tempted any man. Zeb deserved a chance at happiness. They all did.

High fluffy clouds scudded across a vivid blue sky.

The air was warm for mid May, at least Jenny felt it was, but that might be due to her pregnancy. She hadn't felt the need for a coat most of the spring and dreaded the prospect of giving birth again in the heat of high summer. Maybe this one would be easier. She certainly hoped it would be.

"How long has it been since you were here?" Jenny asked as they gazed around at the beautiful setting.

"I came by last fall, before the first snow," Chase replied. There had been too much work for him to sneak away since the snows had melted. Work, family and the chicken pox had cut into what little time he had for enjoying the peace of his surroundings. The lake had always been his favorite place on the ranch, and Jenny could understand why. Crystal-blue water spread out before them, reflecting the rising peaks of the snow-tipped mountains behind. A grove of aspens trailed down to one side, offering shelter to the animals that came to drink.

Chase considered the lake and the area around it to be his own private place of worship. It was where he came to listen for the one true God that his white mother had told him about when he was a lonely boy growing up in a Kiowa camp. He found it easy for his spirit to commune with God when the majesty of His creation surrounded him. Chase had often come to the lake during the years Jenny was missing to pray for her safe return, even though those who knew him would have found it hard to believe he did such a thing. For him, religion was a private matter. He would go to the church in town with Jenny because he knew it made her happy, but he would rather worship in his own way at the lake. This was the place where he sought his answers to the problems that arose. It was the place where he had realized that patience was the best way to win Jenny's hand and heart. And when she was finally his, he had brought her to the lake to share the beauty of this place with her.

His strong arms lifted his wife from the saddle. She laughed with the sheer joy of the moment as he dipped her and twirled her around, his dark hair flying out around his face. He eased her to the ground and handed her the picnic basket and the quilt. He took the time to loosen the bits and girths on the horses' saddles so they could graze on the sweet grass that grew along the gently rolling slope leading down to the shore. Chase hung his gun belt over the saddle horn and slapped the buckskin on the hip. He would not need the weapon today. This was a place of peace and tranquillity.

Jenny spread the quilt and dropped to her knees to open the basket. Chase stopped before joining her, his nose sniffing the air as his eyes surveyed the lake.

"What is it?" Jenny asked, long accustomed to trusting her husband's instincts.

"I smell . . . people. Someone's been here."

"What do you mean?"

"Wood smoke, food cooking and human waste."

"You can identify all those smells?"

"They all go together," he explained as his hawklike eyes scanned the rise behind them. The area seemed peaceful. The birds were calm, and the only sign of life was a prairie dog standing sentinel on a small knoll with his nose twitching at the soft breeze that flowed down from the mountains.

"Maybe someone camped here," Jenny said as she kicked off her boots. She wiggled her toes and with a sigh sank them into the cool dirt beneath the wispy blades of grass.

Chase's eyes roamed around the lake, but there was no sign that anyone had been there beyond perhaps a wild horse or two that had come down to drink. He could walk around to look for signs, but the quilt and Jenny looked extremely inviting. And if someone had been there, they were gone now. The place looked as pristine as the first time he had seen it. But still there was something . . .

Jenny patted the ground and flashed him a mischievous grin. She was in high spirits today. And why shouldn't she be? Her family was back together and everyone was safe and sound with the exception of Caleb. But she had found something positive in his broken leg, too. It gave her a chance to try her hand at matchmaking.

"Most likely," he said, answering her earlier question. Chase dropped to the quilt next to Jenny as she went back to unpacking their lunch. She was starving, as usual.

"I don't understand where you put it all," Chase said as Jenny bit into a sandwich. Except for the roundness of her belly, she was still as lean as ever.

"I'm sure it will all show up in a month or so," Jenny replied. "And if Zane opens his mouth to comment on my figure this time, I won't waste any time with a mop, I'll just go ahead and geld him."

Chase flopped back and laughed. When Jenny had been large with Chance, Zane had the audacity to moo at her like she was a cow. A sopping-wet mop in his face had quickly put an end to his teasing.

Jenny put her sandwich down and leaned sideways across him, placing her hip up against his. Chase's face was relaxed, his dark eyes narrowed to slits against the sun and his mouth smiling widely.

Jenny dropped a kiss on the corner of his smile. "I love you, Chase."

His hand crept up under her shirt and rubbed against her spine. "I love you, Jenny." He tugged on her braid, which had fallen over her shoulder, and pulled her down for a long, lingering kiss.

Jenny's appetite quickly turned from food to something more. How long had it been since they had done anything more than fumble quietly in the dark before falling into an exhausted sleep? Now that Ty was home, some of the pressure would be off Chase. And as soon as Caleb healed, the ranch would be fully staffed and no one would have to work such long hours. They had all survived the years of war. Now it was time to celebrate.

Jenny sat up and slowly unbuttoned Chase's shirt. She spread it open, her hands moving crisply across the smooth skin of his chest. Chase propped his arms behind his head as a pillow, and his eyes glowed as he quietly allowed her to enjoy herself. Jenny plucked a long blade of grass from behind his head and trailed it down his forehead, along the length of his nose before gently switching it against his lips, which he held firmly in check, knowing that it would give her a victory if he smiled. The blade of grass dipped over his chin, stroked his neck and then traced the valley between the muscles of his chest before it found the hollow of his navel. His face remained impassive, but Jenny knew well how to stoke the fires of her husband's passion.

Not that they really needed stoking, she noticed with a smile as her fingers worked the buttons of his pants.

And obviously he was going to make her do all the work. Chase seemed quite content to lie on his back and let her undress him. Rising to the challenge, Jenny decided to take a slower approach. She undid her braid and shook the blond locks loose until they cascaded to her waist. She turned her back to Chase and combed her fingers through her hair. Jenny smiled to herself in satisfaction when she felt the soft touch of Chase's long fingers trailing through her hair. She stood and slowly lowered the pants she was wearing, an old pair of Jamie's that had served her through her first pregnancy. She kicked them free with her back turned, and was satisfied to feel the touch of a hand on her calf. Chase slid his fingers up the length of her leg. She slowly unbuttoned her shirt, another castoff of Jamie's, acting as if she were more interested in the pair of Canadian geese that circled the lake than the perfect example of manhood sprawled on her quilt.

Chase's dark eyes flew open in surprise when he saw that she was wearing nothing underneath her clothes but her silver locket.

In one quick, graceful motion, Chase sat up and

pulled her down beside him, holding himself above the roundness of their child. Jenny slid the shirt from his broad shoulders and lowered his pants down over his hips as he poised himself over her, kissing the tip of her nose, the corners of her eyes, the fullness of her lips. Her lips chased after his as he teased and nibbled at her features. Her hands reached for his fullness, ready to guide him . . .

"Get your filthy red hands off her, boy!"

The business end of a shotgun pushed against Chase's spine. With his great strength and grace, Chase rolled into the feet of the man holding the gun. As he turned, he grabbed the barrel, and the shell blasted harmlessly into the air as the man landed on his back. Before his attacker could draw a breath, Chase seized the shotgun from his grasp, leaped to his feet and pointed the gun at the man's forehead. Jenny quickly pulled the quilt around her body as she scrambled to her feet, spilling their lunch onto the grass.

Chase cocked the gun. "You're trespassing, mister. You'd better have a good reason for being on this property."

"This property is mine," the man said. He lay in the grass with eyes full of hatred. His clothing was shabby but clean, and the shotgun showed signs of care. "You're the one trespassing on my land." His eyes narrowed as he looked over at Jenny. "And on a white woman."

Chase's jaw went rigid. Jenny placed a calming hand on his arm as she saw the old demons stirring. Why did this have to happen now, when finally everything was as it should be?

175

"This man is my husband," she said, never taking her eyes off Chase. "And the child I carry is his."

"You don't have to explain us to anyone," Chase ground out from between clenched teeth.

The look on his face was frightening, even to one who knew him as she did. The man on the ground showed no fear, only a growing hatred. He must have his reasons for hating. But why did his virulent emotion have to spill over onto them? Jenny moved her body between Chase and the man on the ground, shoving Chase's arm away.

"This land belongs to my grandfather, Jason Lynch," she said. "He's owned it for years."

"I've got a piece of paper that says different," the man snarled. He moved to his feet, warily keeping an eye on Chase. "And your grandfather can't be much of a man if he let you marry a stinkin' Indian."

Jenny slapped him.

"Touch my pa again and I'll kill you!"

Jenny and Chase both turned to see a scrawny boy who couldn't be more than fifteen holding a rifle on them. Hunger and desperation showed behind the teenager's false bravado. Chase was still holding the shotgun, and Jenny's position shielded it from the boy's view. She sensed Chase raising the gun behind her and stepped away so the boy could see, once again, that Chase held the weapon on the man.

Her heart jumped into her throat when she realized that the boy before them was terrified. His terror combined with the obvious hostility that the father felt for

Chase meant they would be lucky if this episode ended without someone getting hurt. Or killed.

"I think the best thing for us to do is leave." Jenny hoped her voice sounded calm. "I'll have my grandfather come out and look at your paper."

"He can look all he wants to. The land is mine." The worn eyes in the haggard face were brimming with loathing.

"And we'd be within our rights to shoot you where you stand," the boy added. A sharp glance from Chase set him back a step, and his hands trembled on the rifle.

Chase whistled for his horse. "Jenny, get our stuff," he instructed. His voice was quiet, deadly, terrifying in its flat calm. Jenny quickly went to the basket and stuffed their clothes inside with one hand, while holding the quilt secure around her with the other. The buckskin sidled up, and as she hung the basket on the horn, she grabbed Chase's gun from the holster and his knife, the knife that had belonged to her father, just so she would have weapons of her own. She moved up behind Chase, which was difficult since she was trying not to trip over the quilt with her hands full of weapons. She handed him his gun and he handed her the double-barreled shotgun.

"Spend it," Chase barked with his gun held steady on the father.

Jenny blasted the shot into the sky, startling the geese. They angrily honked their protest before settling back into an easy glide on the lake. Jenny flung the shotgun toward a patch of high grass as they backed away from the men.

The boy approached his father as they moved toward their horses. Jenny had to tighten the girths while Chase held the gun. Then she had to mount, which was difficult since she was pregnant, naked, awkward in the quilt, and trying to hold on to the knife. She put the knife back into Chase's belt and was finally able to find the stirrup with her bare feet and mount.

"Go on," Chase said and slapped her mare on the flank. He kept his gun leveled on the father, who was seething, until he was sure Jenny was a safe distance away. Chase grabbed his saddle horn and in one fluid motion mounted the buckskin, his gun still held on the man. He bent low over the horse's neck and they took off at a run.

Jenny was waiting for him over the next rise. "Did they follow?" she asked. Her golden blond hair was wild about her shoulders from her ride.

"Not yet," Chase said as he looked behind them. "I don't think they will." He was still full of fury. The buckskin could feel it and tossed his head, chewing on the bit that had been hastily slid into his mouth. Chase handed Jenny the basket. "You'd better get dressed."

He turned the buckskin to watch the trail behind them as Jenny slid to the ground and hastily dressed in the privacy between the two horses. A cramp chased its way across her stomach and she bent with it, placing her hand on her side to relieve the stitch.

"Do you want your shirt?" she asked when she was able to straighten up.

"No." Of course not. He had become the savage again. The one who killed to protect what was his. The one who sought revenge against those who wronged him and the ones he loved.

She mounted and took off, her hand still on her side. He did not notice her pain. She felt Chase behind her but knew that his eyes were ever going back to make sure they weren't being followed.

He had left her again.

Her dreams that night proved it.

Chapter Fourteen

"Daddy, don't go," Cat said as she wrapped her arms around Jason's waist from behind and laid her head between his shoulder blades.

"Catherine," Jason said, turning back to hug his daughter. "We won't be gone long."

"That's not it," Cat continued. "I just have a really bad feeling about this." She looked up at her father with green-gold eyes full of concern and love. She had missed him so much these past few years. He always had a way of making things right, no matter how bad the problem. She was amazed that she had survived the war years without having his steady presence there day after day to calm her rashness and keep her on a steady path. She had the sudden realization that she had grown more like him in the past few years.

"Nothing is going to happen. We're just going over to

talk to the man." Jason patted his pocket, making sure that the deeds and map of his property were secure.

Cat looked over his shoulder to where Chase and Ty waited with the horses. Both had the look she had learned to dread. They were going to fight to protect what was theirs. Weapons had been checked and rechecked. Cat wondered if it was a good idea to take Chase along. His fury had barely been contained when he and Jenny had returned from their ruined picnic the day before. He was deathly quiet, and they all knew him well enough to know that silence was not a good sign for those who crossed his path.

"But we only just got home. I want to spend time with you."

Jason dropped a kiss on his daughter's forehead. "We'll be back before lunch. That will give you time to figure out what you're going to do with that flock of yours," he said, his blue eyes twinkling. He stepped off the porch onto his horse, and the three of them rode down the drive. They planned to approach the lake from the opposite side just to see if anyone else had settled on Lynch land.

Cat watched them go with a sinking feeling in her heart. She shook her head, chastising herself for making her father worry over her now that she was finally home. She was just being silly and selfish. She had missed her father, and after not seeing him for so long, she wanted to keep him close at hand.

And why was he so worried about her sheep?

* * *

"I'd forgotten how far you can see out here," Ty commented as they rode. Chase said nothing, his jaw rigid, his eyes hard and his body wary.

Jason looked at the rolling plains that unfolded in the distance toward the east, remembering the first time he had seen the land. His land. The dream he had been building for over forty years. On a beautiful clear day like this day, you could see for miles. You would always know what was coming if you watched for it.

"It is beautiful," Jason replied. "And it's amazing to think how far this prairie goes rolling on."

"And how different the landscape is here from the country back East," Ty added. "You can go miles here and not see anyone. I like the openness of it. Back home I always felt like something was closing in on me."

"Could have just been the war," Jason said wisely.

Ty nodded. How long would it be before he could ride and not be looking around, waiting for an attack?

Chase kicked the buckskin and pulled ahead of Jason and Ty.

"Jenny said that the man who attacked them had a few things to say about Chase and her being together," Jason commented as they watched the proud set of Chase's shoulders.

"Why should some ignorant homesteader's opinion matter to the two of them?"

"It matters because that's always been Chase's insecurity about Jenny. That he's not good enough for her. That he's holding her back."

"Chase Duncan is a better man than most," Ty protested angrily, his blue eyes snapping.

"That's because you know the man inside," Jason said in his usual logical way. "Most people can't get past what they see on the outside."

"Jason, if half the people in this country were as smart as you, we would not have wasted the past few years fighting that dang war."

Jason smiled at his son-in-law. "So maybe you should be the one to help educate them."

Ty gave Jason a quizzical look.

"You've always wanted to study the law, Ty, and you let other things get in your way. Your father, coming west, the war, Catherine." Jason went down the list.

Ty shook his head. It was amazing how Jason could suddenly get to the heart of a matter. It was also amazing how well Jason knew him. Of course, the older man had taken the time to know him. It was more than his own father had ever done.

"I don't see anything standing in your way now," Jason continued. "And it's not like my library isn't full of books. We could get started on it tomorrow."

Ty laughed. "Is this because you want your daughter married to a lawyer instead of a cowboy?"

"It's because I want both of you to be happy. I don't want you to wake up twenty years from now and say 'what if.' "

"I'll do it," Ty said. He had wanted to do it ever since he could remember. He had just let too many things get in the way.

"Good," Jason replied with his gentle smile. "That was easier than I thought."

Chase was returning to them at a gallop, his face grim.

"What is it?" Jason asked.

"Sod hut, built into a hollow," was his clipped reply. "The lake is right on the other side of the rise."

"Best we come in from the front," Jason said. "We don't want them to think we're sneaking up on them."

Chase pulled out his pistol to check the load one more time.

"Chase—" Jason put a hand on his arm. "We're not going to need that."

Chase slid the gun back into his holster, but his face remained set and grim. His jaw was clenched so tight that every line of it stood out vividly beneath the bronze of his skin.

"We're just going in to talk, that's all," Jason reminded them. That was why he had decided to take only two men with him. Any more and it would seem like an attack. Diplomacy was the best tactic under the circumstances.

They splashed across a wide and shallow stream that was the eastern border of Jason's property and rode into the homestead through low ground so the inhabitants would have plenty of time to see them coming. Jason rode in the lead, with Ty and Chase behind and on either side, their eyes darting right and left to make sure they weren't riding into an ambush.

"Do you see anything?" Ty asked Chase calmly.

"No," Chase said. But there was a chill on his spine that would not go away.

Jenny had been restless, her sleep disturbed by dreams the night before. She had attributed her restlessness to being troubled over the incident, but he knew that she was worried about something happening to him. And she knew that he had to go out and face whatever threatened their happiness.

"Stop right there!" The voice rang out as the man who had accosted Jenny and Chase the day before stepped out of his hut, shotgun ready. The dwelling was small and the area around it neat, with a scarred wooden table holding a cracked pot full of spring wildflowers. A few chickens pecked in the dirt, and a cat dashed into the dark recess of the hut as the man stepped out.

Jason, Ty and Chase halted their horses. Jason placed his hands in the air to show that he was unarmed.

"Doesn't appear like this guy is the friendly type," Ty said under his breath.

Chase didn't answer. His eyes were busy searching for the son.

"My name is Jason Lynch," Jason began.

"So?"

"You're standing on my property," Jason finished.

"Am not," the man spat out in protest. "Got a piece of paper that says it's mine."

Jason slowly dismounted, holding his hands up again to show that he meant no harm. "So do I," he said. "Why don't we compare them and see if we can figure out what the problem is, Mr. . . ?"

Jason opened his coat so the man could see that there was nothing inside but a packet of papers, then pulled them out. He slowly walked to the table and slid the flowers to the side so he could unfold his maps and deeds.

"Potter. Charlie Potter." The man leaned his shotgun against the hut and then hollered, "Betty! Bring out my deed!"

A worn woman quickly appeared with two small boys hanging onto her patched skirts. She handed the paper to her husband and then hustled the boys back into the hut without saying a word.

"The boy's around here somewhere," Chase said to Ty.

"Think he's got a rifle aimed at us?" Ty asked, already knowing the answer.

"Wouldn't you?"

Chase kept scanning the homestead while Ty kept his eyes on Jason.

Jason leaned over the table with his map. His finger traced the borders of his property, specifically pointing out the lake and the stream they had come through as the eastern border. The man seemed confused as he looked at his own deed.

"I think I see the problem," Jason finally said. "I believe you're on the wrong side of the road." He moved the map around so the man could see it better. "On the south side of the road, there's another lake, quite a bit smaller than this one. You see how the stream runs down into the lake. The lay of the land is about the same. You're just a bit north of where you should be."

"Don't listen to him, Pa!" It was the teenager. His voice came from above. The sod roof of the hut slanted from front to back toward the rise it was built against.

The boy had stationed himself below the roof line with the rifle in his arms.

Chase started for his gun, but Ty laid a hand on his arm. "Let Jason work it out," he said quietly.

"I know you and your family have put a lot of work into this place. I've got plenty of hands. We'd be happy to help you get another place built," Jason suggested.

"I don't need no charity," the man said. "And I ain't so sure about you, neither. Lots of big cattlemen think they own the entire country out here. Could be there's another lake and could be there's not. I'll let the land office tell me who's right and who's wrong."

Jason sighed. Apparently, there wasn't going to be an easy answer to the situation. "When would you like to go?"

"Don't tell him, Pa. They could set up an ambush and get rid of you the easy way."

Ty shook his head. Jason was the most generous man he knew. No one who was acquainted with him would accuse him of such a thing.

"Why don't you leave now and take that Indian with you?" Potter said. "I don't need the likes of him sneaking around here stealin' me blind."

"Be careful what you say," Jason said, his voice calm and steady.

Ty couldn't believe it. It was the first time he'd ever seen Jason even close to losing his temper, except maybe a few times with Cat.

The boy stood and cocked his rifle, aiming it straight at Jason.

"You best be leaving, mister."

Jason calmly folded his papers. "I'll tell the land office to expect you, Mr. Potter."

"Don't do me no favors."

"Fighting a losing battle, Jason," Ty murmured. "Let's just get out of here."

Jason started toward his horse. The boy followed him with the rifle. "Don't to anything," Jason said as he walked toward Chase and Ty. "Just ride on out. I'm right behind you."

Ty and Chase turned their horses as Jason took his reins.

At the last minute, Jason turned to go back, to make one last attempt at a peaceful solution. He opened his coat as he turned to stick the papers back inside.

"Watch out, Pa!" the boy cried out and fired his rifle.

Jason spun around, a look of disbelief on his face as blood seeped out of the hole in his chest, right where his heart was beating.

"No!" Ty screamed and bolted from his horse, catching Jason in his arms as he sank to the ground. Jason grasped at Ty's arms as his eyes looked up at him in shock, and he gasped for words. "Jason," Ty said. The blue eyes stared vacantly past him, looking up into the heavens. Ty ran his hands over the lids, closing them for the last time.

Chase kicked the buckskin forward, ducking as the boy fired again. Potter went for his shotgun, but Chase kicked him in the face, and then reached up to the low roof and in one quick motion flung the boy over his head onto the ground. Chase was off his horse in an instant, hauling the boy to his feet and slamming him against the wall.

"Chase!" Ty yelled.

Chase pulled his knife from his belt and held it to the boy's throat.

Ty grabbed him from behind. Chase pushed him off without taking the knife away. Ty came back, this time butting his head into Chase's kidneys while wrapping his arms around his waist. They both went down into the dirt. Ty landed on top of Chase and punched him in the jaw, knowing it was the only way to penetrate the red haze that consumed his friend.

"He's just a boy, Chase."

Chase looked up at Ty, his dark eyes full of pain and dread.

"I've seen enough boys die needlessly," Ty said, his chest heaving for air. "Leave this one for the law."

"Jason?" Chase asked, knowing the answer. Hating it.

Ty looked back to where Jason lay in a patch of trampled grass. He choked back the bile that rose in his throat. "He's dead." Ty stood and extended a hand to Chase, who took a moment to test his jaw before Ty hauled him to his feet.

The boy had crawled to his father. The sobbing wife held her husband's head cradled in her lap, dabbing at the blood on his face while the two little boys cried behind her.

Chase found his knife and walked back to where Jason lay in the grass.

"You killed a good man today," Ty said to the boy. "You murdered him in cold blood." His voice trembled. He looked at Chase, who was kneeling next to Jason's body. "I probably should have let him kill you. It would have been easier for everyone. It would have been easier for you."

The boy burst into tears. Ty looked at him hard. He was just a boy, probably hadn't even seen his first whisker. And yet how many boys like this had he seen in the war? How many had learned how to kill? How was this boy any different from Willie, who had ridden to war with them and died along with so many others?

"He was my wife's father," Ty said, his voice hoarse as he turned and walked away. "He was a father to me," he whispered.

Ty knelt on the other side of Chase.

"How are we going to tell them?" Chase asked, pain haunting his dark eyes.

"I don't know," Ty sighed. He pinched the bridge of his nose, trying to will back the tears. "Oh, God," he said and wept.

Chapter Fifteen

The ride back was the longest trip of either of their lives. And yet neither wanted it to end. Ty and Chase both grieved silently, angrily, knowing it would be up to them to be strong, that Cat and Jenny would need them to be strong.

And yet the day was beautiful. The air was warm without being oppressive, and a gentle breeze caressed the tips of the grass and lifted the ends of Chase's hair.

'He deserved better," Ty said. They had not spoken a word since they had placed Jason over the saddle of his horse, which Ty led. "He should have died in his bed, surrounded by his family."

There was no sign that Chase agreed or disagreed. He was thinking of his own mother and father and how they had died, both violently, apart from each other, just as Jenny's parents had died. And her brother. And now her last living relative. Her grandfather.

"There will be a trial," Ty continued, using words to keep his tears at bay. "We'll have to testify."

Chase remained silent.

"I should have let you kill him," Ty ground out from between clenched teeth.

Chase looked off toward the mountains. Snow still capped the tall peaks that faded into shades of blue and purple as they marched into the distance. What would it be like to take Jenny and the boys and disappear into the mountains, away from the hatred and bigotry that came with the ever swelling tide of people moving west? How could he protect them from such violence when it came onto their land, into their homes, to their most special place?

"It would have been easier on all of us," Ty continued.

"Then I'd be the one standing trial," Chase said finally. "You saw that man. He hated me. A lot of the people in town hate me because of my Indian blood. More so because I married Jenny. It wouldn't take much to stir them up against me. Especially now that Jason's . . ."

Both men were silent as they fought for control of their emotions.

"You probably saved my life . . . again," Chase said.

"We'll have to tell the sheriff."

"Let Jake do it."

"Should we get him involved?" Ty wondered, remembering Jake's violent temper.

"He's changed, Ty. Shannon's changed him. He'll be all right."

"I wish Caleb could go with him."

"Caleb would be good," Chase replied. They pulled

up before the long drive to the main house. Both men looked at the rooftop showing in the distance. The tips of the cottonwood tree out front swayed gently in the breeze. "I'll go down and get Jenny. That will give you and Cat time to . . ."

"Thanks," Ty said. No sense in putting it off. Delay would only make it worse. He pulled on the reins of Jason's horse and moved slowly down the drive to give Chase time to find Jenny.

"God help me to be strong for Cat," he prayed as he moved up the drive with his sorrowful burden.

Amanda stood at the open window of her room, brushing her hair. She had taken time to wash it after cleaning up the breakfast dishes. She hummed a tune as she worked, one of the songs that Shannon had sung a few nights before at the welcome-home party for Cat and Ty. It had a catchy tune and the lyrics had been amusing in a sly sort of way. Shannon had told them that her brother Will had written it.

Shannon's brother had been killed in the war, fighting for the North. And her husband, Jake, had fought for the South. They had put such differences aside. If only the rest of the country could do the same. But Amanda had her doubts. The latest editorial in the paper had her worried about the punitive measures the government might inflict on the South. If only Lincoln were still alive.

If only. Wouldn't it be nice to get through a day without an "if only"? If only her life hadn't been so . . . changed from what it should have been.

The branches of the cottonwood swayed in the breeze that freshened the air of the upstairs rooms. Amanda and Cat had opened every window wide to catch it and cleanse the house of the stale odors of winter. The nest that Amanda had watched being built was finished, the female meadowlark patiently protecting her eggs. The male sat in the higher branches, watching for any predators that might threaten his family, keeping them safe from harm.

Amanda felt safe, too. How long had it been since she had felt that way? She had even forgotten the feeling until she felt it surrounding her as she'd sat on the footstool in front of Caleb at the homecoming celebration, looking at the smiling faces of the people around the room. Even after she came here, the Fear had been present, haunting her waking hours. But now it was almost as if she were too busy to think about it. Her days were full of tasks, and most of the time she fell into an exhausted sleep at night.

Sometimes she still dreamed she was back in New York, locked in her room high above the street. She was waiting, as she always was, for someone to come. It didn't matter who—they all blended into one faceless presence because of the opium.

But it was Caleb who showed up at her door in these recent dreams.

Amanda dropped her brush in mid stroke as she saw the rider coming up the drive. It was Ty. He had ridden out earlier with Jason and Chase. So who was stretched out across the saddle?

"Oh, my God," Amanda whispered. She ran from the room just as a crash sounded from the room below.

"Daddy!" Cat's screams filled the stairwell, echoing off the walls.

Caleb was standing in the doorway of his room, leaning on his crutches. "What is it?" he asked as he looked toward the stairway.

Amanda couldn't speak. She looked up at him, her eyes brimming with tears.

Caleb took her arm as she started for the stairs. "Amanda, what's wrong?"

"I think Jason is dead."

"What?" A mixture of fear and dread swept across his handsome features as he looked down at her.

"Ty is bringing a body," she whispered, afraid that she would scream if she spoke any louder. "It isn't Chase."

The sobs that drifted up the stairs were heart-wrenching in their agony.

"Amanda, I need to get this splint off."

Amanda looked down at his leg in confusion. "It's not time yet." Why was he worried about his splint?

"I've got to get downstairs." Days of frustration merged together with the urgency of realizing that everyone's life had just changed. "I can't wait for someone to come help me down."

Amanda went to her room for a pair of scissors. She knelt before him, her hair spreading out in a shiny curtain across her shoulders as she cut the bandages up the side of his leg. Caleb flexed his hand and then placed it on the back of her head, the tips of his fingers disappearing into the strands of her hair.

Amanda felt his touch. Her body was shaking, but whether from the feel of his hand in her hair or the shock of knowing that Jason was dead, she could not tell. She pulled the bandages away as Caleb combed his fingers through her hair, and then she removed the splint from his leg.

She stood still, holding the splint in her hands. Caleb's fingers moved across her shoulder as she looked up into his eyes. His fingers pressed across the ridge of her shoulder, gently moving and massaging the muscle.

"Amanda?" What was he asking her? He looked at her as if he could see into her soul.

The sound of the back door slamming made them jump. Both looked down at Caleb's broken leg, almost as if they were surprised that it was no longer splinted and bandaged. Caleb placed his foot on the floor and leaned on it, checking to see if it would support his weight.

"Maybe you shouldn't," Amanda said.

"Go on." Caleb jerked his head toward the stairs. "I'll be fine."

Amanda started for the stairs but then stopped, instead going into Jason's room. Ty would need someplace to lay the . . . body. She found a sheet in the linen chest and spread it over Jason's bed.

Caleb was dressed when she met him in the hall again. He was wearing his own pants, and both of his boots. He was pale around the mouth and he leaned on one crutch, halfway supporting his broken leg.

He looked at the staircase.

"Do you need help?" Amanda asked.

"No."

She went down before him, knowing him well enough now to know that he didn't want her hovering and worrying that he might fall.

Through the front door she could see Cat, Jenny, Ty and Chase. Jenny and Cat were kneeling on the porch with their arms around each other, crying. Chase and Ty stood watching, their faces grim because they knew there was nothing they could do to relieve the pain of the women they loved.

Everyone else had gathered at the back door as if waiting to be invited in. None of them were looking inside; instead they looked down toward the valley, giving those related to Jason by blood a chance to grieve privately. Amanda went to the back door.

"Do you know what happened?" Cole asked quietly.

Amanda shook her head. She could hear the halting progress of Caleb on the stairs behind her.

"Are you sure he's . . . dead?" Grace asked. Her brown eyes were red and swollen. She felt her own share of grief over Jason's death. They all did. He had made a difference in all of their lives.

"I ha . . . haven't talked to any of them," Amanda said. "But I'm sure."

They filed in through the door—Cole, Grace with Jacey, Jake, Shannon, Zane, who was sniffling and wiping his eyes with his sleeve, even Dan and Randy, who seemed a bit shy about coming in.

"Zeb took the boys out to see the sheep again," Shannon said as she came into the house. "He doesn't know."

Cole went down the hall toward the front door, meeting Caleb as he stepped down from the last stair. Grace handed the baby to Shannon and followed him.

Everyone else stood in the hallway as if they didn't know what to do.

"Why don't you go into the parlor," Amanda suggested.

"We could make some coffee," Shannon volunteered as Caleb came down the hall toward them.

"Quick recovery?" Jake said to Caleb as he joined them. It was strange to hear everyone whispering.

Shannon handed Jacey to Jake, who looked at his wife in surprise as he held the baby at arm's length. "What am I supposed to do with her?" he hissed under his breath.

"Bounce her if she cries," Shannon hissed back as she followed Amanda into the kitchen.

They could see Grace on the porch now, holding Cat in her arms. Cole, Chase and Ty were lifting the body off the horse. Jenny stood with her hands wrapped tightly around the swell of her stomach.

Amanda went to the door and held it open for the men as they came through with Jason's body. They moved on up the stairs with Jenny following behind. Grace and Cat remained on the porch, Cat still inconsolable in her grief.

"What do you suppose they'll do about Jason's murder?" Shannon asked as Amanda came into the kitchen. There was no doubt in anyone's mind about how Jason had died.

Amanda shook her head, totally bewildered. She went to the hutch in the dining room and found the silver coffee service as her mind tumbled about in confusion. Had it just been this morning when she had stood as her window brushing her hair and marveling at how "safe" she felt? Was this all part of some gruesome nightmare? Was she being punished because she had forgotten about the Fear? How could any of them feel safe when the very foundation of their lives had just been taken by some unknown evil? She carried the tray to the kitchen while her mind raced around the happenings of the day.

Why was Jason, who was good and kind and generous, dead when she was the one who had wished to die for so long? Why couldn't it have been her instead? She had nothing to offer, and he had so much to give.

The sound of a baby crying swept through the house. Shannon stopped stacking the china cups onto the tray and poured coffee from the pot on the stove into the silver service.

"Dolt," Shannon said. Amanda smiled shyly. She knew Shannon was talking about Jake, who undoubtedly thought it was a miracle he had kept Jacey quiet this long. Shannon picked up the coffee tray and hurried to the parlor.

Amanda followed, but stopped with head bent out of respect for Cat as she went up the staircase with Grace supporting her.

Jacey's crying had stopped as quickly as it had started. Amanda assumed that Shannon had taken her, so she was a bit taken aback when she went into the parlor and saw Caleb bouncing her against his shoulder. She was sucking on her fingers and watching Zane make silly faces at her behind Caleb's back.

"Caleb's got a way with her," Shannon observed as she poured coffee into the delicate china cups.

Without even thinking about it, Amanda went and sat beside Caleb on the love seat. Shannon joined Jake on the sofa. Zane flopped down on one of the wingback chairs. Dan and Randy both stood uncomfortably in the doorway, all of them ignoring the coffee.

Except for Chase. He strode into the parlor and picked up a cup, taking a long gulp, to the amazement of those watching. It had to be hot; there was steam rising off it.

They all knew he was delaying, searching for words.

"Jake, can you go for the sheriff?" he finally said.

Jake nodded, his pale blue eyes icy as he leaned forward on the sofa, knowing Chase would have more to say.

"What happened?" Zane asked.

Chase told the story, his words concise, without elaboration.

"Whether the shooting was intentional or an accident will be up to a jury to decide," Chase said in conclusion.

"What do you think?" Caleb asked.

Chase walked over to the window seat and looked up at the single grave on the ridge. Soon another one would join it. "I think things are going to get a lot worse before they get better," he said finally.

"I reckon I need to get the undertaker, too," Jake said as he stood.

"Yes." Chase kept his back to the room, his eyes focused on the ridge.

"There's still work that needs to be done," Zane said, suddenly standing. "The ranch is still here even if Jason . . . isn't."

Caleb handed Jacey to Amanda and pushed himself up, without the aid of his crutch. "Jake," he said. "I'm going with you."

Everyone looked at Caleb, even Chase, who had just moments ago closed himself off. Caleb was standing up straight, both boots planted firmly on the rug. His mouth was set in a thin line, and his eyes dared them to say no.

"I'll saddle your horse," Jake said.

"I'll get your gun and hat," Zane added as he followed Jake.

Amanda watched as an almost imperceptible sigh of relief loosened Caleb's shoulders. It had been less than a month since he had broken his leg. Should he be riding? Should he even be standing on his own? They had given him over to her care, was she being negligent by letting him go off with Jake?

He walked with halting steps toward the door.

He needed to go. He needed to do this. He needed to be a part of this.

Shannon started gathering the cups onto the tray,

mumbling under her breath. "Stupid dolt." Clink. "Wind up in worse shape." Clank. "Men." Clink.

"Should I stop him?" Amanda asked.

Shannon looked at Caleb, who had made his way to the back porch.

"No," she said and whisked the tray out of the parlor.

Amanda carried Jacey out to the porch, balancing her against her hip as the baby sucked on her fingers. Caleb stood, determinedly not leaning on the post, looking down at the valley.

"I'm moving back into the bunkhouse," he declared without looking at her.

Amanda stood silently beside him.

"Thank you for taking care of me."

She looked up at him. It seemed as if he wanted to say more—at least his eyes made her think so. She waited, wondering if he would speak, but he said nothing. Finally he turned back to look at the valley.

Jake was riding up the hill, leading Caleb's horse.

"I'll bring your things down later," Amanda said as they watched the progress of man and horse up the hill.

Jake handed Caleb his gun and hat. He quickly put them on and then took the reins from Jake. He took a moment to greet his gelding, a shiny black with a deep blaze, proud tail and high stockings. He grabbed the horn of the saddle and, using his arms, swung himself up.

A grimace of pain moved across his features. Amanda saw it because she was watching. She hoped his thigh had mended enough for him to be riding. She knew him well enough to know that he wouldn't slow down, or expect Jake to wait for him. Indeed, he hadn't; Jake had already taken off around the house.

Caleb reached down to guide his left foot into the stirrup and then adjusted his hat, pulling it down over his eyes against the midday sun.

"Caleb?" Amanda said before he moved his horse out.

He looked down at her from the saddle.

"Be careful."

He smiled at her, but his eyes were lost beneath the brim of his hat. He took off and disappeared around the house. The last thing she saw of him was the flick of his horse's tail.

Chapter Sixteen

"You're in love with her," Jake said. After a quick and silent ride into town, they were sitting on their horses in front of the sheriff's office, waiting for the man to finish his paperwork, as he called it, before they went out to the homestead. They had stopped by the undertaker's before they went to the sheriff. They still weren't exactly sure that the sheriff was trustworthy in matters of local politics. He had failed them before, and had a bad habit of being unconcerned about the "lesser folk" of Laramie.

"I guess Jason was never able to prove that the sheriff was in on that railroad deal with Petty, was he?" Caleb asked, quickly changing the subject to the man who had kidnapped Shannon and Grace in an attempt to gain possession of Jason's land before the railroad came through.

204

"No changing the subject," Jake said. "You're in love with Amanda."

"What makes you think I'm in love with Amanda?" Caleb asked as he looked everywhere on the street but at Jake. The people of Laramie were going about their business as usual, unconscious of the loss that had just struck the community. Caleb knew the news would soon be all over town and the paper would be full of it tomorrow. He just hoped folks had the decency to let Cat and Jenny mourn in peace.

"I've seen how you look at her," Jake continued when Caleb refused to give him an answer. "Especially when you think there isn't anyone watching."

"Since when have you turned into such a romantic?" Caleb asked, quickly turning the tables.

"It's a good thing you have a broken leg or you'd be lying in the middle of the street right now."

"For what?" Caleb asked incredulously. "Your threat would sound a lot more serious if you hadn't been acting like a whipped dog ever since you brought Shannon home."

"So?"

"So what gives you the right to say how I feel about Amanda?"

"Aha!" Jake exclaimed. "You are in love with her."

"I never said that," Caleb insisted.

"You don't have to, I can tell just by looking at you." Jake's pale blue eyes were dancing with glee beneath his hat.

"What's that supposed to mean?" Caleb yelled.

"Why are you yelling at me?" Jake yelled back, his temper rising. They both knew their testiness was because of Jason. They were having trouble dealing with their grief.

A woman on the street paused to look at the two of them as they sat on their horses screaming at each other. The sheriff walked out at the same time.

"Am I going to have to arrest you two for disturbing the peace?" he asked.

"Sounds like a good idea," Jake growled. "Then you wouldn't have to waste your time going after a murderer."

Caleb watched as the sheriff's eyes narrowed. Surely the man wasn't foolish enough to try something against Jake, who was known for his fast draw. The man just stood there, glaring at the two of them.

"The longer we fool around, the better chance the kid has of getting away," Caleb said finally. "I imagine the newspaper would have something to say about that."

The sheriff smiled suddenly as if he didn't know what the problem was. "One of the witnesses should have come in to swear out a warrant," he said as he mounted his horse.

"They're both a bit busy right now," Jake barked. They took off at a canter, Jake and Caleb letting the sheriff lead the way. It wasn't as if they wanted to talk to the man.

Was the sheriff worried about how he would look in the newspapers, or about the men behind the newspapers? Caleb let Jake move ahead a bit. He rubbed his thigh as he rode, hoping he had given it enough time to heal. Perhaps he had been foolish to take off his splint, but he couldn't stand to sit in the upstairs room anymore and do nothing. Who knew where he'd be right now if Jason hadn't come into his life? Where would any of them be?

Caleb swiped at his eyes as they rode back toward the ranch and the trespassers who had brought them a world of trouble.

And why did Jake think that he was in love with Amanda?

"I'm not so sure that was a good thing," Caleb said later as they rode back to the ranch.

Jake didn't say anything, but that was typical of him. He'd been seething with anger ever since the sheriff had come out of his office.

"But it's not like we could let him off, either," Caleb continued. He was trying to work the problem out in his mind. The sight of young Charlie Potter Jr. being led off while his father stared them down with eyes full of hate made Caleb feel as if he had been the one guilty of murder. And the cries of the mother had been as heart-wrenching as Cat's. The boy had tried to be strong, but he was terrified. He couldn't hide it.

Caleb had to admire him, though. He could have run. He could have gone to the mountains and hidden, hoping to escape from the posse that would have come after him.

Chase would have found him before the day was out.

So now there was going to be a trial. Chances were pretty good that the jury would be made up of cattlemen who would quickly bring a verdict of guilty. The boy would be hanged.

That wouldn't bring back Jason. Caleb also knew that if Jason had survived the shooting, he would never have approved of hanging a boy. He would have taken care of the boy, and he would have taken care of the family, too.

Caleb's mind drifted back to the first time he'd met Jason. He was fourteen and had been on his own since his father had died back in the mountains of Georgia. The bank had taken the store and their home above it, leaving him homeless and penniless. He'd gone west, doing odd jobs to earn money to buy paper and pencil, then drawing quick sketches of people on street corners to make enough for food and a dry place to sleep. He was wearing clothes that were too small, didn't own a coat and hoped to make enough money to buy a new pair of shoes before winter set in. Jason had been passing through town on business. He'd given Caleb some money and told him he could choose to spend it on himself, or buy a stage ticket to Wyoming, where a job would be waiting for him on the ranch.

Caleb had wisely chosen the job. And he'd been lucky. He had grown up knowing the love of a father, and had soon found out that Jason took care of everyone who worked for him in the same way.

The pain of losing Jason wasn't any less than the pain of losing his own father, thirteen years earlier. Except now he was a man, and men weren't supposed to cry.

But that didn't mean he didn't want to.

Chapter Seventeen

The house was hot with the crush of bodies and still they came, pouring in from the outlying ranches and home-steads. The house couldn't hold everyone who came; part of the crowd had spilled out onto the front lawn. Grace had set up a table under the tree for the food people brought, because the dining room table couldn't hold anything more. The father bird protested the arrangement mightily, squawking from his perch while the mother nervously watched the intruders below.

Everyone in the county must be present. Amanda had given up trying to keep count long ago. There were officers from the fort, ranchers, homesteaders, towns-people, all gathered to pay their last respects to Jason Lynch. If she could have had her way, she would have locked herself in her room. But that was just the Fear talking. She was needed, if only to shuttle dirty dishes to the kitchen for Cleopatra to hastily wash and set back out again to be used once more.

Agnes had come back and tearfully taken over the kitchen for the day, telling Cat that she would soon be leaving for good. Her daughter was pregnant again and needed her. She was moving in with her family. The poor woman had dissolved into tears then and had to go to her room to compose herself.

Zeb made himself useful and kept the boys out of the way by enlisting their help in taking care of the innumerable horses and wagons that came down the drive. It was a job he knew; he had done it many times when Ty's family had held parties at their plantation. He set up a line in the pasture in front of the house and took the reins of the animals as the guests arrived, handing the horses over to Pharaoh.

Pharaoh and his daughter had proved to be a godsend. A former butler, he quietly moved about the house, bringing guests into the parlor where Jason's body was laid out. He would escort them into the room and announce them to Cat and Jenny, who stood beside the coffin receiving the mourners. Ty and Chase stood guard behind them. Chase's presence intimidated those who only knew him and Jenny by reputation. They would quickly murmur their condolences to her and then move on to Cat and Ty, who were familiar.

Everyone was gracious and properly subdued when they spoke to Jason's family. They shook hands and shared anecdotes and talked about what a wonderful man Jason had been . . . what an asset to the community. . . . how he would be missed.

But outside of the parlor, things were different. The cattlemen had gathered in the dining room and were holding whispered conversations about the murderer, young Charlie Potter, and the sheep. From what Amanda could hear as she circulated among the crowd picking up cups and plates, the cattlemen considered the herd of sheep to be a serious affront to their way of life. Out on the lawn, where the homesteaders had gathered, there were concerns about which way the wind now blew for them. Jason Lynch had always been fair in his dealings with them. But he was the only one. There was also worry about the boy who had shot him. Talk about the poor boy's family filled the air. From what Amanda could tell, the Potters were the only people living in the area who were not present.

The townspeople seemed to float between the two groups, their major concern the upcoming trial.

Amanda shared their concern. She had read the newspaper account, which was skewed, of course, to reflect the cattlemen's point of view. Poor young Charlie Potter had already been tried, condemned and sentenced to hang in one article. No wonder the homesteaders were worried. With the jury mostly made up of cattlemen, the poor boy didn't have a chance.

What would it serve to hang a fifteen-year-old boy? It wouldn't undo what had been done. It wouldn't bring Jason back. Caleb had said that the boy was terrified. Caleb had felt guilty about helping the sheriff arrest him.

Nothing good could come of this. Amanda was afraid that Chase had been right. It was going to get a lot worse before it got better.

The house was stifling. The fabric of the dress Cat had lent her stuck to her back. Amanda made her way through the crowd to the kitchen with her heavy tray. She checked the tall case clock as she went by. Two hours until the funeral, and she was already done in.

Caleb appeared before her. If she was hot, he had to be hotter; he was wearing a brown jacket and tie. He had gotten a haircut, too. Yesterday, his dark locks had curled around his ears; now the sides were trimmed up and the top was combed back off his forehead.

"Let me have that," he said, taking the tray from her hands. "Wait here," he instructed and gently pushed her into the curve of the banister.

She did as she was told, taking time to fan her face with her hand as she watched his wide shoulders move through the crowd. His limp didn't seem to be as pronounced today. Or maybe it was just because he barely had room to walk.

He returned quickly, each hand holding a glass of iced lemonade. He tilted his head toward the back porch and she fell in behind him, letting him blaze the trail through the press of people.

"Where did you find this?" she asked as she gratefully took a glass. Caleb touched her elbow and they moved away from a group of men standing on one end of the porch.

"There are a couple of blocks of ice in the bathing room. Agnes is standing guard over them. They're for us, the ones who live here, along with the lemonade. Everyone else gets punch."

Amanda sipped the lemonade gratefully. She had tasted the punch. It was tepid and too sweet.

"I thought you could use a rest." Caleb smiled at her as he leaned against the porch rail.

"How's your leg?" Amanda couldn't help noticing he had taken the pressure off both of his feet.

"Still attached," he replied with a cheeky grin as he took a deep drink from his glass.

"You're not pushing too hard, are you?"

"Amanda. Jake and Zane will hardly let me turn around without yelling at me to take it easy. One reason I came looking for you was so they would quit nagging me."

"One reason?" Her gray eyes glowed at him over her glass.

A wide grin split Caleb's face. Was she actually flirting with him? "One reason," he said, closely watching her face. "I had others."

"And they were?"

"I miss talking to you."

Amanda looked down at the ground, but she took a step closer to him, placing her hand on the painted rail. Her shy smile teased the corners of her mouth. Caleb placed his hand over hers, gently squeezing her fingers. She glanced sideways at him, let her smile bloom, and he returned it in full. Her hair was damp around her face, and he smoothed back a tendril that stuck to her cheek.

"You've got pretty hair," he said as he moved the stray. "I love how it shines. I don't know how I'd draw it, it's so shiny."

Amanda blushed at his compliment. "Have you been drawing?" she asked.

Caleb quickly dropped his hand from her hair. "No." He paused, collecting his thoughts. "I don't know why I said that. I guess I was just imagining a picture of you."

"You're a wonderful artist, Caleb. You shouldn't give it up."

Caleb looked out over the ridge at the pile of fresh dirt. It sat there, just waiting to cover the coffin after they carried it up. He dreaded the thought of Jason's final journey before they laid him to rest next to Jamie. So many visions of the man filled his mind that he ached to hold a pencil, yet he couldn't bring himself to pick one up. He was afraid of what he would see on the paper.

"I didn't realize that I had given it up." His gaze went back to Amanda. "Until now."

Amanda looked up into his deep brown eyes and realized that Caleb knew about the Fear. She had been so wrapped up in her own version of it that she had not noticed that other people had it, too. He had lost a part of himself, just as she had. He had to deal with the fact that he would never be whole again. But still he got up every morning and did his job, even though it was hard for him and he had to struggle to keep up with the others. His perseverance didn't make the Fear go away, but perhaps it kept it at bay. He was going about the business of living, which was more than she could say for herself.

But he still wasn't drawing. Maybe it was because he

was afraid of what he would see if he started. Just as she was afraid of what would happen if she gave in to her tears. They were both holding on tightly to whatever control they still had over their lives, since other parts had been taken from them, without their volition. They were both victims of circumstances. They were both in the wrong place at the wrong time, and fate had not been kind to them.

It all suddenly became very clear to Amanda as she stood on the porch while Caleb held her hand. In the instant that the ice in her glass clinked as it melted from the heat of the day she realized that her life was once again her own to control. Just because fate had taken years from her did not mean that she could not make something out of the years she had left. Wade Bishop had stolen part of her life. She wouldn't let him have the rest of it.

"I think it would be a shame to let a talent like yours go to waste," she said as she looked up into Caleb's warm brown eyes.

A shout was heard from the front yard, followed by a crash. The men who had gathered on the opposite end of the porch took off around the house.

"Sounds like a fight," Caleb said. "We'd better go see what's happening."

They walked back through the house. Those inside had already started moving toward the front yard. The sight of Chase moving through the crowd before them was not an encouraging one.

A glance toward the parlor showed a few women left

inside, along with Grace, Cat, Jenny and the minister, who must have shown up while Caleb and Amanda were on the back porch. Ty joined them and shoved his way through the press of bodies.

"It's a fight," he tossed over his shoulder at Caleb. "I don't suppose you've got your gun on."

"No," Caleb said. None of them did. It was the one thing they had not expected to need on a day such as this.

Amanda ducked into Jason's study. The door had been kept closed to keep out the visitors. This room was too much a part of the man to open it up to be viewed by everyone who passed by. The study also provided a refuge for Cat and Jenny when the day became too much. Amanda went to the gun case and got out one of the Henry rifles that Jason had kept there. Boxes of shells were in a drawer, and she quickly loaded the gun. By the time she was done, the hallway was empty and she quickly went to the front porch.

The fight had taken over the lawn. Several men were involved, and it didn't take a genius to see that it was a battle between the cowmen and the homesteaders. The men of the ranch were caught in the middle of it. Amanda saw Cole, Chase, Jake and Zane taking punches and returning them as they tried to separate the more vicious of the fighters. The food table had been turned over and the lawn was being trampled beneath feet, food and assorted pieces of broken dishes. Ty was shouting at the sheriff, who seemed to be in no hurry to break up the fight. Caleb was next to them and caught a body that came flying in his direction.

Amanda cringed when she saw the man crash into Caleb, but he stood his ground and shoved him back into the fight.

"Dolts!" Shannon exclaimed from beside her. "Best give that gun to someone who knows how to use it," she added.

Amanda agreed with her and wondered what would be the best way to get it to Ty, since her Uncle Cole was right in the middle of the melee. It would be dangerous trying to approach him, since most of the men who had shown up for the funeral were now involved in the fight. The rest stood on the porch or beyond the boundaries of the brawl, and some had even gone upstairs and were leaning out the bedroom windows. How did they dare go into the family's private rooms?

Before she had a chance to move, she felt a hand on hers. Cat took the gun from her, stepped to the edge of the porch, and fired it in the air. Some of the fighters stopped, but a few didn't, and the next bullet landed in the dirt before two of the more serious combatants. Heads flew up, some men dropped to the ground, and everyone turned to see who was doing the shooting.

"You shame his memory!" Cat shouted. "I want all of you off my property now!" Jenny stepped out of the house, carrying a rifle of her own. Cat looked up at Jenny, who was considerably taller than she. "Off our property," Cat repeated as Jenny raised her gun. Jenny looked as if she were in pain, but her gaze was steady, along with her aim.

A few of the older cattlemen, who had let their hired hands get into the melee, stepped toward the porch to make peace with Cat.

They found themselves looking down the barrel of her Henry.

"Now, Miss Lynch—" one of them began.

"It's Mrs. Kincaid, and this is my niece Mrs. Duncan. I know there are some of you who won't give her the right time of day, and you're not welcome here, either." Cat's righteous indignation seemed to grow with her tirade. "Now I am about to bury my father. And I would like to have his service reflect the dignity with which he led his life. Something that the rest of you seem to have forgotten." Cat's green-gold eyes leveled on various faces in the crowd, and some of them hung their heads in shame.

Amanda could not believe she was standing shoulder to shoulder with Cat and Jenny. Even though the other two women held guns and she did not, she could feel the strength emanating from them, and it gave her strength, too. She felt even stronger when she saw Caleb looking straight at her as he followed Ty through the crowd toward the porch. Beyond she could see Uncle Cole, Jake, Chase and Zane all shouldering people aside to get to the women who were making a stand.

"You'd better pick your friends today," one of the cattlemen said.

"And get rid of those sheep!" someone called from the back of the crowd.

"You seem to forget that this is Lynch land, not free range," Cat said firmly. "I can graze whatever I want on it."

"And ruin it for the rest of us!"

"This is *Lynch land!*" Cat shouted.

"You'd better do something about your wife, Kincaid," someone muttered.

Ty stepped nearer to the porch. "I think she's doing pretty well on her own," he said, looking up with a smile at Cat. The rest of the Lynch ranch men joined him, making a wall between the disgruntled guests and the women on the porch.

"Some of you were Jason's friends," Cole said. "And we appreciate your being here. But the family would like to be alone now. The fellowship is over. Go home."

The crowd began to disperse, some of them muttering under their breath, some of them coming by the porch to offer apologies for the trouble. Cat handed the gun back to Amanda and became the gracious hostess once again, receiving sincere overtures with her own heartfelt apologies.

"Do you even know how to use a rifle?" Caleb asked Amanda as he came up beside her.

"My uncle used to be a Texas Ranger. Of course I know how to use one."

To her surprise, he dropped a quick kiss on her forehead. "I'm proud of you," he said as he took the rifle from her hand. "Jake and I are going to check for stragglers." He flashed a smile at her and went into the house after Jake, who had taken Jenny's rifle.

"Pish on the lot of them," Shannon said under her breath to Amanda. "At least now we can catch up with the dishes."

Chapter Eighteen

Clouds were gathering over the mountains as Jason's family, and those who were considered family, gathered on the ridge to pay their last respects. The coffin had been lowered into the ground, adjacent to the grave site of Jason's grandson. Jamie Lynch, twin brother of Jenny, was still sorely missed after four years by all who'd known him. He would no longer be alone on the ridge. Another headstone would join his.

The minister's voice rang out, accompanied by the booming of thunder in the distance as he read from Psalms, 112:

Praise ye the Lord. Blessed is the man that feareth the Lord, that delighteth greatly in his commandments.

His seed shall be mighty upon earth: the generation of the upright shall be blessed.

Wealth and riches shall be in his house: and his righteousness endureth for ever.

Unto the upright there ariseth light in the darkness: he is gracious, and full of compassion, and righteous.

A good man sheweth favor, and lendeth: he will guide his affairs with discretion.

Surely he will not be moved for ever: the righteous shall be in everlasting remembrance.

He shall not be afraid of evil tidings: his heart is fixed, trusting in the Lord.

His heart is established, he shall not be afraid, until he see his desire upon his enemies.

He hath dispersed, he hath given to the poor; his righteousness endureth for ever; his horn shall be exalted with honor . . .

A stiff breeze swirled around the mourners, catching up the skirts of the women and lifting their hair. A bolt of lightning flashed in the west, casting a fierce light against the horizon. The storm was moving quickly across the prairie, deepening the sky to shades of gray, purple and deep blue.

The minister had chosen his passage well. Jason had never shown fear of anything, but went about his business with calm assurance. He had been a man at peace with himself and who admitted his mistakes and imperfections.

Caleb looked around the circle at the faces that had turned pale in the eerie light before the storm. How would they survive without Jason's steady guidance? To his left, Jenny already looked as if she were about to crumble. No wonder, since she was far along in her pregnancy, and Jason had been her last living relative. She was leaning heavily on Chase and held her hand at her side as if she were in pain. Chase's face was impassive, almost rigid. Caleb knew that Chase held himself responsible for Jason's death. But his arm around Jenny was tender and protective. What would become of Chase if something happened to Jenny? Once again, the lesson had come home to them that life was fragile. Chase would certainly be lost without her, as would the small boys who stood in front of their parents, silent and serious. Jason had adored them and spoiled them. They would miss him terribly.

Cat stood in front of Ty, taking strength from his presence. His hands were on her upper arms, as if holding her up. After her initial outpouring of grief, she had taken on her role as the heir, drawing on an inner strength that no one knew she possessed. But the fight had seemed to weaken her, and silent tears rolled down her cheeks as her curly hair tossed in the gathering wind.

Jake held tightly on to Shannon's hand as the minister, standing on his right, raised his voice to be heard over the wind. Zane stood on the other side of Shannon, occasionally dashing at his eyes when he was certain no one was watching. Dan, Randy and Zeb stood behind them, heads bowed as the service continued.

The circle was completed with Cole, Grace, Amanda and Caleb, who had taken up his position close to Amanda.

223

"Ashes to ashes, dust to dust," the minister intoned. The pages of his Bible flickered in the wind and he held them with his hand.

As the thunder boomed, they could hear the cry of Storm Cloud ringing over the wind. Amanda's hand brushed against Caleb's and he grabbed hold of it, clenching it tightly. Her fingers folded over his, holding on as if she were afraid the wind would blow her off the ridge. Caleb took a step closer, sheltering her from the assault with his body. She eased back until her spine was against his chest and her skirt wrapped around his legs as the wind swirled around them. She placed her free hand on her hair to keep it from flying up around her face, but part of it escaped and lashed against his cheek.

Agnes and her son-in-law stood behind them. The son-in-law was worried about the weather, and the elderly woman whispered to Grace that they would have to leave. Grace nodded as the minister began his benediction.

"May the Lord bless you and keep you. May the Lord lift up His countenance upon you and smile upon you. May the Lord give you peace. Amen."

The minister looked up at the sky, which was now boiling with clouds and high flashes of light.

"God welcomes home one of His own with a mighty fanfare," he said. "The angels are rejoicing as Jason enters the fold."

"Amen," they said as one. Dan and Randy headed slowly down the ridge.

"Daddy?" Chance whispered. "What do we do now?"

Zeb circled around and took the two boys by the hand and led them toward the house, answering their questions in a hushed voice.

The weather became more threatening, but no one else wanted to leave. Jenny leaned heavily against Chase as the wind buffeted them from behind.

The minister stepped close to Ty, who bent his head and nodded. The minister followed Zeb to the house, where Cleo and Pharaoh were taking care of Jacey and cleaning up the mess.

"Shannon," Jenny said. "Will you sing something?"

Shannon nodded as she looked at the expectant faces around the grave. Her clear soprano voice lifted over the wind.

My hope is built on nothing less than Jesus' blood and righteousness.

I dare not trust the sweetest frame, but wholly lean on Jesus name.

On Christ the solid rock I stand, all other ground is sinking sand, all other ground is sinking sand.

She moved into the next verse, the wind carrying the song out onto the prairie, sailing it over the tips of the grass that were flattened by the heavy wind.

Amanda shivered against Caleb, and he wrapped his arms around her from behind as she leaned into his sheltering warmth.

Lightning flashed, blinding them. Shannon's song stopped in mid-sentence as the thunder boomed, shaking the ground beneath their feet.

"We'd better get inside," Cole said.

"We can't leave him," Cat cried, looking at the grave.

Ty pulled off his coat and placed it over her shoulders. "Go inside," he said. "We'll take care of him." He picked up one of the shovels that had been left to fill the grave.

Grace took Jenny's arm. "Are you all right?" She had to shout to be heard over the wind.

Jenny nodded, but her hand stayed at her side as if holding back the pain.

"Cole," Chase said. "Take her inside." He placed his coat around Jenny and went to join Ty as Zane and Jake came to help.

Amanda's teeth were chattering as she looked up at Caleb. He pulled off his jacket and wrapped it around her. She took the lapels in her hands and pulled it close without saying a word. The sky opened up, bringing a torrent of rain that instantly blinded them and plastered their hair to their heads.

"Go on," Caleb said. Amanda turned to look at Cole and the women who were trying to hustle Jenny to the house.

"I'll wait," she said.

"You'll get soaked," Caleb shouted above the rain.

"I don't care." Her face was pale and her eyes huge with raindrops clinging to her dark eyelashes. "I'll wait for you."

The slush of shovels hitting dirt bought them back to reality. "I've got to help," Caleb said.

"I know."

He took a few steps backward, watching her, then

stumbled when a marble-sized piece of hail hit him on the shoulder. Amanda reached for him as he stumbled, but he quickly righted himself.

"Please go," he said. The hail pinged around them, so she pulled his coat over her head and held it under her chin. "Go." He was torn between her and his duty to Jason.

On the porch, Cole and the women stopped to wring some of the wetness from them before they went into the house. Jenny bent over at the waist, trying to catch her breath as a cramp moved across her back and side. Shannon went to help her and Jenny leaned heavily on her as she straightened up, her hand pressed once more against her side.

"Look," Shannon said as she stood. The two women looked up at the ridge. The men were shoveling as quickly as they could, their shirts plastered against their bodies. Lightning flashed around them as the rain poured down in thick sheets, almost blocking them from view. Amanda stood alongside Caleb, but then turned and ran for the house as he went to the grave.

"You were right about those two," Shannon continued.

Jenny nodded in agreement, unable to speak as Shannon helped her into the house.

The men were covered with mud and soaked through when they came in. The thunder and lightning blew through, but the rain settled in, turning the late-afternoon sky dark and dreary. Cleo had coffee and towels waiting for them on the back porch, and they stripped down to their pants as they dried off as best they could. They padded into the parlor on bare feet with towels wrapped around their shoulders.

"Where's Jenny?" Chase asked.

"We put her to bed upstairs," Grace replied. "She's exhausted."

Chase quickly checked on the boys, who were playing with their soldiers on the rug, and then silently went up the stairs to see Jenny.

She lay lying on the bed Caleb had used, in the room that had been hers when she first came to the ranch. She was lying on her side, facing the window that looked out over the ridge.

"At least he won't be alone anymore," she said when Chase sat down on the edge of the bed behind her.

"No, he won't." Chase did not like to speak of the dead. It was part of his Kiowa upbringing. Speaking of them would disturb their spirits from their rest. But he also believed that Jamie's spirit was still with them somehow, protecting them from harm.

"I always felt he was waiting for me to join him there," Jenny said. Her voice sounded disjointed and distant, as if she were speaking to him from another place.

Chase placed his hand on her side. "Don't."

She turned to look at him. "Don't what?" Her sapphire-blue eyes were weak, with great dark circles beneath them. Her face, usually touched with gold from the sun, seemed very pale against the black of her dress. Her cheeks, which a month ago had been full with pregnancy, were hollow and drawn. Chase had seen her look this way before. It was after she had been taken and abused by the man who had murdered her parents. She had almost died then. Almost.

"Don't talk that way. Don't leave me."

"I'm not going anywhere." She tried to flash her grin at him, but it was empty. She was empty.

Chase stretched out next to her on the bed and wrapped his arms around her. She snuggled up against him, her round belly feeling tight against his abdomen. Her right hand found its place over his heart, felt it beating against her palm.

"Chase, I want to go home," she mumbled against his chest.

"We will," he said as he kissed her brow. "As soon as the rain stops, I'll take you home."

"Chase," Ty said from the doorway. Chase looked at the window, trying to determine how much time had passed since he'd fallen asleep with Jenny in his arms. The rain was still pouring. It could have been morning or evening, it was hard to tell from the deep gray of the skies. His stomach said evening. He couldn't remember eating breakfast.

"We need to read the will," Ty said. In his hands were Chase's shirt and boots, which he placed on a chair.

The Will. The word washed over Chase like the rain had earlier. How much of his property had Jason given Jenny? What would be Cat's reaction, after being the only heir for most of her life?

"We'll be down in a minute," Chase said.

He looked down at Jenny. Her eyes were wide and fearful. "All we need is the cabin," she whispered as if she were afraid to ask for even that.

All we need is the cabin. He didn't even need that much. He could provide a home for his family. But Jenny deserved more than he could give her.

"It will be fine," he assured her.

She nodded as if that were all she needed to hear. Chase quickly dressed and helped Jenny up. Her hand, as usual, was placed against her side. He rested his hand over it.

"How is my daughter today?"

"I don't know," Jenny said. "I honestly don't know." She looked up into his dark eyes. "I haven't felt the baby move all day."

"She's just as tired as you are," he assured her.

Jenny sighed and let him support her as they went down the stairs to the study.

Cole sat behind the desk in Jason's chair. He motioned Jenny and Chase to the two empty chairs in front of the desk. Cat and Ty were in the other two, which had been carried in from the dining room. Grace was sitting also, with Jacey in her lap, while Jake, Zane, Zeb and Caleb stood around the perimeter of the room.

"Jason asked me to witness his will a few months ago," Cole began. "And he also appointed me executor. As you probably know"—he was looking at Cat—"every January he would review it. For some reason, this year he was a bit late doing it." Cole looked at Jake. "I think he was waiting for you to turn up, because once you did, he wrote a new one."

Jake shifted uncomfortably.

"This is the last will and testament of Jason Cameron Lynch, dated March 1, 1865," Cole read.

"To my daughter, Catherine, and her husband, Tyler, I leave the house, its contents, and the ten-acre grounds surrounding it, with the exception of the two cabins.

"To my granddaughter, Jenny, and her husband, Chase, I leave the cabin that they now occupy and the property known to them as the lake with ten acres surrounding it."

Chase squeezed Jenny's hand at the news.

"The remaining property and its profits are to be shared between Catherine and Jenny equally, with Catherine having control over the cattle business and Jenny control over the breeding stock.

"To Cole and Grace Larrimore, I leave the cabin now occupied by them and the sum of five hundred dollars cash.

"To Caleb Conners, Jacob Anderson and Zane Brody, I leave the sum of one hundred dollars each and the hope that they will continue to consider this their home. To the man known as Zeb, I leave the sum of fifty dollars and the knowledge that he will always have a home on Lynch land."

There was more—a cash token to Agnes, Dan and Randy; some mementos for the boys; things to be put aside for any future children that Cat and Jenny might have. Cole completed the reading.

Chase couldn't believe it. The lake was his, his and Jenny's. But then, he still had the problem of having squatters on it. Jason was dead and the problem had not been solved.

Things were surely going to get worse before they got better.

And how would Cat feel about sharing her inheritance? She had remained silent throughout the entire proceedings, as had Jenny.

"Any questions?" Cole asked. The rain droned against the window, making the awkward silence inside more noticeable.

Cat stood up, and Jenny blinked as if waking from a trance. She awkwardly pushed herself up, her hand once again going to her side.

"As far as I'm concerned, nothing about the ranch has changed," Cat began. "I want it to be as it has always been, all of us working together." She took Jenny's hand in her own. "I want this ranch to be a tribute to my father. I want his legacy to continue for those two little boys playing in the other room and the child that Jenny is carrying, and the children that Ty and I hope to have." She stopped for a moment as her voice trembled. "But if we don't, then it will all go to Jenny's children, because they carry my father's blood. Lynch blood." Her voice was strong again, full of her spirit. Her father's legacy to her.

"We all have our strengths where this ranch is concerned. I hope that each of you will continue to contribute your strengths to make it bigger and better. To make it everything my father dreamed it would be," she continued. "I consider everyone in this room to be family. I don't want any of you to leave, but if you do, I'll"—she looked at Jenny, who nodded—"we'll understand."

Cat looked at each person in the room, who were all smiling back at her, each one sharing in the collective sigh of relief that life would go on as before. They would be sad and they would miss Jason, but they would pick up the pieces and go on.

Zane waved his arm. "I've got a question," he said.

"Well?" Cat asked.

"Are we going to have to herd sheep?"

Chapter Nineteen

Dawn had not yet touched the eastern horizon when Jenny woke up with the pain. It wasn't like the beginning twinge of a cramp that had led up to Chance's birth. This was a gut-twisting, take-your-breath, red-hot flash of pain that curled her up into a ball as she cried out in agony.

Chase, as always instantly awake at the slightest sound, pulled her closer to him in their bed in the cabin.

"What is it?"

"The baby. The baby is coming. Oh, God, Chase, it's too early."

"Are you sure?" Chase lit the lamp.

Jenny gasped as another pain hit her, and she nodded against his chest. "It's coming fast and hard," she cried. "It's too soon."

"I'd better get help." He eased his body from under hers and pulled on his pants and boots.

"Hurry," Jenny gasped.

Chase placed his hands at the sides of her face. "Jenny," he said, lowering his head so he could look into her eyes. "Everything will be fine."

She nodded in agreement, not because she believed him but because she needed him to believe it.

He kissed her forehead and took off.

Had she ever told him about her baby sister? The one who had died because she was born too soon and wasn't strong enough to breathe on her own.

How far along had her mother been? Jenny tried to remember as she raised herself from the bed. She needed to change into an old nightgown. She needed to put an old sheet over the bed. She needed to check on the boys. A pain doubled her over, and she grabbed the bed post. This was not right. This wasn't the way it should be. The pain was too hard, too fast and too intense. She took a step and realized that she was standing in something wet. She looked down at the floor where a dark, oily substance was pooling.

Her water had broken. But what she saw wasn't red-tinged water. It was blood. Another pain grabbed her, circling her stomach with a hot iron band, squeezing her until she couldn't breathe and jagged silver lines danced before her eyes. She slid to the floor as darkness overcame her, her mind screaming . . .

It's too soon. . . .

* * *

The pounding of the rain lulled Amanda into a half sleep. She had the strange sensation of floating outside her body and watching herself as she lay on the sofa in the parlor with a forgotten book on the floor beside her. She had been unable to sleep in her own bed, even after all the happenings of the day. She had felt like an intruder in the room upstairs that was adjacent to Cat and Ty's. It was just the three of them now in the house, and she knew that Cat needed some privacy. Cat shouldn't have to make polite conversation with a houseguest or worry about being overheard. Amanda had even considered moving into the small room off the kitchen that had belonged to Agnes, but she felt strange about that since the woman's things were still inside. Instead she had gone to the parlor with a blanket and a book, which she ignored to just stare into the remnants of the fire as the rain continued its assault on the house.

Caleb . . . The beginning of a dream teased her senses. She felt herself floating, and a moment of panic almost overtook her as she thought she was back on the boat that had carried her to New York. Amanda knew she was dreaming and the Fear was trying to take control. She wouldn't let it. The floating felt good, and she could still see herself outside the dream, safe in the parlor with the golden embers of the fire glowing in the fireplace and the house strong against the onslaught of the rain. She let the sensation of the dream carry her away.

She was standing on a precipice in the pouring rain. Even though she had felt herself floating toward it, her chest heaved as if she had climbed the highest mountain to reach it. She looked behind her and saw darkness and the swirl of a heavy cloud. Hands jabbed through the clouds, large and gnarled, with long, bony fingers reaching for her, trying to grab her heels and pull her back down into the dark. She shivered at the sight, even though the rain was warm and soft on her skin, and took a step away from the chasm.

She found herself teetering on the opposite edge and threw her arms out for balance. She could feel the sway of her body, back and forth, as her toes ground into the wet earth and fought to keep her safe. She looked up at the sky as she swayed and the rain pounded against her face, but she felt nothing more than the gentle wash of it over her skin.

She finally recaptured her balance and peered over the edge to see what fate would have awaited her at the bottom.

Caleb . . . He was smiling and waving at her. He motioned with his arm for her to join him. But she didn't know what else was down there. All she could see was Caleb. There was nothing else at all. There was no ground beneath him, nothing supporting him, just Caleb.

She couldn't move. She couldn't go to him, even though he smiled and waved and called out to her. She wanted to go. She wanted to take the step and let herself fall into his waiting arms. She knew he would catch her.

But something was holding her back. She looked down at her feet and saw a chain attached to her ankle and snaking back into the darkness behind her. Something or someone was tugging on it, jerking at it as if trying to pull her into the pit.

It was the Fear. The Fear was holding her back. If only it would let her go, but it wouldn't. It just came closer and surrounded her, pounding against her desire as the rain pounded against the house.

The pounding continued, and Amanda shook off the dream and ran to the back door as the present came rushing back to greet her.

"Uncle Cole?" Amanda quickly unlocked the door and let him in.

"Jenny's gone into labor," he said.

"Isn't it too soon?"

"Yes. Grace and Shannon are with her. Dan and Randy went to town for the doctor. We thought Cat would want to know."

"Of course," Amanda said.

"Everyone is waiting at our place, if you want to come," Cole added as she went upstairs to rouse Cat and Ty and change into her clothes.

They both met her in the hallway, their faces etched with concern.

"I pray that she doesn't lose this baby," Cat said as they all went down the stairs together. They put on slickers and went down the hill, Cat heading toward Jenny's cabin and Amanda going with the men to Grace's.

The stove door was open so the fire would chase some of the night dampness away. Justice was curled in front of it, his tail thumping against the wood floor in greeting as she came into the cabin. The door to Grace and Cole's room was ajar, and Amanda saw the boys in the bed and Jacey in her cradle.

Caleb, Jake, Zane and Zeb all sat around the table,

each one solemn at the thought of Jenny losing the baby. Ty joined them while Amanda went to the sink to begin making coffee, feeling a bit out of place when she realized that all the women were helping Jenny.

"When was the baby supposed to come?" Zane asked.

Apparently, it wasn't the first time he had asked the question. "July," Jake replied, his temper short. "Jenny said July, just like Chance."

Zane started counting on his fingers. "What part of July? The beginning or the end? It could make a difference for the baby, couldn't it?" Jake slammed his fist on the table and stalked out the door.

"What's wrong with him?" Zane asked.

"He's worried about Shannon," Ty replied.

"Why?" Zane asked, clearly confused. "Shouldn't he be worried about Jenny?"

"Because someday it will be Shannon having a baby," Cole explained. "And we can't take the pain for them, even though we would. You know it's coming and you know that the woman you love can die during childbirth, along with the baby, and there is nothing you can do." Cole's gray eyes turned to Amanda. "There's nothing worse than watching someone you love suffer and knowing there's nothing you can do to make the pain go away."

Her uncle Cole had suffered over what had happened to her, Amanda realized. There was pain in his eyes now that had not been there years earlier. He had never stopped looking for her, no matter how hopeless the search. And he had found her.

But he couldn't make all the pain go away. He couldn't return the years that she had lost.

But he had never given up, he had found her, and he had sat by her side and held her hand when the need for opium had twisted her body inside out and she begged for death. He had brought her to a kind and gentle place, and he had given her time to heal.

The enamel coffee pot clattered in the sink as Amanda ran across the room and threw her arms around her uncle's neck.

"It wasn't your fault," she cried against him as Cole wrapped his arms around her.

"I never stopped looking," Cole said, squeezing his eyes shut against the sudden powerful emotion that had overcome him.

There was a scraping of chairs as the five men sitting at the table realized that they were caught in the middle of a private moment. Suddenly the stock needed checking and firewood needed to be carried, and were Pharaoh and Cleo staying dry in the barn? They each had a task to take care of as they faded out into the rainy night.

Amanda and Cole sat at the table and Cole told her of his search and his fears while she had been missing. He told her about what her mother had gone through, and without malice toward his sister, he told Amanda about the anger Chloe had turned on him when he could not find her daughter. He had left Texas to give her peace. His presence was a reminder of his failure to find Amanda.

"She left you some money, you know," Cole said

when he had talked himself out. "She made a good living as a midwife. And I sold the house and most of the furniture after she died. I had all the personal things stored, books and such and some things that had been in the family for a while. It's all waiting for you in Laredo when you're ready. But the money is here." He went to the bedroom and returned with a small pouch. It was stuffed full of bills, and in the bottom was her mother's wedding ring and a gold locket.

Amanda knew the locket well. She didn't have to open it to know that it held a likeness of her and her father.

"I had the jewelry sent to me," Cole explained. "I've been waiting to give it to you until you were . . . ready."

Amanda nodded in agreement as she opened the locket. "I wish I had a picture of Mother," she said as she gazed at the handsome face of the father she barely remembered. She couldn't look at her own likeness. She didn't want to remember how full of hope and excitement she had been, looking forward to her future as if it were a great treasure just waiting to be discovered.

"You do," Cole said. He pulled his watch from his pocket and opened it. Inside were two miniatures, one of her and one of her mother.

"But that's yours," Amanda protested.

"You take it," Cole urged. "I don't need it. You're so much like her that I see her face every time I look at you."

"I'm sorry that she was angry at you when she died," Amanda said, squeezing his hand.

"I'm sorry that she died not knowing what happened to you."

Amanda squeezed her eyes shut, willing the tears that threatened to go away. She didn't want to cry. She didn't want to think about her mother dying alone and full of fear about her fate. She was afraid that if she started crying, she would never be able to stop.

"Amanda?"

She gave Cole a weak smile. "I'm fine. Really, I'm fine," she assured him.

"How about we get some coffee on? I'm fairly certain the others are ready for some about now," Cole said, tilting his head toward the front door and the porch where they could hear the hushed voices of the men talking.

Amanda shook her head and swiped at her eyes to make sure there weren't any rebellious tears sneaking through. Satisfied that her emotions were under control, she went back to her task while Cole jerked the door open.

"Are you going to stand there all night or come in here where it's warm and dry?" he growled at the men with mock fierceness.

They filed in and went back to the table, except for Caleb, who joined Amanda at the sink.

"Need any help?" he asked.

"The sugar bowl needs filling," she replied. "Have you heard anything?"

"No, nothing," he said as he found the sugar tin and poured some into a small crock. "Zane said the first time, she screamed her head off."

"You were away fighting then?"

"Yes. We were." Caleb took the mugs from the shelf. "Jason wrote and told us about Chance's birth, and finding out that Jenny was his granddaughter, but when we got the letter about Fox . . ." Caleb shook his head at the memory. "It was such a wonderful thing, Jason knowing that Jamie had a son, that . . ."

"He had a legacy," Amanda finished for him.

"Yes. A legacy."

"How long has it been?" Zane asked from the table.

"A couple of hours," Cole said, checking his watch.

"I'll go find out if there's any news," Amanda volunteered. "The coffee should be ready soon."

"I'll go with you," Caleb said. "It's pretty wet out there."

No one mentioned that Caleb stood a better chance of falling than Amanda did. The two of them put on their slickers and left the cabin. Cole went to get the coffee to hide the smile that came over his face as he watched Caleb hand Amanda her slicker and open the door for her.

Jenny had recognized them as two people who needed each other. Both of them scarred from tragedies they'd had no control over. Both of them victims of chance. Jenny had managed to throw them together, but the rest would be up to them.

Cole was pretty sure that Caleb was in love. He had seen the way his friend looked at Amanda. But was he brave enough to act upon his feelings, or would the loss of his leg hold him back? And what about Amanda? What if she was falling in love with Caleb? Would she be strong enough to express her emotion, or would she run from the physical aspects of the relationship?

He couldn't imagine Caleb accepting anything less. What man would?

Cole shook his head at his meanderings. He had a tiny daughter sleeping in the next room, and the thought of a man touching her, even in love, was enough to drive him insane. And just a few years ago he would have said the same thing about Amanda. She was too good for the average man. It would have to be someone really special to deserve the love she had to give. How many times had she teased him about frightening away her potential suitors? But now he couldn't help hoping that she would feel that way about Caleb. He hoped she wouldn't give up on life, or on love. She had so much to offer a man, if only she realized it. It wasn't too late for her.

Caleb held on to Amanda's arm as they splashed through the puddles with heads down against the blowing rain. Even though it was morning, the windows of Jenny's cabin glowed with light, guiding them to their destination through the gloom.

Chase was behind Jenny on the bed, holding her up against his chest as she labored silently. Her gown was pushed up over her stomach, leaving her lower body exposed. Her face was as white as the sheets around her, and her hair was wild around her face. Cat held on to her hand and was talking to her in soft tones while Grace had a hand on her stomach, moving it about as if searching for something.

Shannon met them at the door. "The babe isn't positioned as it should be," she explained quickly. "It doesn't have its head down."

"Can Doc do something when he gets here?" Caleb

asked as he took Amanda's slicker and hung it on the door.

"It needs to be turned," Amanda said. "He'd have to turn it."

"How?" Caleb asked.

"You just reach inside. I watched my mother do it once," Amanda explained. "She was a midwife. She delivered most of the babies in Laredo."

"Can you do it?" Chase asked. Amanda looked up in surprise. She had not realized that he was listening.

"I don't know," Amanda said. "I never really helped her. I just watched."

"We've got to do something," Chase said. "She can't stand much more of this."

Amanda went to the bed to look at Jenny. She was barely conscious. Her breathing seemed shallow, except when a pain came. Then she didn't breathe at all. It seemed to catch her and hold her in its grip, squeezing the life from her.

"I'm afraid for both of them," Grace said.

"And the good Lord only knows how long it will take the doctor to get here in this weather," Shannon added.

Amanda looked at the faces around her. Cat seemed terrified. She was holding on to Jenny's hand for dear life. Grace was worried also, the lines on her face evident in the light of the lamp. Shannon had her hands on her hips; she had been present when Jacey was born, but Chase had handled the actual delivery. From what Amanda had heard, he was the one with the most experience delivering babies. She looked at his face, the face that had at one time frightened her. Now he was the one who was scared. He was terrified. What would he do if he lost Jenny? The two of them could go on if they lost the baby, but if he lost Jenny . . .

Caleb placed his hands on her shoulders from behind as Jenny moaned softly, weakly. Chase bent over her face, his hair cascading around them, sheltering them, as he spoke to her, words of encouragement, endearment and love.

What had her mother said as she turned the baby? Amanda thought. She had always been good at explaining things as she worked. *You just close your eyes and imagine what a baby looks like. You find its head and you find its bottom and you turn it so that its head is down, watching out for the cord, making sure that it doesn't twist itself around the baby's neck.*

Could she do it? What choice did she have? The baby might already be dead, and Jenny surely would be before too much longer. Amanda had to try.

Caleb squeezed her shoulders. "You can do it," he said softly.

"I . . . I need to wash my hands," Amanda said.

Shannon produced a pan of hot water and a towel, and Amanda rolled up the sleeves of her shirt.

Please, God, let me do this right, she prayed. But why was she praying? Hadn't God ignored all her prayers for all those years? But this prayer wasn't for her. It was for Jenny and for Chase and for their baby. *Guide my hands, Lord. Help me.*

"You might have to hold her . . ." Amanda swallowed hard as she sat down on the side of the bed. She looked at Chase.

"I'll take care of Jenny," he said. "You take care of the baby."

Amanda placed her hand on Jenny's stomach. It was tightly drawn, hard to the touch as her womb fought to bring the baby out.

Amanda took a deep breath and inserted her hand. Jenny gasped, her eyes fluttering. Chase held her.

"Hold on, Jenny. It will be over soon," he said.

Amanda closed her eyes. She could hear Shannon behind her, quoting the Lord's Prayer as she held on to one of Jenny's legs and Grace held on to the other.

Amanda envisioned Jacey as her hand moved into Jenny's womb. Tiny arms, tiny legs, a precious face with rosebud lips and a swirl of brown hair. She touched something, and her hand carefully inched up to where it joined with the body. A leg. It had to be, because the other one was so close; there was no chest separating it. As the realization of what she was touching came over her, Amanda couldn't help smiling.

"What is it?" Cat asked, incredulous that Amanda was smiling.

"I think it's a girl," Amanda said without opening her eyes.

Knowing that it was a baby girl inside Jenny made the task even more urgent. The baby had an identity. It was a daughter. It was Chase and Jenny's daughter. Amanda's hand touched the cord. *Keep it away from the baby's neck.* She heard her mother's words and she saw her performing this same operation. Her arm was in deep now, up to her elbow. Did she have enough leverage? Could she use the hand on top to guide the baby's head down?

She eased her hand up, knowing that she was touching the front of the baby. She didn't want to damage the face. What does she look like? Her hand found the head and Amanda twisted her arm so that her palm held the back of the baby's head.

"I'm going to try to turn her," she said. She moved her other hand to the top of Jenny's stomach and used it as leverage as she guided the baby down.

"Look," Cat gasped, and Amanda saw the movement, just as she imagined it, as Jenny's stomach rolled and she lurched up. An inhuman sound passed her lips, and Amanda wondered if Jenny would have the strength to get through the rest of the birth.

Amanda gently guided the baby into the birth canal. Then there was nothing more she could do. She stumbled back from the bed and into Caleb's chest. He quickly wrapped his arms around her from behind.

"You did it," he said into her ear. "I knew you could."

"Bless your heart," Shannon said as she wiped Amanda's arm. "You're a brave woman."

"I can see her," Grace announced. "Jenny, can you push?"

"Come on, Jenny," Chase said. "You've got to do it."

Amanda watched from the shelter of Caleb's arms as Jenny managed to rouse herself. She braced her back against Chase while Shannon and Cat held her knees.

"Push," Grace said, and Jenny did. The baby was so small that she slid out in an instant, landing in the blanket that Grace held to catch her in.

"Is she alive?" Jenny asked. "Is she breathing?"

Grace held the baby up to her breast and quickly

wiped her face and then wiped out her mouth and nose.

"Grace?" Jenny asked. She had collapsed against Chase, and both of them looked at Grace expectantly.

"Come on, baby," Grace said. She placed two fingers on the tiny chest and pushed.

The tiny head jerked, the mouth stretched open, and a thin wail came out. She was alive, but just barely.

"We've got to get her cleaned up and keep her warm," Grace said as a collective sigh of relief filled the cabin.

Shannon, Cat and Grace all went to work, cleaning the baby, wrapping her up, washing Jenny. The bustle of the women and their concerned voices swirled around Amanda like leaves in a whirlwind. She watched the circle of life spin around her; she felt her heart leap in her chest as Chase bent over Jenny and kissed her tenderly, assuring her that the baby would be fine, even when he wasn't so sure himself. Amanda felt the solid presence of Caleb behind her. She felt the thud of his heart beating against her shoulder. She felt the comfort of his arms encircling her.

She felt safe.

Chapter Twenty

"You turned that baby on your own?" Dr. Green asked Amanda after he was done with his examination of Jenny.

Amanda nodded, fearful of getting a stern lecture for practicing medicine without the proper training.

"Your mother must have been very good at her job to teach you to do something like that," he said. "I couldn't have done it." He held up his hands. "My hands are too big." He turned back to Chase and Jenny, who was holding their daughter. "You owe your life and the life of your daughter, if she survives, to Amanda," he said.

Amanda felt her face flame with embarrassment.

"We know," Chase said. "That's why we've named the baby Faith Amanda. We know she'll need a strong name to survive, so we named her after two strong women."

Why do they think I'm strong?

"Faith was my mother's name," Jenny said. "And we have faith that this little one will survive."

"Try tempting her with some sherry, cream and sugar water. If you can get her to swallow that, then you should be able to get her to nurse, eventually, if she doesn't starve to death first." Not only was the doctor efficient, he was direct. "At least she's breathing on her own. Keep her warm and keep her inside. For all we know, some of that chicken pox might still be floating around." He snapped his bag shut in his usual way. "I want you two to think long and hard about having any more babies," he said, once again looking at Chase and Jenny. "You might not be so lucky next time. Now, if someone will find me some breakfast, I'll be on my way."

"I'm sure we can scrounge up something," Shannon said. Satisfied that she had done all she could for Chase and Jenny, she left with the doctor. Caleb had gone shortly after the birth to give everyone the news. Dr. Brown had arrived at the same time that Jacey had summoned Grace with her cries to be fed. Cat had gone along with her to help fix breakfast, leaving Shannon and Amanda to take care of Jenny and the baby.

"Amanda, wait," Chase called out as she pulled on her slicker.

She stood in the doorway as he came to her. She still found him intimidating. Perhaps it was his size, or the reminder of the violence she had witnessed when she killed Bishop. But she was no longer frightened of him. She had seen his capacity for love, and knew he would protect her if the need arose. It was nice to know that there was someone else who would be there for her besides her Uncle Cole . . . and Caleb.

" 'Thank you' is not enough," he said. His dark eyes were piercing as he looked into hers. She saw within them the depth of his passion for his family. It sent a shiver through her to witness the intimacy she had seen between Chase and Jenny. What would it be like to feel something that . . . desperate?

"We'll never forget what you've done for us," he added.

Amanda looked beyond him at Jenny, who was bent over the baby, her blond hair now neatly tamed into a braid; she was cleansed and dressed in a fresh gown, full of hope that the tiny life she held in her hands would survive.

"Faith is a strong name," Amanda said.

"Both of her names are strong," Chase replied. "You're a survivor. I hope you passed some of that strength on to her."

Words failed her. Why did they think her strong?

The rain was over. The heavy clouds had turned fluffy and white, powered by a warming wind that promised to quickly dry the landscape. The puddles were fairly steaming with heat as the morning sun touched them with its bright rays. Amanda picked her way through the swamp of the yard as she hurried toward breakfast.

She was exhausted, but for some reason she didn't want to sleep. The day held too much promise.

Apparently, someone else felt the same way. Caleb was leading his horse from the barn.

"Going somewhere?" Amanda asked.

"Yes." He smiled at her over the saddle, looking as if he had a delicious secret that he was dying to share. "Want to come?"

The sound of laughter drifted from Grace's cabin. Amanda didn't want the others looking at her and asking her about what had happened. She didn't want to be the heroine of the day.

"It's been a while since I rode," she said.

Caleb swung into his saddle and slid his left foot into the stirrup. "I won't let you fall off." He held out his hand.

Amanda looked toward the cabin. She could go in, eat breakfast, help with the dishes, then go up to the house and try to stay out of Cat and Ty's way.

Or she could be independent and mischievous, the way she used to be. She could be the girl who had at one time had the audacity to think she could write for a newspaper.

Caleb was waiting. She took his hand and he swung her up behind him. She adjusted her skirt, and then her hands crept around his solid waist as he looked over his shoulder at her.

"All set?" he asked.

Amanda nodded and they took off, his horse settling into an easy canter.

"Where are we going?" she asked.

"You'll see."

Amanda had never seen this part of the ranch before. She hadn't set foot out of the small valley that sheltered the cabins and barns since her arrival last fall. They rode east out of the valley and crested a ridge; the entire prairie lay before them. The rolling plains were covered with deep grass that moved beneath the wind like waves on the seashore. The wind was at her back and it tossed her dark hair around her face and Caleb's wide shoulders, whipping the strands into her eyes.

Caleb saw her predicament and laughed as he pulled a bandana from his pocket. "Tie it back with this," he suggested as they stopped on the ridge.

She made a face at him, but twisted the fabric into a rope and tied her hair up behind her.

"At least you have a hat," she said.

"So next time we'll plan better," he replied.

Next time . . . Amanda took a firm hold again and they set off, the horse seeming to enjoy the day as much as she was.

"What's his name?" she asked.

"Who?"

"Your horse."

"Banner."

"Banner?"

"Look at his tail."

She twisted around and saw the black tail riding high behind them, like a banner in the wind. "Guess it's better than Flag," she laughed.

Caleb laughed with her. "Jenny gave him to me last summer. I think she was trying to get me back on a horse and knew that he would tempt me. He's still young and a bit green, which is one of the reasons I wound up with a broken leg."

"One of them?"

"I guess maybe I was trying to prove a point," Caleb

explained. "Sometimes I get the feeling that they expect me to stay safe at home while everyone else is doing the hard work."

Sensing that he didn't want to talk about his handicap, she asked, "Are we still on the ranch?"

"The ranch extends as far as you can see. It runs all the way to the mountains to the north and several miles east and west. We're pretty close to the southern border right now. We're on our way to the south pasture."

"Isn't that where the sheep are?"

"Yes, it is."

He was being mysterious, so Amanda remained silent, letting him have his secret, whatever it was. They rode on, Banner's tail flying high behind them, the bright sunshine quickly warming her beneath the slicker. Her face would most likely be sunburned before the day was out, but at the moment she didn't care. And as long as she kept her cheek against Caleb's back, his hat offered her some shelter from the strong sunshine. It was also nice to feel the movement of his body against her and to know the strength that it contained.

They crested a rise and Banner came to a stop, tossing his head at Caleb's command. He still wanted to run. Pharaoh's dog, Sally, ran up the hill to them with tail wagging. She sniffed around Banner's feet and then took off toward the wagon below, barking as she went.

Pharaoh and Cleo waved in greeting from the wagon, and Caleb and Amanda waved back. Amanda wondered if they were just going to sit there or go down and say hello.

Halfway down the hill a lamb hopped straight up in

255

the air, like a jack-in-the-box springing out of a bale of cotton. Another one followed suit, and soon there were lambs hopping all over the place. The ewes bleated at their antics, and the ram bleated at the ewes while the lambs kept hopping.

Amanda laughed at the ridiculous sight and Caleb laughed with her.

"Are you hungry?" he asked as the lambs finally settled down.

"I seem to have missed breakfast," she replied.

Banner was off again. Amanda waved toward the wagon as they rode through the sheep, which baa'd at the interruption of their meal. They continued up the other slope and toward a stand of cottonwoods along a stream.

"This is the end of the ranch," Caleb explained as they rode into the patch of trees. "North of here is the lake, and the road to town is south."

Amanda nodded. She knew about the lake.

He offered her his arm and she used it to dismount. She knew that dismounting would be difficult for him so she pulled off her slicker and walked toward the stream while he got off his horse. She listened as he tested his foot against the ground behind her, then heard his halting footsteps as he came to join her by the stream.

He was holding his saddlebags and a blanket. Amanda looked at him suspiciously. Had he planned this, or was it truly an impromptu picnic? He threw his saddlebags over his shoulder, placed the blanket over her arm and took the slicker from her hand.

"The ground's still a bit wet." Caleb spread the slicker out under the trees in a spot close enough for them to hear the gurgling of the stream and then placed the blanket over it. He hung his hat on a branch, took off his gun belt and then settled down on the blanket, placing the saddlebags beside him as he stretched his legs out with a satisfied sigh.

Amanda watched him with a bemused expression on her face.

"I've got breakfast," he said and opened his bag. "It's not much."

He was right. All he had were two biscuits with sausage and a jar of milk.

"I guess you weren't expecting company," Amanda said as she sat down next to him.

"No, but I'm glad to have it." He handed her a biscuit and she took a bite. She quickly decided that it was the most delicious thing she had ever tasted and had to stop herself from wolfing it down.

"So what were your plans, before you had company?" Amanda asked as she picked the crumbs off her skirt.

Caleb took a drink from the jar and wiped away the foam from his upper lip. He handed her the jar and then stretched out on the blanket, folding his arms behind his head as a pillow.

"My plans were to enjoy the day." His face showed her that he was going to do just that, whether she did or not.

Amanda took a drink of milk and replaced the lid on the jar. She wrapped her arms around her knees and settled her chin upon them.

"How's your leg?" she asked after a moment.

"Fine."

She twisted to look at him. His eyes were closed, the long dark lashes lying against his cheeks. He hadn't shaved since yesterday, and dark stubble shadowed his jaw. His hair was untamed, too, the careful grooming of the day before lost in the subsequent rain and interrupted sleep of the night.

Amanda touched her own hair and wondered if she had even taken a brush to it since yesterday morning. She had, she recalled, but she was sure it was wild from the wind and their ride. She pulled the bandana away and combed her fingers through it, quickly checking to see if Caleb was watching her.

He was. A slight smile lightened his face and his dark eyes were laughing at her. She flung the bandana at his face, and he laughed out loud.

Banner snorted at the noise and moved away, browsing in the sweet grass along the bank of the stream. Birds chattered in the treetops as the wind swayed the branches to and fro, showering the remnants of raindrops down on their heads. Caleb mopped his face with the bandana and handed it back to Amanda.

A movement on the other side of the stream caught her eye, and she watched as a rabbit stuck his head out of a hole dug into the bank. It remained motionless, moving nothing but its nose as it tested the air to see what sort of creature had invaded its home. Amanda silently watched as the rabbit moved back and forth, pulling its head in like a turtle and then sticking it out again. She silently urged him to come all the way out. To ignore its fear. To enjoy the day with her.

The stream gurgled and Banner chomped at the grass. The wind, gentled by the trees, caressed Amanda's cheek and the sun drifted through the treetops, warming her head and shoulders. She blinked. Had the rabbit moved? A yawn followed.

Her eyes were heavy with sleep. She leaned back, and with another yawn, lay down and stretched her legs out beside Caleb's. He didn't move. Amanda looked up at the treetops swaying against the blue of the sky, and her eyes closed, as all the emotional turmoil of the past day finally caught up with her.

When she rolled over on her side and curled her legs up so that her knees hit against his leg, Caleb opened his eyes. He had been lying silently, praying that she would fall asleep. He knew she needed rest after what she had done, but he also had his own selfish motives.

He had planned to enjoy this day. So much had happened lately that he just wanted to get outside and clear his mind. He needed time to think. He needed time to figure out his place in the world. But mostly he just needed time to think about Amanda. It was all he did anyway.

He couldn't stop thinking about her. At first he had thought it was because they were both stuck in the house together, but even after he had moved back into the bunkhouse, he still thought about her. When he slept, he dreamed about her. Which led to the painful waking in the mornings wanting her. Luckily, no one had yet noticed the "tent" that appeared every

259

morning in his bunk, but he was fairly certain it wouldn't take Zane long to spot it and then make it the main topic of conversation for everyone within hearing distance.

But that wasn't the worst of it. The worst part was, he couldn't keep his hands off her whenever they were together. Whether he was smoothing back a silky tendril of her hair or caressing the soft skin of her hand, he couldn't help himself. He felt drawn to her like the proverbial moth to the flame. So what was he going to do about it?

Even more important, how did she feel? The fact that she had agreed to come with him on his impromptu ride had to mean something.

And she had wanted to stay with him at the grave yesterday, even though hail was dropping out of the sky like buckshot.

Was it possible that she had feelings for him? Yesterday she had let him put his arms around her. He hadn't even thought about it when he did it. The protective gesture had been instinctive: the wind was blowing, a storm was coming, and she was shivering. Caleb recalled the feel of her body melting against his as she'd leaned against him. Her spine had been against his stomach, the top of her head right beneath his nose. It had taken every ounce of his willpower to control his longing for her. He had focused on the coffin, on what it contained, because it would have been way too easy to lose himself in thoughts of Amanda.

When he had seen her coming toward him this morning, it was if a dream had come true. His plan had been to spend the day thinking of Amanda. But to actually spend the day *with* Amanda . . . The touch of her hands against his stomach as they rode had burned clear through him.

Caleb quietly opened a saddlebag and pulled out his sketch book and box. Hands that hadn't held a pencil in nearly a year suddenly ached to go back to what they knew. He had been thinking about drawing her ever since she'd appeared at his door in the middle of the night. It was the first time he had thought about drawing since he came home from the war.

With the first swoop of his hand, he caught the curve of her hair falling back from her face. Her head was cradled on her hand, and he recorded the contrast of light and dark, the smooth skin of her cheek against the line of her hands that faded once again into the hair.

Her features were relaxed, not guarded as they usually were. She even held a slight smile upon her lips. Caleb longed to see the spark of a smile within her eyes, but they remain closed, so he concentrated on the arch of her brow and the curve of her eyelashes against her cheek.

Her hair was difficult, as he'd known it would be. How could he impart the shine by just using shades of gray? Especially now when the sunlight filtering through the treetops touched it, bringing out different shades of brown and even a hint of red.

But Caleb had never been one to give up on getting something right. His pencil moved over the page, the wind occasionally drowning out the soft sound of the lead against the paper.

He stopped to look at the drawing and was pleased with his work, but somehow the subject demanded more. He flipped over the page and began another drawing, this one coming from his memory.

It was Amanda on the night they had celebrated Cat and Ty's return. She was sitting on a footstool with the fire lighting her hair and her face full of laughter.

The next page showed Amanda standing on the porch with Jenny on one side and Cat on the other. Jenny and Cat's images faded into the paper as his pencil captured Amanda's steady gaze and the courage that she had shown that day. He smiled at the thought of her holding the Henry.

Caleb let his muse lead him as the next drawing took life. Amanda stood in a doorway. His memory recalled a modest white gown with long sleeves and a high neck, but his imagination called for something more. His pencil flew, and her shoulder was bared as a mere slip of a gown slid down her arm. Her dark hair tumbled over her shoulders and down her back, disappearing into the darkness behind her. Her gray eyes glistened beneath half-lowered lids, and her mouth . . .

Caleb glanced at Amanda to make sure she was still sleeping. His thoughts, were once again being controlled by his rampant desire instead of his brain. His hand had drawn the Amanda of his dreams, the one who haunted him from the time he closed his eyes at night until he woke up the next morning, painfully frustrated.

Maybe he should go jump in the stream. It came

down from the mountains, so it had to be cold. He hoped it was freezing.

Could he get up without waking her? She seemed to be deeply asleep, but he was anything but graceful when trying to rise. Maybe he should have thought of that before he plopped down on the blanket.

Caleb struggled to his feet, careful of Amanda. Her forehead was creased with a frown, and he wondered if he had disturbed her. Perhaps she was caught up in a dream. Should he wake her? He wasn't sure if he'd be able to restrain himself if he happened to look into her eyes, so he walked away. He felt scorching hot, even with the breeze, so he pulled his shirt out of his pants and unbuttoned it as he went to the stream.

The bank had caved in at some point, leaving a series of steps down to the water. Caleb dropped his shirt on the grass and stepped down to the stream. He knelt and splashed water on his face and across his chest, letting out a hiss as it trickled down his stomach and into the front of his pants. He scrubbed his wet hands through his hair until the dark ends stood straight up.

He leaned back on his good leg and placed his arm across the other as he surveyed the meanderings of the stream. The wind had blown the remaining the clouds away and the sky was as blue as he'd seen it in a long while, washed clean by the rain.

"Caleb!"

It was Amanda. Her voice sounded fearful, so he quickly scrambled up the bank, wondering if some wild animal had happened upon her. If so, he wondered why Banner wasn't kicking up a fuss.

She was standing at the edge of the trees, her hair wild about her face and her eyes terrified.

"Amanda?" Running was difficult, but he managed it.

She was trembling. Much to his surprise, she threw her arms around his neck and he quickly caught her against his body.

"What's wrong?"

"Nothing. I just didn't know where you were." She didn't mention the dream that had awakened her.

"I'm here." There was no place else he would rather be. He reveled in the feel of her in his arms, the touch of her cheek against his chest, the caress of her hair under his chin. He felt every inch of her against him.

Surely she felt it, too? How could she not? His desire for her was obvious to the point of embarrassment.

She nodded at his assurance and leaned back against his arms, placing her hands on his shoulders as she looked into his face. Her gray eyes were moist with tears, and her upturned face plainly showed her trust in him.

It was his undoing. His mouth swooped down and caught hers as his arms crushed her against his chest, pinning her arms between them.

She gasped, and he deepened the kiss, moving his hand up to catch her head as his other hand moved down and pressed her hips against him.

Blood roared in his ears as passion and longing filled him. He was caught up in a whirlwind that threatened to carry him away. And he wanted Amanda to go with him. He needed her to go with him, to be with him. He was incapable of thinking of anything or anyone else.

She moved against him, which was nearly impossible since he was holding her so tightly against his body. He wanted more; he needed more. His mouth moved down her cheek, slashing a path to her neck.

"Caleb," she gasped, breathless from his kiss. "Don't. Please stop."

He couldn't. He knew she'd spoken but he could not grasp her words.

Her nails dragged across his chest, breaking the skin, and his head flew up in sudden comprehension as she pushed him away.

"Don't!" She spat out the word.

They both stood with chests heaving, staring at each other for what seemed an eternity. Blood oozed from four slices in his skin, right over his heart. Caleb looked down at the wound and touched his fingertips to the blood. It was a wonder that it wasn't pouring out on the ground, the way his blood still pounded, thumping against his temples until he thought he would explode.

She had wounded him.

But how much more had he wounded her?

He reached out his hand, his fingers tipped with blood.

She jumped back, fearful of his touch.

"Amanda," he gasped. "I'm sorry."

She folded her arms over her chest and looked down, her hair forming a curtain around her face. "Can we go now?"

Why didn't someone just shoot him? Caleb turned

and found his shirt. He stumbled back down to the stream to wash off the blood, to catch his breath, to give her time.

What had he been thinking? He was no better than any of the other animals who had crawled all over her. What made him think he would be any different? Why did he think she might possibly have feelings for him? Why would any woman? Why would a woman want a damaged man when she could have a whole one? Why would a woman want any man when she didn't want a man at all?

He didn't need to worry about anyone shooting him. He was fairly certain Cole would kill him with his bare hands when he found out.

"Dang," he said to the stream. He had left his sketch book lying by the blanket. She would see what he thought of her. Everyone would see.

A rifle shot sounded, ripping through the quiet of the afternoon. Before he was up the bank, there was another report. Amanda was standing by Banner. She had packed up their picnic and held his hat and gun. He quickly strapped on his gun belt and checked his load. He checked his rifle also and then swung up into the saddle. Banner tossed his head as another shot echoed.

"I might have to leave you somewhere," he said as he held out his hand to Amanda. Without a word, she found the stirrup and scrambled up behind him. His back was rigid as she placed her hands on his hips, determinedly not leaning against him. But Banner made it impossible for them to remain apart as he took off with a hop, throwing Amanda against Caleb's back with a jolt.

"Hang on," he said, and they took off at a run toward the gunshots, both of them wondering what fate had thrown against them now.

Chapter Twenty-one

His spine was as rigid as a tree trunk and just as solid. Amanda kept a firm grip around Caleb's waist as Banner settled into an easy run, quickly eating up the ground between the grove and the sheep.

There was no doubt in her mind that the sheep were under attack. The gunfire came closer with every movement of Banner's hooves. Everyone knew that sheep were unwelcome in cattle country. It seemed to her that there was enough room for both. She hadn't seen one cow on their ride; surely there was plenty of pasture for both breeds.

But she wasn't really worried about the sheep, although concern for Pharaoh and Cleo had crossed her mind.

Caleb pulled Banner to a stop by a huge boulder that had been left from an age before memory.

"The flock is just over that rise," he said. "Stay put until I come back for you."

Amanda slid off Banner and made for the boulder. Caleb pulled his rifle from the stock.

"Be careful," she said, shielding her eyes with her hand as she looked up at him.

His face was grim and he gave no sign that he heard her as he urged Banner up the rise.

Amanda plopped down on the boulder, frustration and anger consuming her as she watched him ride away. What was wrong with her?

She knew the answer. It was the Fear. But knowing the answer did not justify her actions in her mind.

Her first instinct upon waking had been to find Caleb. She had been dreaming again. The same interrupted dream as before, when she had stood on the precipice looking down at Caleb. The chains had grabbed her around the ankles from behind and were pulling her into the pit. She had reached out for Caleb, knowing that he was beside her, and had found him gone. The blanket was empty except for his sketch book and the remains of their picnic. She had called out to him.

And he had come charging up from the stream at her call, as she'd known he would. He had come to her and given her comfort, made her feel safe.

Then he had kissed her.

Her fingers went to her lips, still swollen, still tingling from his assault on her senses.

Lord, she had never been kissed. Not really. There had been awkward pecks by sweet young beaus, and the slobbery attacks that she had tried her best to avoid, but never anything like this. Never had she been carried away, swept up into something so beyond . . . control.

It had been wonderful, yet she had fought it. It had been a gift, and she had thrown it in his face.

She had hurt him desperately. She'd seen it in his eyes. And like a fool she had looked away and asked him to take her home.

And all because of the Fear.

He'd had his sketch book with him. Amanda's eyes widened with the realization of what Caleb had been doing while she slept. He had been drawing. He had overcome his fear.

A shot sounded beyond the rise, and she crawled up the grassy slope on her belly. Her head crested the top, and she watched as Caleb and Banner charged up the opposite rise. He was firing the rifle at a pair of men who were riding away as fast as their horses would carry them. Caleb had both hands on the rifle; the reins were loose around Banner's neck, but the horse responded to the guidance of his knees.

Caleb might not be able to walk well, but he sure could ride.

Another pair of riders came in from the north. Amanda rose up, ready to scream a warning to Caleb until she realized they were Chase and Ty.

Caleb stopped Banner at the top of the rise and continued firing until the riders were out of range. Chase and Ty rode through the flock, scattering the sheep, which were bleating in terror.

Some of them were dead. As the sheep moved,

Amanda saw the bodies lying about. One ewe was struggling to rise, and her lamb stood next to her, bleating encouragement. Pharaoh and Cleo crawled out from beneath the doubtful safety of their wagon, Pharaoh holding on to a rifle and Cleo, the dog. Cleo released the snarling and lunging animal, which immediately took off up the rise, barking viciously as she ran.

Amanda ran to the flock as the three men consulted on the rise before they rode back down. Cleo and Pharaoh moved about the sheep, checking the ones on the ground. When they came to the wounded ewe, they both knelt by her side, then Pharaoh mercifully shot her. Cleo gathered up the lamb and took it to the wagon as Amanda ran through the milling flock.

"Anyone hurt?" Ty asked as the men rode down into the basin.

"No, sir," Pharaoh said. "But some of these sheep are dead."

"Do you know who it was?" Amanda asked.

"Does it matter?" Chase replied. "No one cares but us." He looked at Amanda as if he had just realized she was there. "What are you doing out here?"

"She's with me," Caleb barked.

Ty and Chase exchanged glances at the bitterness of his tone.

"Looks like we're stuck in the middle of more bad news," Ty said as Amanda looked anywhere but at Caleb. "We went out to talk to the Potters."

"They accused us of stealing their land," Chase added.

"But that's not true," Amanda said.

"No, it's not," Chase replied. "But they sure know how to make you feel bad, even when you're right."

"You can't let them stay there," Caleb growled.

"No." Chase looked from Caleb to Amanda, obviously sensing the tension between them. "But I can't really run them off, either, when their son is sitting in jail waiting to see if he's going to hang or not."

"I should have let you kill him," Ty said. "Then they'd be gone by now."

"I can't believe you just said that," Caleb said, looking at Ty.

Ty took off his hat and scrubbed his hand through his hair. "You know I didn't mean it." He looked around at the dead sheep. "I'm just tired of all the fighting and killing. I was hoping I'd seen the end of it."

Caleb and Chase nodded their heads in agreement.

"Do you think those riders will come back?" Ty asked his friends.

"I think they were just making a point," Caleb said. "Or maybe they were just a couple of cowboys out on a drunk. They skedaddled pretty quick when I showed up."

"It looks like we're going to be eating mutton for the next few days," Chase said.

"Guess we ought to move the herd closer in," Ty said.

"I think it's called a flock," Caleb pointed out.

"What's left of it," Chase added.

"We'll have to send back a wagon for the carcasses," Ty said. "Get packed, Pharaoh, looks like you're moving again."

Ty and Chase turned their horses. "Do you herd sheep like you herd cattle?" Chase asked Ty.

"Mostly you let the dog do it," Ty said as they rode toward the wagon. "It's pretty easy. You just get them turned in the direction you want them to go and they go. All you've got to do is watch out for fools with guns . . ." Their voices faded as they rode out of earshot.

Caleb looked at the dead sheep lying on the ground. He looked up at the late-afternoon sky. He watched Sally circling the flock with her nose to the ground, trying to discover which predator had attacked her charges. "I'll see if there's room for you in the wagon," he finally said to Amanda. He turned Banner, and with a flick of his tail they took off.

Amanda gathered her skirts and silently trudged after them.

I don't want to ride in the wagon. I want to ride with you.

But the Fear kept her quiet as he lifted her up onto the back of Pharaoh's wagon.

Chapter Twenty-two

Caleb made it all the way to Saturday without anyone noticing the scratches on his chest or the other problem he was having. Of course it had to be Zane who said something.

They had just finished their chores Saturday morning and Caleb had managed to get to the shower first. He stripped out of his clothes, which were filthy from mucking out stalls, and was grateful for the cold water from the barrel that washed over his steaming body.

He let the water pour over his face as he propped his stump against a low stool that had been placed there just for that purpose. No one had made a comment about it; one day the stool simply appeared and he had quickly figured out how to use it. It was much better than hopping around or hanging on to the wall.

Why did I have to kiss her? He knew why, but he was still agonizing over it days later. He had totally lost control that day. He hadn't given a thought to what he was doing; he was only thinking about what he wanted. He wanted Amanda. She was all he ever thought about. He saw her in his dreams, and he looked for her when he was awake, although he hadn't seen anything of her except the twitch of her skirt as she went down to Jenny's or Grace's while he was coming or going. He was sure she was timing her visits for when she knew he wouldn't be around.

The water pounded against his chest and slid down his stomach, temporarily cooling the ache that had settled below his waist.

He was also pretty certain that Cole wanted to kick his tail, although the man hadn't said anything to him directly.

Or maybe he just thought he should take a beating for what he had done. Having Cole take a swing at him couldn't hurt any worse than the mental punishment he'd been heaping on himself since that ill-conceived kiss.

What had made him think that Amanda would even consider kissing him, or any man, for that matter? But especially him. He had nothing to offer her.

Except his heart.

But she didn't want it. She didn't want him. Maybe someday she would want someone, but not him.

Caleb picked up the bar of soap and scrubbed it over his chest. The cuts had healed over, leaving a long trail of scabs. He couldn't keep dwelling on his mistakes. He had to get over Amanda and get on with his life.

So what was he going to do? A one-legged cowboy

wasn't exactly an asset to the ranch. He was young and he was strong, in spite of his handicap, but would he be able to keep up ten years from now, or twenty? He was smart, but he didn't have any real education. He knew the people around him cared for him, but he couldn't just live off their generosity and kindness.

Satisfied that he was clean, Caleb turned off the spout and grabbed his towel from the wall. Now that the water was off, he could hear the normal everyday sounds of life on the ranch. The chickens scratched around in the dirt behind Grace's. Bits of conversation drifted from the open window of the bunkhouse. Chance and Fox were playing in the yard.

Things had been relatively peaceful since the incident with the sheep. Ty and Chase had decided to keep the attack quiet and see if anyone in the area remarked about it. Zane had graciously volunteered to go hang out in the saloon and whorehouse tonight to see if anyone was bragging about taking potshots at the sheep. Zane had his talents and knew how to use them.

The sheep were now grazing just over the ridge behind the cemetery. Pharaoh had moved into the bunkhouse and Cleo into Agnes's old room. Cat had hired her as housekeeper, which was fine with Zeb. At least those two had a pretty good chance for a life together, for love and happiness, Caleb thought. Even Justice and Pharaoh's dog Sally had taken to frolicking together around the yard and lying side by side on the porch. Everyone would probably be tripping over puppies before too long.

Caleb pulled on a clean pair of pants, put on his

socks and then stomped into his boots. He flipped his towel over his shoulder, opened the door and ran smack into Zane.

"What happened to you?" Zane asked, pointedly looking at Caleb's chest.

Caleb's hand moved to the four lines that stretched over his heart.

The sight of his fingers dragging over the cuts made everything clear to Zane.

"Amanda shut you down."

"Shut up, Zane."

"You must have been moving in pretty close to have your shirt off and get . . . wounded . . . like that."

Caleb stepped past him. "I mean it, Zane. Shut up."

"It was the day with the sheep, wasn't it?" Zane fell in beside him. "I wondered where you snuck off to. You took Amanda out to make advances on her."

Caleb whirled and grabbed the front of Zane's shirt. "Don't say another word about her," Caleb forced out between clenched teeth.

"Come on, Caleb. You just need to get rid of some of your . . . frustration," Zane said, shaking him off. "And I don't mean on me."

Caleb wondered if he could drop Zane with one punch.

"You look like you're ready to explode. How long has it been?"

"None of your business!"

"Just what I thought. Too long." Zane hung an arm over Caleb's shoulder. "We're going to town, and you're going to get laid if I have to hogtie you to the bed."

"I can't," Caleb said as he looked up at the big house.

"She shut you down, didn't she? What difference does it make if you go to town? Why should she care? She doesn't want you."

Amanda didn't want him. She had made that point perfectly clear. She didn't want any man, much less one with half a leg. What difference would it make to her? He might as well go.

Caleb was avoiding her. And why shouldn't he? He had given her a wonderful gift and she had thrown it in his face. He had found her desirable, even after knowing what she was, what she had done, all the men she had been with.

Amanda had tried to be near the bunkhouse when she knew Caleb would be there. She had hoped to catch him alone, but he was usually riding in or out, or with one of the other hands when she came down to visit with Grace or Jenny. He hadn't spoken a word to her since he had lifted her up into the wagon to ride home with Pharaoh and Cleo. He hadn't even spoken to her then really, just grabbed her around the waist and set her up on the back of the wagon before he swung up on Banner and cantered off.

So what should she do about it? Say, *I'm sorry, Caleb; would you kiss me again, please? I promise I won't scratch you or kick you, or do anything else totally stupid, because I really want you to kiss me.*

But that was foolish, because she knew she couldn't control the Fear and it might prompt her to do any number of things.

So she kept her feelings to herself while trying to remain sociable. The last thing she needed was for Uncle Cole to ask her what was wrong with her, after he had been so happy to see her becoming a part of things.

If only she could sleep. But sleep brought the fog and the chains slipping around her ankles and the falling into the pit. Caleb was still waiting for her on the other side, but it was hard to see him now. She wasn't so sure that he would catch her.

Amanda hated the Fear.

She went down the hill toward Jenny's, checking to see who was about. She spotted Caleb walking with Zane from the shower. He wasn't wearing a shirt. She drank in the sight of the white towel thrown carelessly over his shoulder, the smooth skin of his back, the way his dark hair stood on end as if he had carelessly dried it and then just left it alone.

Her fingers ached to roam through the thick locks and smooth them down into place.

The Fear laughed at her.

Amanda had seen Ty and Chase ride out earlier. Cat had said they were going to town to see if the circuit judge had shown up. They were uneasy about the trial and wanted to talk to him. Chase and Jenny had decided to leave the Potters alone until after the trial. Everyone hoped the squatters would just decide to move on their own. If young Charlie was spared, it would be best for them to move, and if he wasn't, well, there was time enough to worry about that when it happened.

Amanda read the newspapers. She knew there was

no chance that young Charlie would be spared. As far as the cattlemen were concerned, the boy had been tried and found guilty, and the only thing left to do was build the gallows.

Cat just wanted it all to be over with. She had started the long process of going through her father's papers and spent her days in his study.

Now that Cleo was the official housekeeper, Amanda was uncertain as to her own place in the scheme of things. Even though she felt most welcome in the house, she was still an outsider.

She went to visit Jenny every day. For some reason, Amanda felt that Jenny knew what she was going through, what she had been through, though they had never really talked about anything beyond the mundane.

And it was wonderful to see how baby Faith was thriving. She was nursing now, putting on weight, and her cries were strong instead of the weak mewling she had made on the day she was born.

Amanda knew that Jenny was still worried about her daughter. One of the baby's legs looked different from the other. It was almost as if it had been turned the wrong way at one time. As Amanda came into the cabin, Jenny was holding the leg in her hand while the baby nursed. Jenny had recovered from the birth, though she was still weak and sore. Her face had finally recovered its golden glow, and the deep circles under her eyes were gone.

Jenny was beautiful. Amanda was greeted by her dazzling smile when she walked in. Jenny patted the bed beside her, inviting her to sit down and talk.

"How is she today?" Amanda asked.

"Hungry as usual," Jenny replied. "For someone who supposedly couldn't swallow, she sure did get the hang of eating fast."

"Maybe she's looking for some more sherry."

"I can't believe he prescribed that," Jenny said.

"But it worked."

"Yes, it did. And now it seems she can't get enough to eat."

As if in agreement, Faith made a gulping sound, a big noise from such a tiny mouth. The women laughed and then settled into silence, listening to the smacking of Faith's mouth against Jenny's breast.

"Jenny," Amanda asked. "How did you get that scar?"

Jenny looked down at the scar that showed over the soft blond fluff that covered the head of her daughter. "I did it," she said.

Amanda turned on the bed to face Jenny. "Why?"

"To remove the past."

Amanda looked at her in confusion.

"Before Chase and I were married, something happened to me. Something horrible."

Jenny looked down at the baby, who had fallen asleep while she nursed. She wiped a drop of milk from the corner of her rosebud mouth. "Would you?" Jenny asked, handing the baby to Amanda. "I know it might seem silly, but I don't want her to hear this."

Amanda took the precious bundle and gently placed her in the cradle at the foot of the bed. Jenny buttoned her gown and carefully moved off the bed. Amanda followed her awkward gait to the chairs in front of the fireplace.

"When Jamie and I were thirteen, our parents were murdered by a man named Randolph Mason. Jamie was burned in the attack, and it left horrible scars on his face." Jenny ran her hand down the left side of her face as she spoke.

Amanda looked up at the picture of Jenny, Jamie and Chase on the mantel. She could not imagine a scar on the handsome face of Jenny's brother.

"We were sent to an orphanage. That was where we met Chase." Jenny's sapphire-blue eyes glowed with the memory of it. "Soon after Chase came, I was sold off to a family moving west. It broke my heart to be separated from my brother. I was finally able to escape them, but that was when I ran into Wade Bishop."

Amanda nodded. She knew what it was like to run into Wade Bishop. She had lost years of her life because of it.

"I finally got away from Bishop in Texas. By then I had been gone for almost a year. I went back to find Jamie, but he and Chase had left the orphanage to go looking for me. We were lost to each other."

The loneliness of those years started to settle on Jenny and she shook them loose. They were in the past. She had a family and friends and she would never be lonely again.

"Four years later I found the two of them here," Jenny continued. "And Chase and I fell in love, although it took me a while to figure that out," she said with a smile.

"Jamie and I decided to go back to our old home, to say good-bye to the place and see if we could find our mother's quilt." She pointed to the blue double-wedding-ring quilt that graced the foot of the bed. "Mason was there. Mason and several of his men. He had moved into our house after killing my parents. He hated my father that much."

Jenny's voice changed as she spoke of that terrible time. "We couldn't fight him. I stayed so Jamie could escape. It was the only way to save his life."

Mason had threatened to finish the job of burning her brother. There was no doubt in Jenny's mind that he would have done it if she had not have offered herself as a sacrifice.

Jenny slowly stood and went to the mantel. She looked into the likeness of her brother's face, captured so perfectly by Caleb's hand. "I was there for three days before Jamie returned for me. It took that long for Jamie to find Chase and the others and come back. I knew I could hang on for as long as it took, because I knew they would come." Jenny looked at Amanda. "I was lucky. I had that to count on."

If only Amanda had been that lucky. If only she had known that someone would come for her. Amanda tightly gripped the arms of her chair.

"Mason liked to brand his property. I guess it went back to my father stealing my mother away from him on the eve of their wedding. He took his knife and carved his initials into my skin." Jenny looked down, once more seeing in her mind's eye the horrible image of the monogram as it had appeared on her skin.

"After they rescued me, Jamie and Chase brought me back here. I wanted to die. I think I would have, but

Chase wouldn't let me. I kept seeing myself in hell, and Mason was there. Chase had killed him. . . ." The image of what her husband had done to the man was not something she would ever forget.

"But I got better. Chase was fixing this place up for us." Jenny's arm gestured around the room. "But then I thought that I might be pregnant by Mason. So I ran away." Jenny sat down again, stiffly. "Finally I realized that there are some things you can't run from. So I came back and we waited to see." Jenny smiled at the memory of the relief she'd felt when she knew she wasn't pregnant. She remembered the sheer joy of the moment when she told Chase and she lay on top of him in the field while he looked up at the sky. "I wasn't pregnant." She leaned over the arm of her chair to make sure Amanda was paying attention. "But there was still something else standing in our way."

"The brand," Amanda said.

Jenny nodded. "I couldn't stand the thought that every time Chase looked at me, he would see it. He would know that another man had had me first. Even though I knew that he loved me and understood and it didn't matter, I had to get rid of it. Kind of like a clean slate, I guess. I took Chase's knife and placed it in the fire and burned it off."

"Did it hurt?"

"Yes, it hurt. But I knew that Jamie had survived worse than that. And when it was done, it didn't hurt anymore."

"You were lucky to have Chase and your family,"

Amanda said, her gaze focused on the empty fireplace instead of on Jenny.

"I know that what happened to me does not compare to what happened to you."

"But it does."

"No, not really. You see, I always had hope. And even though Cole desperately wanted to find you, he didn't know where to look."

Amanda looked down at her lap, her dark hair falling around her face, shielding her emotions from Jenny's wide blue eyes.

"But you still have a chance, Amanda."

Amanda turned her head.

"You have a chance to be happy . . . with Caleb."

"Caleb?"

"He loves you."

"He can't," Amanda whispered. But he did. She knew he did. It was in his eyes every time he looked at her. It was in his kiss.

"Why can't he?" Jenny asked.

"Because . . ." Amanda's hand went to her lips. He might have loved her, once, but he didn't now. She had turned him away. She had hurt him, deeply hurt him. She would never forget the look on his face after she pushed him away. He couldn't love her, not now.

"Because you're soiled goods? Because you've been horribly used? Because you were the victim of an evil man's lust and greed? Where would I be today if I let my doubts get in the way of my happiness?"

"I don't know." Amanda looked down at her hands,

once again clasped in her lap. Jenny rose again, ignoring the pain, and knelt in front of Amanda, taking her hands into her own.

"Amanda. Not everyone has a chance to be loved, and I mean truly loved. My parents had it, and it was something I desperately wanted for myself. I could have used what happened to me as an excuse not to feel . . . anything. I could have told Chase to walk away and find someone else. But he loved me. He loved me enough to let me figure it out in my own mind, but I have no doubt that if I had left, he would have run me down and brought me back kicking and screaming. We're lucky that we have this place to live in, because not everyone out there is as accepting of the two of us as the people who live here. But if it meant living in a cave and having nothing to eat and nothing to wear, I would live with him, and I will love him until the day I die."

Amanda pulled her hands away and Jenny leaned forward, placing her hands on the arms of the chair so Amanda could not escape. "What happened to you was horrible, and I'm sorry, but good things have come out of that pain." Jenny pointed to the cradle. "Faith and I would probably be dead now if you hadn't been here. But you wouldn't have been here if Bishop had passed you by. Cole wouldn't be here, either. You'd all be fat and happy and living in Texas."

Jenny continued. "If my parents had not been murdered, I never would have met Chase. Believe me, I miss my parents more than anything, but I wouldn't have known what loving Chase was like. I wouldn't know his love for me. I wouldn't have these wonderful children."

"Caleb loves you, and I believe that you love him. Any fool can see it just by looking at the two of you. You're just too scared to admit it. And he probably is, too. But once you do, nothing can stand in your way. You can be happy. You can have a long life full of love and happiness. It is right in front of you. All you have to do is reach out and take it."

A tear appeared in Amanda's eye. It swelled over her lashes and slid down her cheek. Amanda quickly wiped at it as if embarrassed that Jenny had seen it.

"Don't hide your tears, Amanda. God gave them to us for a reason."

"Why?" Amanda whispered.

"They cleanse our souls and wash away the pain." Jenny's hand went to the scar on her breast. "The pain of crying might be unbearable for a moment, but then the moment is over and you can go on. Have you cried at all since you came here?"

Amanda briskly shook her head as she jumped up from the chair, rocking Jenny back on her heels. She bolted from the cabin, nearly plowing into Chase, who was coming up onto the stoop.

"What's wrong with her?" Chase asked as he helped Jenny to her feet.

"She asked me about my scar," Jenny replied as she melted into his arms.

Chase placed a kiss on top of her blond head. "So you were comparing horror stories?" he asked with a half smile on his lips.

287

"You might say. Actually, I just gave her a swift kick. Told her to take notice of something wonderful that's right under her nose."

"Caleb?"

"Mmm," Jenny said against his chest. "I might have scared her."

"You couldn't wait for her to figure it out for herself?"

"I'm not as patient as you."

"Really?" Chase swooped her up in his arms.

"What are you doing?"

"Taking my wife to bed."

"I hope you remember that your wife had a baby just a few days ago."

"I remember. She gave me a beautiful baby girl who looks just like her." Chase placed Jenny on the bed. "And I would just like to spend some time with her now and tell her how much I appreciate the effort. That's all I plan to do." He lay down on the bed next to her and pulled her into his arms. "I love you, Jenny."

"Thank you for loving me. I love you too."

Chapter Twenty-three

Caleb and Zane ran into Ty and Chase as soon as they hit the road to town. They reported that the circuit judge had been delayed by a trial in another town. The sheriff was gone and the town was rumbling. Folks were anxious for a hanging. Ty looked grim and Chase frustrated. Like everyone else, they just wanted it to be over.

Further down the road, Caleb and Zane met Agnes and her son-in-law. The woman was on her way to pick up her things and went into a tizzy when they told her about Jenny having her baby early. Zane began to give her all the details, even though Caleb had been the one who actually witnessed the birth.

Caleb didn't feel much like talking about Amanda's part in it all, but Agnes was sweet and caring, so he told her what had happened. After they went on their way, Zane occasionally looked at him as they rode silently along. They had known each other a long time. Zane might bluster, but he knew when to be quiet. He was a good friend, in spite of his nonsense.

Maybelle's hadn't changed much since the last time Caleb had visited. How many years had it been? Four. Four years since he had lain with a woman. Dang, but he needed a drink. He should have talked Zane into going to the saloon before Maybelle's, but Zane had different priorities. Caleb stood in the middle of the main salon as the chatter of the women and the laughter of several men surrounded him.

The girls he remembered had aged a bit and wore face paint to disguise it. They couldn't be any older than Jenny or Cat, but they looked different from his two friends. Was it the difference in the way they lived their lives? Jenny and Cat had been through hard times, but their eyes were still soft and had a spark. Some of these women looked at life through eyes that were dull and hard.

Caleb did not recognize the girl that Zane was with. She must be Missy, the one he usually talked about. Caleb suddenly felt self-conscious when he saw her whispering to a Chinese girl who looked as if the top of her head would barely reach his shoulder. Both of them looked down at his legs as if trying to decide which one he had lost.

Zane grabbed the Chinese girl by the hand and pulled her across the room to where Caleb was standing. "This is Toy," he said proudly. "Toy, this is Caleb."

Her eyes were as dark as night and heavily painted with kohl to enhance their exotic look. Her hair was twisted into an elaborate knot on top of her head and was held in place by two ivory picks with butterflies carved into them. She wore an elaborately embroidered robe that was held in place by nothing more than a sash.

"We go upstairs," she said.

Zane grinned and smacked Caleb on the arm. "Don't worry, buddy, this one's on me."

Caleb didn't answer; he just followed the brightly colored robe as if he were bewitched by the contents.

"You didn't tell me he was so good-looking," Missy said to Zane as she hung on to his arm.

"He's nothing next to me, sweetheart." Zane grinned as he pulled her up the stairs.

Why was he here? Caleb wondered as he sat on the bed with his legs stretched out before him, watching Toy light a long stick of incense and place it in a delicate porcelain bowl. The scent of sandalwood filled the air.

She pulled the ivory picks from her hair and it cascaded down her back in an ebony waterfall that ended at her knees. As she walked toward him, she untied the sash and dropped the silken robe from her shoulders. Caleb drew in his breath when he realized that she was completely nude beneath her robe.

"You like?" she asked, her black eyes almost disappearing as she smiled.

What was not to like? She glided to the bed on graceful feet.

"In China my feet would be bound," she explained. "I would not be wanted there." Toy stepped onto the bed and straddled Caleb's legs, slowly sinking down onto his lap. The heat of her body settling on him hit him with a jolt, and he felt the rising tightness against the buttons of his pants.

"Here men want me," Toy whispered in a husky voice. She leaned forward and licked his face from the corner of his mouth to the corner of his eye. Caleb sucked in air. He felt as if he had been punched in the gut.

He buried his hand in her hair and gently pulled her head back. Her eyes held a glittery glaze. She avoided looking him in the eye. The scent from the incense was overpowering, filling his senses until he felt as if he were viewing himself through a haze from a distance.

What am I doing here?

"What's your name?" he asked.

Her nimble fingers worked at the buttons of his shirt. "I am Toy."

"Your real name," he insisted as her hands grasped his chest and squeezed hard before they roamed across the muscles and dipped down around his waist.

"I am Toy," she said. "But I can be another if you wish."

Her hands moved to his fly and released the buttons, one by one. She reached inside and grabbed him, freeing him from the constraint of his pants. Toy raised her body, ready to impale herself and take him inside her warmth.

Caleb wrapped his hands around her waist and set her aside. He rolled off the bed and quickly and painfully buttoned his pants with trembling hands.

"You no like?"

"No. Yes." He ran his hands through his hair. "It's not you. It's me."

"You no like girls?"

"Yes, I like girls." Caleb swallowed hard. "I like girls very much. It's just that . . ."

Toy jumped from the bed and put on her robe. "You not tell Maybelle?" She went to the dresser, pulled out a dark brown bottle and took a swig, surreptitiously glancing over her shoulder to see if Caleb was watching.

She was drinking laudanum. Caleb's stomach turned. It could be Amanda in this room.

"I won't tell Maybelle," he said, stepping to the window. Night was quickly falling. The moon, fat and full, had made its appearance in the deepening sky.

The saloon was coming to life across the street; he could hear the tinkle of the piano and the sounds of laughter floating out. Poor Charlie Potter could probably hear it, too, from his jail cell. The sounds of groans and creaking bedsprings pounded through the walls on both sides of Caleb. He heard the slide of the drawer again. He didn't have to look to know that Toy was nipping another drink from her bottle.

It could be Amanda in this room.

What am I doing here?

Amanda had been walking all afternoon, trying to escape Jenny's words. She swiped at the tears that wouldn't stop. It wasn't time for them. She didn't have time for them. In spite of what Jenny said, Amanda knew the tears were part of the Fear.

Jenny knew about the Fear.

Jenny had defeated the Fear.

Where was she going? What was she doing? Without

really knowing it, Amanda had returned to the ranch house. She reached the back porch and hung on to a post, panting hard.

She had run away from Jenny because Jenny had placed the truth before her. She hadn't said anything that Amanda didn't already know, but hearing the words out loud was totally different from trying to convince herself in the wee hours of the morning that things were going to get better.

Things *were* better—at least, they had been until she had totally messed them up.

So what was she going to do about Caleb?

Amanda looked into the valley. Peace had settled over it like the dusk of the evening. The chores were done for the week, and the few people she could see down below were taking their time, enjoying the end of the day.

Dan and Randy were mounting their horses, undoubtedly going to town for a Saturday-night celebration. She could see her Uncle Cole as he appeared and disappeared with the movement of the porch swing. Jacey was in his arms. Amanda wondered if he sang the same nonsensical song to her cousin that he had sung to her.

The top of Zeb's head was visible over the shower stall. No doubt he was getting ready for a night of courting Cleo. Chase came out of his cabin and hollered for the boys, who charged across the yard and flung themselves at his legs, joyously wrapping their arms and legs around his strong limbs for a ride.

Jake and Shannon were nowhere to be seen, but she

had a pretty good idea of where they were. Their love was still fresh and new. And Shannon really wanted a baby.

Voices carried through the house behind her. Ty and Cat were working in the office. Cleo was singing as she prepared dinner. Life on the ranch—the cycle continued, going forth, moving on. Everyone fulfilled a purpose. But what was her purpose?

As she hung on to the porch post, Amanda considered her part in the story that took place every day. Where would she be now if fate had not stepped in and carried her away from her childhood home? Would her life be better at this exact time? Probably. Would it be better tomorrow? Or ten years from now? Her mother's life would certainly have been better. She would most likely still be alive and delivering babies in Laredo.

How about Uncle Cole's life? He was truly happy with Grace, and had a child. Amanda didn't think that would have happened before. He never would have found such happiness if he had not left Texas. And Grace would not have Jacey if he hadn't come.

Jenny had said she would be dead now if not for Amanda. Baby Faith would certainly have died if she hadn't stepped in when she did. The fact that they were both alive had a wonderful impact on Chase and the boys. She hated to think what would become of Chase without Jenny.

The very fact that she was here had changed things for so many people. Changed them for the better. And what about last fall when she had gotten the boys out of the house during the attack? They could have been left with someone else that night. Probably Caleb, since his handicap made it difficult for him to go out.

And he would have stood and fought and probably died to protect the boys. He never would have hidden. She knew him well enough to know that he would have stood his ground. The thought of Caleb dead was more than she could bear. Caleb was alive. Caleb had life. Caleb had loved her. Would he, could he, still love her?

Fate had closed doors for her. She had felt abandoned and lost, and, sometimes she had wanted to die. But when one door had closed, another one had opened. She had begged God to end her life, and had not received the answer she wanted. But sometimes when you prayed, you didn't get what you wanted. You got what God wanted. God wanted her to live. God had given her a life and a good place to live it. He had given her a gift.

A precious gift. Some lines of scripture surfaced in her mind.

And therefore will the Lord wait, that He may be gracious unto you, and therefore will He be exalted, that He may have mercy upon you: for the Lord is a God of judgment: blessed are all they that wait for Him.

A passage from Isaiah, chapter 30, verse 18. A tidbit of memory from a sermon she had heard at the church she had attended with her mother. It had stuck with her, though she never knew why. Now she did. She had prayed, but she had not waited for God's answer. It had been a long time coming, but it was here. He had answered her prayers.

Amanda recognized Agnes's voice in the hallway talking to Cat about Jenny's baby.

"Caleb said Amanda saved both Jenny and the baby," Agnes was saying.

Caleb had talked to Agnes. When?

"We saw Zane and Caleb on the road to town," Agnes went on.

He wasn't here. He had gone to town. Amanda hopped off the porch and ran down the hill.

She was going to Laramie.

Chapter Twenty-four

"I need a horse."

Cole stopped rocking and looked at Amanda as if she had grown an extra head. "Why?"

"I'm going to town."

"It's Saturday night," he protested.

"I know."

Grace came out.

"Why are you going to town?" Cole insisted.

"I've got business there."

"Does this have anything to do with Caleb?"

"Why?"

"Because I'm your uncle, that's why."

"Cole," Grace chided him.

"If you think I'm going to let her take off to Laramie on a Saturday night by herself, then you're as crazy as she is right now," Cole protested.

Grace looked at Amanda. Brown eyes met gray in the

light of late afternoon. Grace understood that Amanda couldn't wait for Caleb to come back. She had to find him now. The Fear was gone, and determination stood in its place. "You could go with her," she suggested.

"Grace!" Cole exclaimed.

"I'll help you find a horse," Grace said as she came down the steps and took Amanda's hand. "Zeb will help, too."

"Dang it!" Cole barked and followed after them. He handed Jacey to Grace, who smiled contentedly. He had done exactly what she expected, and he didn't know if he should be angry about it or not.

"Can you at least wait until I get my guns?" he asked as he picked out a mare for Amanda and saddled their horses.

"Be quick about it," Amanda replied saucily.

Cole looked at her, a bemused expression on his face. "Do I get a say-so in this?"

"How about if I promise to let you know something as soon as I know something?" Amanda said.

"It's pretty obvious to everyone where that boy's heart lies, Amanda. I just hope Zane hasn't talked him into doing something stupid," Cole said.

"Why don't you hurry up, then?" Grace suggested sweetly.

"Give me a minute," Cole groused and went to get his guns.

Amanda led the horses out and mounted her mare.

"Everything will be fine," Grace assured her as she grabbed her hand.

"I just hope I'm not too late," Amanda said.

"It doesn't mean anything," Grace said.

Amanda looked at her in confusion.

"Where he is, what he's doing."

Realization swept over Amanda. It was Saturday night. She had grown up in a cow town. What did all single cowboys do on Saturday night? What did soldiers and sailors and longshoremen do on Saturday night?

Caleb had gone to the whorehouse.

Amanda gathered up her reins. The Fear was not going to win. She knew her way around a whorehouse. She'd just go in and drag him out. A self-satisfied smile lit her features.

"That's not what I'm worried about," Amanda said. "But I'll keep it in mind."

The night air hit Caleb with a rush. He sucked it into his lungs as he stood on the porch at Maybelle's. He had stayed in Toy's room long enough to keep her from getting into trouble. Long enough that he'd thought he would never escape the place.

And Amanda had been a captive of such a house for four years.

And survived.

She was too good for him.

He looked up and down the main street of Laramie. He hadn't been to town since the day he'd returned to Wyoming last summer. Maybelle's and the saloon were the same, of course, the bank, the mercantile and restaurant hadn't changed. The church and schoolhouse were still at one end of the street and the livery and blacksmith at the other. A few empty storefronts were scattered among the rest of the buildings that held the newspaper, gunsmith, sheriff's office, telegraph, doctor's office and dressmaker. The dressmaker was probably thrilled that Cat was back in town. Every place was dark except the sheriff's and the saloon.

The saloon was boisterous. Business was booming, and the harsh sounds of male voices disturbed the peace of the night.

It was hard to say how long Zane would be. Caleb stepped out into the street and quickly caught himself. For a moment there he had forgotten about his leg.

There's no shame in it. You lost it in the war. There are soldiers in there, same as you, who lost friends, parts of themselves.

Caleb steadied himself and walked across the street to the saloon.

He was wrong about the soldiers. The place was full of cowboys. Every cowboy off every ranch around must be in town. Dan and Randy waved at him from a table, and he made his way through the press of bodies to join them.

"So how was she?" Randy asked.

Caleb flushed down to his shirt collar.

"That good?" Dan laughed and slapped him on the back. "Randy's just asking because he's too cheap to spring for her. Toy's expensive. Zane said he was going to get her for you."

Caleb decided to give Zane a thrashing tomorrow, preferably before he was totally awake.

"Maybe we oughta go get him and go home," Randy said. "Things are pretty ugly around here tonight."

"What's going on?" Caleb asked as the waitress dropped a beer in front of him.

"Just listen," Dan said.

Caleb leaned back in his chair and sipped his beer, tuning his ears to the conversations buzzing around him.

"Charlie Potter. . . ." "Judge is late . . ." "Everyone knows. . . ." "Oughta go ahead and lynch him and save the time and expense . . ."

"Dang," Caleb said.

Dan and Randy nodded in agreement.

"I don't want to see anyone lynched," Randy said. "But I think they're right."

"He's just a kid," Caleb said. "He's a scared kid."

"A scared kid who shot Jason in cold blood," Dan exclaimed as he slammed his mug on the table.

"Cat and Jenny wouldn't want this," Caleb said. "Jason wouldn't want this."

A crash sounded near the door. A man stood on a table, swinging a rope over his head.

"Why wait, boys?" he shouted. "I've got the solution right here."

"Looks like we're not going to have a say in the matter," Dan said as the crowd roared in agreement and swarmed toward the door.

"*No!*" Caleb shouted as he stood. "We've got to stop them," he said to his friends.

Randy gulped down what was left of his beer. "Stop them with what? There are three of us and a hundred of them. I'm not going to get myself killed over some fool kid."

"We can't let it happen," Caleb insisted.

Dan threw out his hands. "What are we supposed to do, Caleb? It's out of our hands now."

Caleb grabbed Randy. "Go get Zane."

"You're not thinking about trying to stop them, are you?" Randy asked.

"Just get him," Caleb ground out.

The crowd tramped down the street toward the jail, screaming and hollering. Caleb followed Dan and Randy across the street and swung up on Banner as the two cowboys went into Maybelle's.

A crowd had already gathered on the balcony.

"What's going on, honey?" one of the whores shouted down to Caleb.

"Nothing," he yelled back. "At least if I have my way," he said to Banner. Banner swung around in agitation. The horse wanted to escape the noise and the crowd, but Caleb wouldn't let him. He pulled his rifle out and dug his heels into Banner's flanks. Banner surged forward at about the same time that young Charlie Potter was dragged out of the jailhouse.

Where were the sheriff and his deputies? Completely useless, as usual. The sheriff fired a shot in the air in mock protest, pretending to do his job.

Banner charged down the street just as a rope was thrown over the beam in front of the livery stable.

He should have sent one of the guys to the fort, Caleb thought. But they wouldn't have made it in time.

The noose was around Charlie's neck. The boy was terrified, and Caleb couldn't blame him. He was terrified, too.

Some men were stringing the boy up. Charlie's hands

went to his neck, grasping the rope, trying to pull it away as it choked him.

Caleb fired his rifle, unnerving the men holding the rope. Charlie dropped to the ground as the crowd roared in protest. Hands reached for Caleb as he charged through the crowd on Banner.

It was just like being in the war.

Caleb swung his rifle and clubbed someone on the head. He swung the rifle back up and shot at a man who tried to yank Charlie up again.

"Somebody get that fool!" a man yelled.

A shot whizzed by Caleb's head. He ducked over Banner's neck.

God, he loved this horse.

Caleb reached Charlie and pulled Banner to a stop. The horse reared, with hooves reaching for the sky. He landed on his forelegs and kicked out, catching a man who was sneaking up behind him.

It was a miracle Caleb hadn't been shot. So far.

Suddenly every man in the crowd had a gun leveled on him. They all stood a few feet away from striking distance of Banner's hooves.

"We don't want to hurt you, Caleb," someone yelled.

"We got nothing against you," another man said.

"Get out of our way."

"Let us take care of business."

"Stinking homesteaders."

"Murderers."

"I won't let you kill this boy!" Caleb shouted to the crowd.

Where was Zane? Where were Dan and Randy? His eyes scanned the street behind the crowd.

Charlie was kneeling on the ground behind him, crying.

He knew just how the kid felt.

"Sheriff, why don't you do your job?" Caleb asked.

"The way I look at it, I'm just saving the town of Laramie some time and money," the sheriff replied, casually scratching his chin.

With a roar, the crowd agreed with him.

"You're going to have to go through me to get to him." Caleb's jaw was clenched, the words ground out from between his teeth.

He didn't want to die. *Please, God, I don't want to die.* Charlie didn't want to die, either. Or Jason. Or Jamie.

Caleb saw the look in the eyes of his adversaries. He saw the change that comes when a decision is made. He was one against a hundred. He didn't stand a chance.

They wouldn't even waste a shot on him. They'd just pull him off the horse and beat him to death.

The crowd moved as one. Hands reached out. Banner shied and reared. The men were too close for the rifle to work. Caleb reached for his pistol.

Shots ricocheted in the dirt in front of the crowd. Heads flew up in shock, and relief washed over Caleb.

"Need some help, Caleb?" Cole shouted.

"I can't leave you alone for a minute," Zane added.

Caleb quickly changed his mind about giving Zane a beating. He decided to kiss him instead. But what was

Cindy Holby

Cole doing here? Caleb didn't dare take his eyes or his pistol off the threat that still stood in front of him.

"Sheriff, I think I'll take young Mr. Potter here home with me," Cole drawled, brandishing his rifle.

"You can't do that, Larrimore," the sheriff sputtered.

"Really?" Cole said, amusement in his voice. "Who's going to stop me? The liquor's going to wear off pretty soon and these boys will lose their nerve."

A reputation as a sharpshooting Texas Ranger was a wonderful weapon when the odds were against you.

"Amanda, would you mind untying that boy and letting him use your horse?" Cole said.

Amanda? Caleb turned and watched in amazement as she jumped off her horse and went to help Charlie.

"You wouldn't mind giving her a ride home, would you, Caleb?" Cole asked.

Zane, Dan and Randy were all grinning at him from their saddles. They were holding guns, too, but their eyes danced with pleasure. Cole had just given the entire town a beating. It was a thrill and a privilege just to watch him work.

Amanda pulled the rope from Charlie's neck and pushed him toward her horse. The boy scrambled into the saddle, a look of pure amazement on his face.

"Take him to Chase, boys, and tell him to stash him somewhere," Cole instructed. "I know none of you folks want to cross Chase," Cole added to the crowd.

No, they didn't.

"We'll see what the judge has to say about this," the sheriff threatened.

"Tell him to come see me," Cole said. "I can't wait to tell him all about it."

Caleb slid his rifle home and held out his hand to Amanda.

"Any one of you boys that decides to follow me is going to get shot," Cole said to the crowd as Caleb and Amanda rode past. "Any one of you that trespasses on Lynch land is going to get shot. And last time I checked, Charlie's family was living on Lynch land. So why don't you go back to the saloon and figure out if it's really worth it to you. He'll hang just as good in a week or two as he would tonight."

Cole backed his horse away, his rifle still held on the crowd until he reached Caleb and Amanda. They turned together and rode away, Caleb kicking Banner into a run. Amanda's back was exposed. He wouldn't, couldn't chance a shot coming at her that was meant for him.

Her hands around his waist were tightly clenched. She knew they were at risk. Her cheek pressed against his back and she held on tight.

What in the world was she doing here? Caleb wondered.

Chapter Twenty-five

"They're not going to follow us," Cole said when they stopped the horses to let them blow.

Caleb released a sigh of relief.

"That was a brave thing you did back there, Caleb," Cole said. "Especially since you didn't know you had anyone watching your back."

"I couldn't let them hang him."

"It was foolish, too," Cole went on. "You would have been killed if we hadn't showed up." Cole looked at Amanda, who still had her hands wrapped tightly around Caleb's waist.

"So why did you show up?" Caleb asked, knowing Cole well enough to know that he was just blowing off steam.

"I'll let you two figure that out," Cole said. "I'd better catch up with the boys. Knowing them, they'll have Chase and Ty tearing off to town thinking you're dead."

"Uncle Cole," Amanda called out. "Don't wait up."

Cole stopped his horse, started to say something, then shook his head and took off again.

What exactly was that supposed to mean? Caleb wondered.

Banner tossed his head and chewed on his bit. He was ready to run some more, but Caleb held him back to a walk. The moon was high in the sky, casting a surreal glow over the landscape. It was all without color, images cast in black and white, just like Caleb's drawings.

Caleb slowly felt the tension of the night drain from his body. At least, some of it did. One part of him was still quite tense, and it made riding difficult.

The feel of Amanda's soft breasts pressed against his back wasn't helping matters.

"Why did you and Cole come to town?" he finally asked as they rode along.

"Cole came with me," she replied.

Caleb tried to look at her face, but it was hidden beneath the brim of his hat. "So why did Cole come with you to town?"

"I was looking for you. He had some concerns about its being Saturday night."

Caleb pulled Banner to a stop in the middle of the road. The moon illuminated the landscape, showing the road unfolding before them and behind them, disappearing into the darkness. Caleb twisted around, and Amanda leaned back so he could face her.

"Why?" His heart pounded in his chest. There could be only one reason why she would look for him.

"I wanted to tell you that I love you."

309

His arm snaked around her waist and he pulled her up and around so that she landed sideways in his lap with the saddle horn pressing into her bottom. She squirmed around until she found a comfortable seat, while Caleb tried to hang on to his self-control.

Caleb placed his hand under her chin and tilted her face up so that the moon shone directly on it. "Say it again," he said.

"I love you." Her gray eyes were dark pools in the moonlight. "Can you love me? Will you?"

She was the bravest person he had ever met. She had just laid her heart on the line. He hadn't had the courage to do that.

"I've loved you since the first day I saw you," he said.

He wanted to kiss her, but was afraid of scaring her again. She placed her hand against the back of his neck and pulled his face toward hers. His lips caught hers and trembled against them until she pulled him closer, pressing her mouth against his.

She wanted this. She wanted him. His arms wrapped around her and pulled her closer, crushing her body against his as his lips, encouraged by hers, deepened the kiss until they had to break apart because they couldn't breathe.

He held her against his chest as her arms circled his neck. The blood roared in his head, pounding against his temples

"If I don't make love to you soon, I'm going to die," Caleb said, his voice hoarse against her cheek.

"I want you to make love to me. I want to know what it's like." Amanda leaned back against his arms so she could look into his eyes. "I want you to take the bad away and replace it with something good."

"Amanda, the only women I've ever been with were"—he nearly choked on his words—"women I paid."

Her fingers touched his lips and she gave him a wry smile. "And I've only been with men who paid. I've heard that there's a difference."

And he was the one who would have the privilege of showing her. *Don't let me disappoint her.*

Caleb searched his mind for a place they could go. There wasn't a chance of getting any privacy at the ranch. Sneaking into her room would just be embarrassing, and he couldn't take her back to town and subject her to the humiliation of checking into the hotel.

"Let's go back to the grove by the stream," she said. "I want to see the moon."

All those years she had spent locked up looking at dingy ceilings and bare walls. He should have thought of it himself. But he hadn't been thinking much lately. All he'd been doing was dreaming.

"Hang on," he said, and with one arm wrapped around her and the other hand on the reins, he kicked Banner into an easy canter. They left the road and went cross-country, the moon illuminating the prairie as they moved across the landscape, man, woman and horse. Amanda's hair sailed over Caleb's shoulder, looking like Banner's tail. The horse splashed through the stream and scrambled up the other side, Amanda still safe in Caleb's arms.

Caleb jerked his bedroll off the back of the saddle

and loosened Banner's bit before he turned him loose to graze. Amanda took Caleb's hand and led him into the grove. They spread the blanket on the ground and turned into each other's arms.

A step brought them closer together. Amanda peeled off Caleb's hat and flipped it aside. Her fingers teased his hair, already on end from his wild evening. He made use of the time by unhooking his gun belt and dropping it by the blanket. Chances were he wouldn't need it. The violence was over for the night.

Their eyes searched each other's, secrets shared in the moonlight as they found the answers they were looking for.

They were both whole and complete in the eyes of the other.

They kissed again, sealing the promise between them. Amanda plucked at the buttons of his shirt while he pulled hers up, his hands moving beneath her camisole and finding the bare skin underneath. The calluses on his hands skimmed over her tender skin as she spread his shirt wide and let her hands roam over his chest.

He buried his mouth against her neck, and she tilted her head back to give his lips access to the graceful line. But then she wanted to touch him, too. Amanda jerked his shirt down over his arms and off, dropping it on the ground behind him as her lips repeated the same pattern on his skin that he was tracing on hers.

Caleb pulled at her clothes. He had never undressed a woman before, and she gently pushed his hands away to work the buttons and ties that held everything in place.

He watched with indrawn breath as she revealed herself to him in the moonlight. Her skin shone alabaster white, contrasting with the deep shadows of the trees. Her hair hung over her shoulders, teasing him with glimpses of her breasts. Caleb pushed the strands aside with his fingertips, and her head moved back as her body leaned into his touch.

She hooked a finger into the waist of his pants and pulled him close as his hands skimmed over her shoulders and down her back, bringing her close to his desire. She worked at the buttons of his pants, pushed them down his hips and took him into her hand.

Her touch scalded his senses, and his mouth found hers again. His hands roamed over her back and down, pulling her up as she wrapped her legs around his waist.

She was killing him. Could he get them down to the blanket without hurting her? He dropped to his knees and groaned as they fell onto the blanket, Caleb rolling on his side to take the brunt of the fall. Her lips never left his. She knew he would keep them safe.

His hands worshiped her. His fingers traced the lines of her body in feather-light touches to give her pleasure. Her eyes looked up at him with wonder as she felt sensations she never knew existed. Caleb held himself back, not knowing how he did so, except for the fact that he wanted to give her the satisfaction of sweet release. He wanted her to know it.

When at last she reached her peak, when she trembled beneath his hands and arched her back and lost her breath, the tears came. Caleb gathered her against his body and held her tight as the lost years came flooding out. Her body shook with the magnitude of her grief, and he held her tighter, kissing her forehead and anchoring her in the storm that threatened to rip her apart.

The tears slowed finally, the sobs subsided, and she raised trembling lips to his and guided his hips over hers, pushing his pants down and away, and she pulled him in, wrapping her legs around his waist as he sank into her.

He couldn't breathe. He couldn't think. Her hands stroked up his spine and he moved and she told him it was good and she loved him.

Amanda loved him. He closed his eyes—he would never forget the sight of the moon shining on her face—and lost himself inside her.

Amanda put on his shirt and they wrapped themselves in the blanket and watched the moon trace its path across the sky. They talked about their childhoods and the parents that they had lost. Caleb had never known his mother. Amanda had never known her father.

Caleb told her about the war. He told her about the men he knew who had died, and about the ambush when Ty had been captured and he had lost his leg. He told her about the journey back and the surgery done on the table in Ty's kitchen without morphine. He told her about the guilt he felt over Cat losing her baby. He told her about learning how to walk again, about the kindness of his friends and his frustration at feeling inadequate.

They linked hands and shared stories of the past, and when the first light of dawn teased the eastern horizon, they made love again, sharing the passion and discovery.

Caleb grinned sheepishly as they were getting dressed to return to the ranch.

"What's wrong?" Amanda asked.

"We're going to get an earful when we get back," he said as she wrapped her arms around his waist.

"I can handle it," she said and dazzled him with a smile. Caleb dropped a kiss on her lips.

"I'm afraid that Cole might kill me."

"To quote a very brave man," she said, "he'll have to go through me to get to you."

"I'm not brave, Amanda. I'm just foolish. You're the one who's brave."

"Why does everyone keep saying that? I'm the biggest coward in the world."

Caleb picked her up and leaned back, rubbing his nose against hers. "I don't think false modesty will ever be a problem with us," he said with a grin.

"*Us.* That's a nice word. I also like *we*," Amanda replied as she slid down his body until her feet touched the ground.

"How about *together?* And *forever?*"

"Yes. I like those also."

"*Man and wife?*" Caleb asked, his heart suddenly still as he waited for her response.

"As in *married?*"

"*Married, together, forever.* I believe those are my favorites. Along with *I love you.*"

"Really?" Her eyes questioned his as if she thought he was playing.

"I don't know what the future will hold. I don't even know how or where we'll live, or how I'll support you. I do know that I love you, Amanda. Will you marry me?"

"As long as we're together, nothing else matter. Yes, I will marry you."

"With you by my side, I believe we can do anything." Caleb pulled her into his arms, and they sealed the promise with a kiss. When their lips parted, he looked around the grove. "This would be a nice place for a wedding."

"Indeed it would," she agreed. "As long as it happens as soon as possible."

"The sooner, the better."

They didn't want to leave their special place, but responsibility called them. Caleb whistled for Banner and lifted Amanda into the saddle and then swung up behind her.

"I'll talk to Cole as soon as we get back," he said as he picked up the reins. "Maybe it will keep him from killing me."

Amanda laid her head against his shoulder and laughed out loud. She had a nice laugh. He was looking forward to hearing a lot of it.

"Caleb, I have an idea about what we could do," she said as they rode.

"Tell me about it."

"We could start a newspaper."

Caleb pulled up Banner. "A newspaper. I don't know anything about newspapers except that they're supposed to tell the truth and don't, at least the one around here doesn't."

"Exactly. So we could start one that does tell the truth. And I know a lot about newspapers. I was working for one when I was taken."

They set off again, and Amanda explained what they would need to get started and told him about the printing process. She went into great detail, even estimating the cost of a press and how they would fund its purchase.

"All we need is a place to set up shop," she concluded. "In Laramie."

Caleb had quietly absorbed all the information she had given him. It was apparent that she knew what she was talking about. And this was something he could do. They could use his drawings in the paper. Zane had once told him that he ought to take up the trade of drawing wanted posters. He had laughed off the suggestion, but this was a similar concept. He could illustrate the articles. He could do this.

"I saw some empty store fronts last night," Caleb said as he settled things in his mind. "I'm sure we can find a place to set up shop. I've got some money."

"I do, too," she said. "We could be partners. I can write and you can illustrate." Amanda looked over her shoulder so she could see his face. "You could still work as a cowboy, too. If you want."

They had come to the ranch. Caleb stopped Banner,

and they looked at the buildings spread out in the small valley, with the big house overlooking them. This had been his home for a lot of years. The people here were his family. Could he leave them?

But he wouldn't be leaving. Not really. And his friends would always be here. They would understand and support Amanda and him as they went out and made their way in the world. They would welcome them back if they failed and offer them encouragement to try again. They would be here for him.

He could still work as a cowboy if he wanted. He was good on a horse. He could hold his own out on the range.

"I'll help out with the roundups and the drives," Caleb said. "Partner," he added.

Chapter Twenty-six

The small valley was deserted when they rode in, except for Zeb and the boys. "Everyone is up at the big house," Zeb explained. "I'll take care of your horse," he volunteered as Caleb and Amanda dismounted. "I heard the two of you had a big night, Mr. Caleb. Sho' wish I coulda seen it." Zeb led Banner away, with the boys following along, asking about the "big night."

Caleb and Amanda walked hand in hand up to the big house. Voices filtered from the dining room as they came in through the back, and they headed toward the sound, which stopped abruptly as soon as they entered the room.

Grace, Cole, Cat, Ty, Jenny and Zane were all sitting around the table. Chase, Jake and Shannon were missing. Everyone turned a smile on them—everyone except Cole, who narrowed his eyes at Caleb as if he were a murdering horse thief.

"Dang, Caleb. It looks like you saved the day *and* got the girl," Zane said

Caleb rolled his eyes.

"Shut up, Zane," Amanda said, and everyone laughed—everyone except Cole.

"What's the meeting for?" Caleb asked.

"We're trying to decide what to do with Charlie Potter," Ty explained. "Chase has got him stashed in a cave, and Jake and Shannon went to talk to his family."

"Shannon being the diplomat," Caleb offered.

"Yes," Ty said.

"You should have seen that kid's face when we turned him over to Chase," Zane said. "He thought he was going to get worse than a hanging."

"Chase let him think it, too," Ty continued. "I think he's planning on teaching young Charlie Potter a lesson about judging people by the color of their skin."

"A lot of good it will do him if he hangs anyway," Caleb said.

"That's the problem," Ty said.

Cat abruptly rose from the table, brushing past Caleb and Amanda as she ran to Jason's study.

"I guess we've still got a lot of things to figure out," Ty said as he followed her.

"Ty wants us to let him leave," Jenny said. She was still sore from childbirth, so she carefully rose from her chair and went to the window.

"What do you want, Jenny?" Caleb asked.

"I want it all to end," she said, her eyes looking out the window. "I want peace."

It would have all ended tonight if he hadn't stopped

the lynching. It would have been tragic and sad, but in the long run, would the hanging have been a bad thing? For the first time, Caleb doubted his actions. He had been so sure about it when it was happening. The realization came over him now, like a dunking in a cold stream, that he could have died last night. Caleb suddenly felt extremely tired. His thigh ached where he had broken it, and his stump was killing him. He needed to sit down.

Jenny turned back to the faces in the room. Her deep blue eyes caught Caleb's and saw the sudden weariness that filled them, replacing the cautious joy that had been evident when he and Amanda had entered the room. "I'm glad you stopped it, Caleb. Hanging Charlie Potter would just be another mistake. It wouldn't change anything. It wouldn't bring Jason back."

Jenny walked out of the room, stopping to touch Caleb's arm as she left. "He would have been proud of you," she said. "I am."

"I don't think we realized how young Charlie was until we saw him," Grace said to break the awkward silence that filled the room after Jenny's departure. "I'll get you two some breakfast." She went off to find them plates.

"Zane," Cole said, "I think there are some chores that need doing."

"It's Sunday!" Zane exclaimed.

"Then maybe you should go to church," Cole fired back.

"Cole, if you want me to leave, just say so."

"*Leave!*"

Zane backed away from his chair and left the room, waggling his eyebrows at Caleb.

Cole pointed to two chairs across from him and then at Caleb and Amanda.

"Sit!" he commanded, and they obeyed, although Caleb's movements were a bit stiff.

"What are your intentions toward my niece?" Cole demanded.

"Uncle Cole—" Amanda protested. Cole held up his hand to silence her.

"Caleb?"

Caleb knew how the lynchers must have felt last night. He was pretty sure he knew how every criminal Cole had ever arrested felt. Those dime novels that Zane had read about Cole in his Rangering days didn't do him justice. Caleb took Amanda's hand. "I've asked Amanda to marry me."

"And I said yes."

Cole leaned back in his chair and crossed his arms. "Good," he said. "When's the wedding?"

Grace came back in, with two plates in one hand and Jacey on her hip. "Give them time, Cole," she chided as she handed Jacey off to him. Jacey immediately began her favorite pasttime of late, chewing on her fist.

"No," Cole insisted. "I'm not going to have them sneaking off every chance they get."

Grace placed the plates in front of Caleb and Amanda and turned to Cole, putting her hands on her hips.

"Oh, really?" she began. "I seem to recall someone who thought sneaking off was a good thing." She poked a finger in his chest. "I seem to recall someone who didn't even bother to sneak. He just came into my room and made himself at home, got me pregnant and then took off for several months." "Grace—" Cole protested.

Caleb grinned. Cole didn't seem as scary as he had before.

Satisfied that she had put Cole in his place, Grace sat down next to Amanda. "So, when is the wedding?" she asked.

Amanda looked at Caleb, who was suddenly very hungry and attacked his plate. "We haven't picked a when, but we know where."

"We should wait," Caleb said with his fork halfway between the plate and his mouth. It pained him to say it. He didn't want to sneak around. He wanted to spend every minute with Amanda. He wanted to fall asleep with her and he wanted to wake up with her.

But still he said, "We should wait until this is over."

"Why don't you two go upstairs and sleep on it," Grace suggested.

"Grace!" Cole barked. Jacey jumped in his arms and looked around in distress, her lower lip jutting out as she contemplated letting out a good cry.

Grace held out her hands to Jacey, who immediately reached for her mother. "Don't you have some chores to tend to?" she asked Cole sweetly.

Cole gave Grace a challenging look, but she continued to smile at him. He shoved his chair back and left the room, mumbling.

"He's just feeling protective," Grace explained as she followed him out.

"A nap sounds like a wonderful idea," Amanda said.

"Sleep sounds good," Caleb agreed.

"I wasn't really thinking about sleep," she said, laying her hand along his thigh.

Caleb's head fell forward as heat flashed up his leg. He squeezed his eyes shut, amazed that he was already fighting for control.

"But I will let you have a quick nap," she whispered in his ear.

"Can I eat first?"

Amanda picked up her fork. "I plan to," she said and took a bite.

Caleb went back to his meal, watching Amanda as she ate. What had she been like before Bishop got hold of her? Had she had the same spirit that she was showing now? She had been a mere shadow for the months since she had been here, but suddenly she had come to life again.

Was it because of him?

"What?" she asked as she caught his steady perusal.

"I love you."

She dropped her fork and shared a kiss that tasted very much of eggs. "I'm ready for my nap," she said, pulling him up from the table. Caleb grabbed his napkin, wiped his mouth and let her lead him up the stairs.

He had never been in her room. It was plain and simple, with nothing to mark it as hers except for a pile of books on the bedside table and a stack of newspapers on the bureau.

"I have some things," she explained as she firmly shut the door behind them. She instantly noticed his curious perusal. "My mother's. Uncle Cole had everything stored in Laredo."

"We could go get them," Caleb said as he realized that she was suddenly sad. "You could visit . . . her."

Amanda walked into his arms. "I'd like that. I never had a chance to say good-bye to her."

"My father died while I was in school." He had glossed over the details of his father's death earlier. "I came home and found him on the floor behind the counter. The doctor said his heart just gave out. The undertaker came and got him, I went to the funeral and came home to find out I didn't have a home. We lived over the store, and the building belonged to the bank. They let me pack some clothes in a sack, and I was out on the street."

"Didn't you have any friends, or family who could take you in?"

"No family. We had a few friends, but no one who could afford to raise me. I was pretty scrawny, too. I guess they thought that since I was raised in town, I wouldn't be fit to work on a farm."

"That's so sad. Not to have anyone."

"It was scary, but I knew that feeling sorry for myself wouldn't help matters, so I just started walking, wound up in St. Louis, and that's where Jason found me." Caleb kissed the top of her head. "If I hadn't started walking, I would never have met you."

"One door closes, another one opens."

"What does that mean?"

"It's something I realized when I talked to Jenny. She said it was horrible what happened to me, but if it hadn't happened, I would not be here today. Her baby would have died; she herself might have died. I never would have met you. You never would have met me. One door was closed, another one opened."

"If I hadn't broken my leg, we never would have spent time together."

"If Agnes hadn't gone to take care of her daughter, she would have nursed you."

"So fate brought us together."

"It would have been a lot simpler and easier if you had just walked south instead of west."

"I'd have wound up in Alabama," Caleb laughed.

"I think you know what I mean," she laughed with him.

"I do. I'm sorry that you had to go through what you did. I'm very happy that you're going to marry me. I never thought any woman could love me after I lost my leg."

"Caleb, losing your leg doesn't make you any less of a man, or less desirable."

"But—"

"Shhh." Amanda placed her fingers over his lips. "Come here." She pulled him around, pushed him down to sit on the edge of the bed and then knelt before him. She picked up the boot on his good leg and pulled it off, then reached for the other.

"Don't," he said.

Amanda looked up at him. "Caleb. I'm going to be your wife. Do you think you're going to hide this from me for the rest of our lives?"

He had tried not to think about it. Even when he'd asked her to marry him, a part of his mind had nagged at him about his stump. Would she turn away in disgust when she saw it? Could he slip into bed at night after the lamp was turned off and rise before she did? He wanted to be whole for her. But he also wanted her to know every inch of him, and that wasn't possible when he was hiding something from her.

She was still looking at him. Waiting for his permission. He had a feeling, however, that she would press on, permission or not. He nodded his head. Might as well get it over with.

She tugged on his boot, easing it over his calf as if the contents were fragile. She set the boot aside, then rose to her knees and unbuttoned his shirt, then unhooked his gun belt and placed it next to his boots.

"No guns in the house," she said with a slight smile as she eased the shirt over his shoulders and off.

"Yes, ma'am."

Her nimble fingers moved to his pants and quickly worked the buttons. She tugged at the waist of his pants, and he braced himself on his hands as she eased them down his hips, taking his drawers with them, over his thighs, the bend of his knees, reaching his calf, where the left leg ended. Caleb held his breath as she tossed his pants aside and pulled off his socks. He couldn't see her face as her hand touched the back of his left calf. She looked at his stump. Then examined his right foot.

"Caleb," she said. Her voice sounded strange, almost strangled. Caleb felt a flush rise up his chest as he prepared himself for the blow. He would leave. He understood. At least he had given her a moment of happiness. At least he had something wonderful to take with him.

"You have the longest toes I have ever seen," she announced and burst into laughter.

Caleb looked down at the toes of his right foot and gave them a wiggle. "So you've seen a lot of toes in your day?"

"More than I'd like." Hilarity danced in her eyes.

Caleb grabbed her arms and pulled her onto the bed, rolling on top of her. She was trying not to laugh and grabbed the pillow, covering her mouth to keep from disturbing Cat and Ty in the study below. Her eyes sparkled above the white of the pillowcase as he looked down at her.

Caleb tunneled his hands in her hair, nudged the pillow down with his chin and kissed her. Her laughter was lost in his throat as she wrapped her arms around him and pulled him closer.

Caleb broke off the kiss and went to work on the buttons of her shirt while she twirled her fingers through his hair.

"Caleb," she said breathlessly as he eased her clothes away.

He stopped what he was doing, waiting to hear what she had to say.

"I almost feel guilty about being so happy now, with everything that's going on."

"Don't," he said, kissing her again. "You deserve all the happiness you can get."

"I said *almost*," she replied as his mouth moved down her neck. She moved beneath the caress of his hands. "Almost," she whispered.

Chapter Twenty-seven

A sheet was tangled around his legs, a body sprawled over his chest, and hair tickling his nose. A breeze from the open window cooled his body and dusk filled the sky. The chirping of baby birds came from the cottonwood tree out front.

Had he ever in his lifetime been this happy? Caleb smoothed Amanda's hair back from her face; she looked perfectly content in her slumber. He had nothing but happiness to look forward to. *Please, God, give us long years of happiness together. For her.* Happiness, health, prosperity, children. Just being together. Like now.

Except he really needed to relieve himself. Which meant getting dressed. He gently slid Amanda off his body and began to search for his clothes.

The house was quiet. He took care of business, then went to the kitchen, suddenly conscious of his interrupted breakfast and missed lunch. He fixed himself a sandwich, then made one for Amanda, grabbed an apple from the bowl on the table and went toward the stairs.

The front door was open. Deciding he had better close it before some wild thing moved in, he put his food down on the narrow table in the hall.

Cat was sitting on the front stoop. Caleb looked around the porch for Ty but saw that she was alone.

"Cat?" he asked.

"I could hear you walking around," she said.

Caleb went out on the porch. "I guess it's pretty easy to tell it's me."

"Come sit with me, Caleb."

He eased down next to her and waited. She needed to talk. They had known each other a long time but had only recently gotten close. They had forged a bond the past summer.

"When I was a girl, I used to sit here and wait for Daddy to come home. He traveled a lot then when he was a judge. We had a couple who kept house, and she would mark the days off the calendar so I would know when to start looking for him. I would sit here for hours waiting for him to come up the drive on his horse."

Cat stretched her legs out in front of her. "I would always show him how much I'd grown while he was gone by marking where my legs reached on the steps."

Caleb waited, knowing she just wanted to talk. She needed someone to listen. And who better to listen than he after the things they had shared last summer?

"He sent me back East when I got older. I was becoming quite a hoyden, according to Ruth, our housekeeper, so he was hoping my mother's family could give me some culture." Cat grinned sheepishly at the thought. She was still a hoyden when she wanted to be. "But I still waited for him on the steps when I came home. Even when he was working the ranch, he knew I'd be sitting here waiting for him, so he'd come around front instead of going in through the back."

"I remember that," Caleb said. "We used to ask him why he didn't go in the back door. He said it was because you liked to have things your way."

Cat pulled her knees under her chin. "I wish I could have things my way now." Her voice trembled. "I'm out here pretending that if I wait long enough, he'll come home."

"Cat." Caleb put his arm around her and she leaned into his shoulder.

"I keep wondering what we could have done differently to keep it from happening. I begged him not to go. I just had this strange feeling that he shouldn't. I ought to have stopped him. I should have thrown one of my tantrums and cried and pouted until he stayed here with me."

"I'm sorry, Cat," Caleb said gently. "But you can't sit here and punish yourself for what happened. Remember what you told me last summer after you lost the baby?"

"What?" Her voice broke as she tried to get her emotions under control.

"We could spend the rest of our lives torturing ourselves over things that we've done. We all make choices, and we live or die with the results. Jason chose to go;

you chose to let him. He was killed. If he had not been there, it might have been Ty or Chase who was killed. Jason's life and death were in God's hands. It's up to us how we choose to live with what's happened."

Cat nodded against his shoulder and swiped at her eyes. "Knowing that doesn't make it any easier."

"No, it doesn't. And his death will probably hurt for a long time. You've lost a lot."

"Yes. I lost my father and I lost my child, but I still have Ty and I have this place. I have a family here and friends. Good friends. I'm grateful for that."

"I lost my leg but I'm alive, and I'm grateful for that. Amanda lost years and she lost her innocence, but we found each other. I'm especially grateful for that."

Cat nudged him with her elbow. "You should be."

"I never thought love would come to me. She told me that when one door closes, another opens. I guess you've just got to have enough sense to walk through it when it does. I was afraid to go through it. Luckily, she wasn't."

"I'm happy for you, Caleb. I don't know her well, but what I do know is that she's special."

"She is."

"So what kind of door do you think will open for us now?"

"I don't know," Caleb said. "I just know that when it opens, you can't be afraid of it."

Cat nodded in agreement, and they sat for a while, Caleb keeping a comforting arm around her shoulders. His left leg finally cramped, and he stretched it out along the steps. Cat stretched her legs out beside his.

"Even with part of mine missing, my leg is longer than yours," he said teasingly.

"So what?" Cat replied in the same manner. "I can probably run faster."

"That's a given," he said carelessly. "I can ride better. Shoot better, too."

"You might be able to shoot better. I mean, you had to learn since you were in the war," Cat replied. "I know I can ride better."

"What, are you challenging me?" Caleb moved his arm away as the banter continued.

"Sure, why not?" Cat had always kept up with the men on the range.

"Have you seen my horse?"

"My horse can take your horse any day."

"Are you talking about that chestnut you brought back from North Carolina?"

"You mean the one that carried your scrawny behind down the mountain when you were about to die from fever?"

"Well, if someone hadn't whacked my leg off with a sword, I wouldn't have gotten a fever."

"You're right, you would have died and I would have had to carry your body down strapped over the saddle." Cat punched his arm.

"Did you know that Fox and Chance like to play Auntie Cat whacking off legs when they take out their toy soldiers?" Caleb said, knowing how much that information would annoy her.

"I told you that you never should have told them what

333

happened," Cat protested. "They're going to be terrified of me."

"At least you'll be able to make them behave. All you've got to do is wave Ty's sword around."

"I might have to try that sometime," Cat said as she turned serious. "Caleb, is it hard for you? Getting around?"

She still felt guilty, even though it wasn't her fault, the same way he felt guilty about her lost baby.

"No," he assured her with a lie. "Although there is one thing I miss."

"What's that?"

"Going barefoot. I have to put my boots on just to go to the outhouse."

"You should look at it the other way," she said.

"What do you mean?"

"One door closes, another one opens. You don't have to worry about getting snake bit, or stepping on dog poop, or getting a splinter in your foot, or . . ." They dissolved into laughter, leaning against each other as they were overcome with relief. Laughter was a better outlet than tears for now. So much had happened in the past few weeks. It was almost more than a person could deal with, but they had to deal with it, and then they had to move on.

"So, I hear there's going to be a wedding," Cat said when their laughter had subsided.

"We thought we'd wait until the trial is over with," Caleb said.

"You don't have to."

"I know."

They heard footsteps in the hall and Ty joined them, sitting down on the opposite side of Cat.

"Is Chase back?" Cat asked as she leaned into her husband.

"Yes." Ty looked up at the sky and the moon, which was just coming out. "Nice night," he sighed.

"Peaceful," Caleb added.

"If only it would stay that way," Cat said.

Caleb left them then, knowing that he was no longer needed. It had been good to talk to Cat. They had not had a chance to talk since she had gone back to "bust Ty out of the prison camp." The bond they had forged together last summer was still strong.

He grabbed the food from the table in the hallway and carried it upstairs. He was surprised to find Amanda sitting on the floor before the window that looked out over the cottonwood tree.

"I was listening," she said with her shy smile.

Caleb sat down on the bed and handed her a sandwich. "What did you hear?" he asked.

"Confirmation."

"Of what?"

"How wonderful you are." She took a bite and looked up in approval. "You make a good sandwich, too."

Chapter Twenty-eight

Cole and Grace were sitting on the porch swing when Caleb walked by on his way to the bunkhouse.

"How was your nap?" Cole growled.

"Restful," Caleb replied. He and Amanda had decided not to push Cole too hard since he was in a protective frame of mind, so Caleb was returning to the bunkhouse for the night.

"Cole, leave him alone," Grace chided, and Caleb walked on by, grinning sheepishly. He knew he was in for an earful from Zane when he hit the bunkhouse. The good thing was, he didn't care. The teasing would be fun. He was happy.

He was right. Zane hit him with a hundred questions as soon as he walked through the door, starting with what happened with Toy. Caleb realized he had forgotten about Toy, and his face turned a deep red, but not for the reasons that Zane assumed.

Zane, Dan and Randy filled him in on their part of the happenings on Saturday night, while Zeb listened. Zeb had only been to town a few times.

Caleb refused to answer any questions about Amanda, even after the others went to sleep and Zane kept asking. He found his sketch book and box and sprawled out on his bunk.

"You don't have to say a word," Zane finally yawned from his bunk above Caleb's. "I can tell by the way you're acting that you're a goner, just like everyone else around here."

"Yes, I am," Caleb said, smiling. He leaned back on his pillow, and in the dim light of the lamp, he sketched. The drawing took shape—a man, tall and straight, with eyes crinkling into a smile and a touch of gray in his hair. In his arms he held a girl of around seven or nine with a head full of curls and uptilted eyes. The scene had taken place before he had come to the ranch. He had been a boy in the mountains of Georgia helping his father in the store, but he had seen these two through Cat's eyes.

Caleb had never drawn Jason before; it had never seemed right, until now. Now he was making up for lost time. He drew Jason again, on his horse looking out over the ranch. Sitting in his chair with a book, and a boy on each knee. Standing on the ridge next to Jamie's grave.

Caleb's head filled with images. He drew Willie and the other men from his company in the war. He drew Ty as he had seen him during the Wilderness Campaign, screaming a charge as he rode into battle with his sword in one hand and his gun in the other.

Cindy Holby

He drew Jake as he had been in the war, desperately seeking his own death. Then he drew him as he was now, at peace, with Shannon by his side.

Caleb drew Cole, Grace and Jacey. He drew Jenny and Chase. He drew the boys. He drew Zeb. He drew Justice.

And when the lamp flickered with the last drops of oil, he put the finishing touches on a drawing of Amanda. She was wearing a white dress, holding a bouquet of wildflowers and standing in the glade. Caleb fell asleep with the sketch book in his lap as the lamp went out.

In the big house above the valley, Amanda slept also. She hadn't taken a book with her to lull herself to sleep as she usually did. She spent the time in the darkness envisioning a wedding. Seeing a future with Caleb by her side as they worked at the newspaper. As they had children. As they grew old together. And when she did fall asleep, she dreamed of the precipice again. Only this time she shook off the chains and the hands that reached for her. She leaped off the side and slowly fell, with arms stretched out wide as if they were wings. She landed safely in Caleb's arms, and all around him she could see the familiar faces of the people on the ranch. She was safe. She was loved. She had a home and she had a purpose. The Fear was gone.

Amanda was at Grace's the next morning, helping Shannon prepare breakfast. Caleb was surprised to see her

338

there and thought about greeting her with a kiss until he saw Cole's stern visage at the end of the table.

"Mama used to tell me not to make faces because my face might freeze that way," Amanda said to her uncle as she set a cup of coffee in front of him.

"She told me to keep watch over you, too," Cole retorted.

Amanda laid a comforting hand on his shoulder. "And you are. You're doing a good job. Now watch me be happy." She went to Caleb, who had sat down at the opposite end of the table from Cole, and kissed him, then turned to her uncle with a smile. "See?"

Cole scowled at the both of them.

"I pity the man who asks Jacey to marry him," Zane said as he looked around the table.

"She's not getting married," Cole replied. "She's not having anything to do with men."

"What are you going to do, Cole, send her off to be a nun?" Zane asked.

"I just might, to keep her away from the likes of you."

"Cole," Grace said, hands on her hips.

Dan and Randy came strolling in, obviously quite hungry—they began shoveling food in their mouths before they even sat down.

"I guess Ty and Chase made it back home?" Jake asked. The men were taking shifts going to the cave to watch over Charlie.

"Yes," Dan said, grabbing a plate and sitting down next to Caleb. "He wants to talk to you."

"Who?" Caleb asked. "Charlie?"

Cindy Holby

"You're the one who saved his neck," Randy said.

"Maybe he just wants to thank you," Shannon suggested.

"You feel up to taking a ride today?" Caleb asked Amanda.

She smiled. "Sure do. I want to see more of the ranch. Just let me go change."

Caleb gulped down his breakfast and went to saddle the horses. He was just leading them out of the barn when Amanda and Cat showed up. And Amanda was wearing pants.

"Cat gave them to me," she explained when Caleb arched his eyebrows in surprise.

"I told her they were much more comfortable for riding," Cat added as she went into the barn.

"She's going with us," Amanda said. "She wants to talk to Charlie."

Caleb gave Amanda a hand up to the saddle and found himself in the same predicament he'd been experiencing every morning for over a month as he suddenly became fascinated with the way her pants showed off the curve of her behind. The wedding couldn't happen soon enough, as far as he was concerned. Either that or Cole would shoot him for sneaking into her room.

Cat came out with Scarlet, and gave Banner a once-over before she mounted up. "We're ready anytime you are," she said.

Caleb was tempted to teach her a lesson but decided to wait. He didn't want to leave Amanda behind. They rode out north toward the canyon where Chase had hidden young Charlie. The Potter family had joined him there.

Pharaoh waved to the trio as they rode by, and Sally gave them a half-hearted race. They rode over rolling pasture for a while, found the herd and rode through the cattle, which looked up in surprise at the interruption.

"The cows will obliterate our tracks in case anyone comes looking for Charlie," Caleb explained to Amanda.

"Do you think they are?" Amanda asked.

"I'm sure they're thinking about it," Caleb said. "I don't think anyone is going to ride up to the front door and demand we give him back, at least not until the circuit judge arrives, but it wouldn't surprise me if someone was sneaking around, trying to figure out where we've got him hidden."

"We probably should send someone over to the Potter homestead to see if anyone's been poking around," Cat said.

"Jake said he was going to go today," Caleb replied.

"I can see why you three survived the war," Cat said.

"Barely," Caleb said, a bit confused by her remark. "Why?"

"You each knew your role, you knew what needed to be done, and you just did it." Cat rode on ahead, her mind obviously considering several things.

"What was your role in the war, Caleb?" Amanda asked as they rode side by side.

"Watching Ty's back," he said. "Jake went ahead, I stayed behind. Ty had to survive even if we didn't."

"Why was he more important than you or Jake?"

"He had Cat," Caleb said simply. "Besides, she would have killed us anyway if something happened to him."

"She broke him out of prison? I remember Uncle Cole telling me about it, but I wasn't really capable of understanding much at that point."

"She did, along with Jenny, Chase and Cole. That's when Jenny ran into Wade Bishop, which was actually a good thing since that's how they found you."

"One door closes, another opens. I guess it was a good thing for me that Ty was captured."

"And he wouldn't have been captured if I hadn't lost my leg. He sacrificed himself to save me."

"It's all almost more than I can think about," Amanda said.

"Whatever the reasons for our being together, I'm thankful for them."

They both stopped, and Caleb leaned over to give her a kiss.

"I think I like it better when we share a horse," Amanda said when they finally broke it off, breathless once again.

"I'm thinking that this pasture would be a nice place to spend some time," Caleb said suggestively.

"I think we'd shock the cattle," Amanda replied saucily. "I hope this trouble is over soon. I can't wait to be your wife. I want to be with you all the time," she added in a more wistful tone.

"I know," Caleb said. "But I also want it to be a happy day. I don't want everyone pretending just for our sakes."

"You're right, of course,"

"Admitting that I'm right is a good start to a happy marriage."

"Don't think for a minute that you get to be right all the time," Amanda retorted, her gray eyes sparkling in the sunshine.

"Hey, you've already said it," he teased. "You can't change your mind now."

Amanda rolled her eyes and took off after Cat. Caleb watched for a moment as her mare ran to catch up with Scarlet, fully appreciative of the view of her bottom. Then he let Banner, who was anxious to run, have his head. The horse quickly caught up with the women as they began the ascent into the canyon.

Chase had chosen well. The position was easily defensible, had access to water and commanded a good view over the land below. Chase was on a ledge above the cave, and Ty waved to them as soon as they rode into the rift.

"Why did you want to come here, Cat?" Caleb asked as their horses picked their way up to the rim.

"I don't know. I just wanted to see Charlie and talk to him. There wasn't enough time the other night."

"I wonder what he has to say to me," Caleb mused.

"Whatever it is, you've got to admire him for having the courage to say it," Amanda said.

They rode on in silence until they reached the ledge that held the cave. Ty seemed surprised to see Cat, who just shook her head when he asked her about her arrival. She wasn't sure why she had come.

The two younger Potters were playing on the ledge under the watchful eyes of their mother. She called them to her when she saw Caleb, Amanda and Cat. The elder Charlie held his rifle in his arms as young Charlie walked toward Caleb.

"I wonder what happened to that family to cause so much mistrust and fear," Amanda said quietly so only Caleb could hear her.

Caleb gave her a reassuring smile and walked forward to meet young Charlie.

"Caleb Conners," Caleb said, shaking the boy's hand.

"He told me," Charlie said, motioning toward Chase.

"Chase," Caleb said.

"Yeah," Charlie practically stammered. "Chase."

"You wanted to talk to me?" Caleb asked.

"I just wanted to say thanks, for what you did." The boy's brown eyes were watery but earnest. "Risking your life to save mine, after what I did."

"I couldn't let them hang you like that."

"Pa says I'm going to hang anyway."

Caleb looked over Charlie's shoulder at his father, who was watching the two of them with narrowed eyes.

"Let's talk," Caleb said. He led Charlie over to a boulder. Ty, who had been watching, immediately went to cut off his father as the man made a move to follow the two of them.

"Tell me about your life, Charlie," Caleb said as they leaned against the boulder. Charlie looked at him in confusion. "Where do you come from? What brought your family west?"

"We came from the southern part of Ohio," Charlie said. "Close to the river."

"What did you do there?"

344

"Farmed," Charlie said. "I went to school for a bit, until the little ones came and Ma had to take care of them. Then they needed me on the farm."

"Did you like school?"

"I reckon. I liked the reading part. Not much on the numbering."

"So why did you come west?"

"Pa thought we could do better. Have more land. Raise more crops. We had some trouble with the war too."

"In Ohio?" Caleb asked. "I didn't think there was much fighting going on there."

"There wasn't. But the slaves were going through there, on something called the Underground Railroad. Ma's brother got hanged for helping some of them, and people started talking against us, thinking we was helping, too."

"Did you see them hang your uncle?"

Charlie looked out over the canyon. "Yes, sir," he said, his voice trembling. "The slave catchers dragged him out from Sunday dinner. Offered a reward for information on anyone else that was helping slaves escape. That's when people started snooping around the farm. So Pa packed us up and we came west."

"You know the property you settled on doesn't belong to you," Caleb said.

"Yes, sir. I know it. Pa knows it, too. He just won't admit it."

"He doesn't like the fact that it belongs to Chase."

"Something like that," Charlie mumbled. "He said we couldn't trust no Indians."

"Yet Chase brought you to a safe place, even though he has reason to mistrust you."

"Yeah," Charlie mumbled.

"He could have killed you after you shot Jason."

"I thought he was going to."

"Could you blame him?"

"No, sir." Charlie looked at Caleb. "So why are all of you helping me?"

"Because we want to do what's right. We know you didn't mean to kill Jason."

"No, sir. I thought he was going to kill my pa. I didn't even mean to shoot him. I was just scared and the gun went off."

"It was an accident?"

"Yes, sir. But I reckon that don't matter none. The sheriff said that Mr. Lynch was a big man around these parts. He said that everyone in the territory would probably turn out for my trial and my hanging."

"Jason Lynch was a wonderful man. He will be greatly missed. But he was also a fair man. He wouldn't want you to hang for this." Caleb looked for Cat, who was watching them with great interest.

"There's someone else who wants to talk to you," Caleb said.

When Cat came to join them, Charlie looked more scared than he had a few moments before, if that was possible.

"Charlie, this is Cat," Caleb said. "She's Jason's daughter."

Caleb left the two alone. Amanda was standing with Ty, and Chase had jumped down from the ledge to join them. The four of them stepped away from Charlie's parents as Cat and Charlie bent their heads in conversation.

"He didn't mean to kill him," Caleb said.

"That still doesn't change the fact that it happened," Chase said.

"He's not a killer," Ty replied.

"I know." Chase looked over at Charlie's father. "He's not a bad kid. But he might be better off without that one giving him advice."

"He's just trying to protect him, Chase," Amanda said. "Kind of like Uncle Cole growling at me and Caleb."

Chase nodded his head in agreement, a wry smile on his face.

"And Charlie was trying to protect his father," Caleb added. "You can't blame him for that."

Chase, more than any one of them, knew to what lengths a man would go to protect his family.

"So what do we do about it?" Ty asked. "We can keep him here to protect him from the lynch mob, but once the judge hits town, we'll have to turn him over."

"And we'll have to testify in court that we saw him shoot Jason," Chase said.

"No, you don't," Amanda said.

"They'll call on us, Amanda," Ty said. "We won't have a choice. We can't commit perjury."

"They can't charge him with the crime without witnesses. If you didn't see it in the first place, how did you know he did it? Have you two even talked to the sheriff?"

"No," Ty said. He looked at Chase, who shook his head.

"I've been busy," Chase said.

"What did you say when you and Jake went in to get the sheriff?" Amanda asked Caleb.

"I didn't say anything," Caleb said. "Jake told the sheriff that Jason had been shot and he knew where the kid was that did it. We went out there and the sheriff arrested him. That was it."

"We didn't actually see the shooting," Ty said. "We had our backs to Charlie when it happened."

"Jake would have to agree," Chase said. "This plan would make him look foolish, after he led the sheriff to Charlie Potter."

"I don't think Jake will be a problem," Caleb said.

"In the long run," Ty said, "it's all up to Cat and Jenny."

"Jenny would say to let him go," Chase said. "As long as the whole family leaves."

"It would be the answer to your problems," Ty remarked.

"But that shouldn't be the reason for it," Chase said. "It should be because it's the right thing to do."

Cat and Charlie had finished their conversation. Charlie went into the cave, followed by his family, while Cat joined the group on the ledge.

"I can't justify hanging him," she said as she wiped her eyes. "He's just a foolish kid. Daddy wouldn't want it." She looked around at the faces of her husband and friends. "What are we going to do?"

"Let him go," Caleb said.

"Can we?" Cat asked.

"We can," Ty said. "We can send the Potters on their way and make sure that a posse won't go after him."

"It would involve lying," Chase said. "Although where

the sheriff is concerned, that doesn't bother me much."

"I prefer to think of it as misleading," Amanda said. "Just like the local newspaper. I can't wait to see what the editor has to say about the happenings of Saturday night."

"Most likely he'll say that I busted Charlie out of jail myself," Caleb said. "And killed three people while doing it."

"You did shoot some of them," Amanda said. "At a full run from the back of your horse."

"I wounded them," Caleb stated. "If I had wanted to kill them, they'd be dead."

Ty nodded in agreement. "Caleb wounded more than he killed in the war. Jake was always griping about it. He said the doctors would just patch them up and send them back at us."

"Jake only wants to do things once," Caleb added.

"How long do you think it will take the circuit judge to get here?" Cat asked, bringing them back to the subject at hand.

"The sheriff said a couple of weeks," Ty said. "He's got a big trial going on somewhere."

"So the Potters could be well on their way by the time he hits town?"

"Yes," Ty said.

"Do you think they'll agree to it?" Cat asked.

"They'd be foolish not to," Chase said. "But they would have to leave everything behind."

"Or we could pack their belongings up for them," Amanda suggested.

"It's all up to you, Cat," Ty said.

"What about Jenny?" Cat asked Chase.

"She just wants it all to be over," Chase replied. "She wants peace."

"So do I," Cat said. "Let's go talk to the Potters."

Cat and Ty went to the cave, and after a moment, asked Chase to join them.

"Mr. Potter probably thinks I'm going to sneak up on his family and scalp all of them as they make their escape," Chase said with a wry smile as he left Caleb and Amanda.

"I feel good about today," Amanda said. They walked to the edge to give the people behind them more privacy.

"It wouldn't have solved anything to kill the boy," Caleb said. He wrapped his arms around her waist from behind and placed his chin on her shoulder.

"It's easier to forgive than to carry all that . . . hatred," Amanda said.

"Do you forgive Bishop and his sisters for what they did to you?"

"No," Amanda said. "They don't deserve forgiveness. And I'm pretty sure that Bishop is getting his just deserts right now. I don't remember much about that time, but I do remember the sight of him going out that window." She turned into Caleb's arms. "I was carrying a lot of . . . I don't want to call it hate. I think frustration is a better word. I was frustrated with God. I thought He had abandoned me, and I couldn't figure out what I had done to make Him do that. I realize now that He was just using that time to bring me to a better place."

"You are very wise," Caleb said as he kissed her forehead.

"I have plans for Bishop's sisters and their business dealings also," she said as she leaned into his chest. "Have you ever heard of the power of the press?"

"Yes, I have."

"Good. Because our press is going to be very powerful."

"Do you think you can do something before you start writing all these powerful editorials?"

"What would you like me to do?"

"Marry me," Caleb said, his dark eyes warm and glowing.

"As soon as possible," Amanda replied, her gray eyes twinkling with life.

Chapter Twenty-nine

Caleb, Amanda, Jake, Shannon, Zeb and Cleo packed the Potter family's belongings into their wagon that night. They had a bit of trouble with the cat, which hid in a corner under the bed, hissing and spitting the entire time. They removed the mattress, and Jake managed to reach in between the roping and grab the cat by the scruff of its neck and stuff it into a waiting basket. The animal yowled insults to them as they loaded it into the wagon amidst the supplies that Jenny and Cat had provided for the family, along with some money they'd hidden with Mrs. Potter's things. They knew the elder Potter well enough to know that he wouldn't accept charity and figured that the family would be well on its way before the money was discovered.

The wagon was taken to the canyon where the family was waiting. Chase and Jake went along to lead them a safe distance away from Laramie.

The Potters had all summer to travel; with luck they would reach Oregon territory before it was too late in the season.

Chase asked young Charlie to ride with him for a while. Jake lent the boy his dun and took over driving the wagon. They were pressing on as hard as they could push the animals. The Potters needed to get as far away as possible in a short amount of time. And Chase and Jake were eager to get back home. They had a wedding to attend.

"Do you think any of this would have happened if I were white?" Chase asked the boy as he rode nervously beside him.

"What do you mean?" Charlie asked.

"The day your father pulled a gun on Jenny and me, out by the lake. Would he have done the same with a white man?"

Charlie looked back at the wagon. His father sat up on the bench next to Jake, who looked as if he'd just as soon throw the older man off into the first ravine they came to. Charlie's father didn't look happy either. He had only been homesteading on Lynch property for a few weeks, but it was long enough for him to have built a home and to have made a start at putting in a crop. He had lost time. He had also been wrong about a number of things. Young Charlie knew his father didn't want him to hang. But his father was also proud. It was hard for him to admit he was wrong, especially to the people he had wronged.

"I don't know," Charlie said. "Maybe."

"You heard a lot of stories about wild Indians back in Ohio?" Chase asked.

"Yes, sir. We heard about how they was always attacking the wagon trains and settlers and such."

"Did you hear about the Sand Creek massacre?"

"Nope."

"Two hundred men, women and children were massacred there."

"Settlers?"

"Cheyenne and Kiowa." Chase looked at the boy. "My father was Kiowa."

"Your father is dead?"

"Killed by the army."

"Oh," Charlie said. "Sorry."

"If I lived by your father's code, I would have been justified in killing your family."

"But we didn't do anything to you. It was the army."

"I didn't do anything to you either, did I?"

"You was on our la—" Charlie stammered. "No. You didn't."

"My father was Kiowa and was killed by the white man. My mother was white and was killed by the red man. I would be pretty lonely if I hated all men because of the color of their skin, wouldn't I?"

"Yes, sir."

"There are good men and there are bad men, Charlie. You have to learn to see what's inside instead of what's outside."

Charlie looked into the dark, hawklike eyes of Chase. "I'll remember that, sir. I appreciate all that you've done for us, too. I'd be dead right now if not for you and your friends."

"Just don't disappoint us."

"Yes, sir." Charlie's shoulders straightened, as if a heavy load had been lifted from them. "Miss Shannon said your wife had her baby."

"She did." Chase looked at the boy riding next to him. Should he mention that Jenny had almost lost the baby? Should he tell young Charlie that the stress of losing her grandfather had brought on the early birth, and that he had almost lost his wife along with his daughter? Should he say that there are repercussions to everything you do? Jason's death had hurt a lot of people. It had touched a lot of people.

"I hope she's all right."

"She is," Chase said. The boy was making strides. Intelligence showed in the brown eyes where once there had been fear. "We have a little girl named Faith."

"That's a nice name."

"It's a strong name," Chase added.

"I'm sorry that she won't get a chance to know her grandfather."

"We are, too. But we'll tell her about him. She'll know what he was like and what he built."

Charlie nodded as Chase spoke. The boy had learned a lot. He couldn't change what he had done, but he was sorry. He would learn from it.

They couldn't bring Jason back. But they could continue his legacy by giving the boy a chance. They gave him forgiveness.

"I expect to hear great things about you, Charlie Potter," Chase said.

"Yes, sir," Charlie said with a grin. "I'll do my best, and I'll remember what you said."

"Go give Jake his horse. I think you can make it on your own from here."

"So did you teach him a lesson?" Jake asked when he was once again on his horse and they were watching the descent of the Potters' wagon from a high ridge.

"He's a smart boy. I think he'll figure most of it out on his own," Chase said. He raised his hand in farewell to the family as the two small boys waved from the back of the wagon. "In spite of what his father says," Chase added.

"We've got a wedding to get to," Jake said as the wagon faded into the distance.

"If we fool around long enough, we'll miss most of the work," Chase said.

"I'm in no hurry," Jake replied. "They can't start without me because I'm the best man."

Cat jumped into the wedding plans with the same zeal she had used on Jenny's. Amanda was carted off to the dressmaker, where she was pinned into a simple white dress, in spite of Cat's desire for something puffy and lacy.

Amanda had protested that she shouldn't wear white, but since Cat had compromised on the style, Amanda gave in on the color. Every bride wanted to wear white. Wearing it was Amanda's personal victory over the past. Though it could never be forgotten, it could be put behind her. She was moving on into the future with Caleb. She was starting a new life.

The dressmaker added a silver sash that matched

Amanda's eyes, and with the addition of her mother's gold locket, Cat pronounced the ensemble perfect.

Shannon and Grace gathered every wildflower they could find and wove the blossoms into a garland that was hung in an arch over a tree branch in the grove. Zeb braided the remaining flowers along with some bells into the mane and tail of the horse that would pull the buggy Amanda and Cole rode to the grove.

Everyone else preceded them, either by wagon or on horseback.

Caleb wore his brown suit and had his hair slicked into place. Jake was beside him with Amanda's mother's ring safe in his pocket. Caleb tried his best not to look at Zane, who was determined to make him laugh out loud.

Grace and Jenny held their baby girls while Chase rode herd on the boys, who were determined to climb every tree in the grove. He finally gave in and sat them on a low branch where they could easily see the ceremony and would stay out of trouble.

They heard the bells of the buggy, and Caleb arched his neck to see his bride as she came over the last ridge and into the hollow before the grove. Cole helped her down from the buggy and placed her arm through his as he walked her into the grove, past the smiling faces of Pharaoh, Cleo and Zeb, Dan and Randy, Zane and Shannon, Cat and Ty, Chase and Jenny. Grace held Jacey and dashed at her eyes with an embroidered handkerchief as a beaming Cole brought Amanda down the path to where Caleb waited with Jake at his side and the minister behind him.

Amanda's feet felt as if she were walking on air. She was floating again, and Caleb was there, steady, waiting to catch her. Her smile was not shy this time; it was wide, and her gray eyes danced with merriment and joy.

Caleb grinned broadly in return, shaking his head at Zane, who was making faces at him as if he were going to his death instead of a wonderful future. Zane would figure it out someday. Surely there was a woman for him somewhere. And was she in for a surprise.

Amanda looked as she had in his imagination when he had sketched this day. Her gleaming hair was loose and flowing about her shoulders, her dress was perfect even down to the silver sash, and her face glowed with happiness. Her gray eyes were focused on his face.

How many miles was it down the path? It might have only been a few feet, but to Caleb the distance stretched on forever. He wanted Amanda by his side. He wanted to touch her hand and look into her eyes. He wanted her to be his wife.

"Take it easy," Jake whispered. "You've got the rest of your lives to be together."

"Can't happen soon enough," Caleb whispered back as Amanda and Cole came to his side. Cole took Caleb's hand, gave it a hard squeeze while he narrowed his eyes at him and then placed Amanda's hand in his.

The others faded behind them as Amanda and Caleb looked into each other's eyes and somehow repeated the words the preacher spoke. Jake nudged Caleb's arm, and he realized that it was time for the ring. He slid it onto Amanda's finger and grasped her hand in his own as he anxiously awaited the next words.

"I now pronounce you man and wife. You may kiss the bride."

He did—for what seemed like an eternity. Finally those watching began to clear their throats. Caleb came up for air and saw Amanda's eyes twinkling merrily before him. Chance and Fox were watching the disgusting display through their fingers when everyone else broke into applause.

"We have a feast at the house," Cat declared. Everyone piled into the wagon and onto horses for the return trip, leaving the buggy to Caleb and Amanda.

"Have I told you how beautiful you are?" Caleb asked as they slowly rode behind the group.

"No. Not today," Amanda replied as she leaned into his arm. "It was perfect, Caleb. Exactly what I dreamed it would be."

"I'm afraid I don't remember much about it after you arrived," Caleb confessed. "But I have a picture of it. I drew one the night after . . ." He stopped the buggy and drew her into his arms for a kiss.

"I can't wait to see it," Amanda said when the kiss was over. "I want to see all of your drawings."

"You will. I plan on doing a lot more of them, too. You, me, our children."

"Children will be nice."

"I want several, if you're willing."

"The more the merrier," Amanda laughed. "Are you sure you won't miss the ranch?"

"No," Caleb said as he looked at the rolling prairie that surrounded them. "Maybe a little. But I can't really keep up with the others, and they know it." He slapped the reins against the horse's back. "Zane's upset about my leaving. He acts like I'm deserting him."

"Zane needs the love of a good woman."

Caleb laughed. "That is someone I cannot wait to meet. The woman for Zane. As if there could be only one."

"If only he could have his way," Amanda laughed with him. "And speaking of only one woman for one man, if I ever catch you near Maybelle's again, I will make sure that is one activity you never participate in again."

"Me?" Caleb protested. "What makes you think I would ever go anywhere like that?"

"I know why you went to town that Saturday night."

"You knew where I was going to be and you came after me anyway? What exactly were you planning to do?

"Knock down the doors and drag you out."

Caleb stopped the buggy again and pulled Amanda into his arms. His hand smoothed her hair down the side of her face as he looked into her eyes. "I admit I went there for some . . . er . . . relief, as Zane put it. But nothing happened. I couldn't go through with it. I couldn't stop thinking about you."

"I love you, Caleb."

"I love you, Amanda." Caleb said. "I plan on spending the rest of my life loving you."

"I can't wait," Amanda replied as he kissed her again. "We're never going to get back for dinner," she sighed against him.

"I think we should skip dinner and get straight to the wedding night," he said with an evil grin.

"Exactly where are we spending our wedding night?"

Amanda asked. "Are we going to the hotel? Are we going to have some privacy?"

"Yes," Caleb said.

"Which?"

"We'll have plenty of privacy."

"When will I find out?" "When we get there," Caleb said with a mysterious smile as he urged the horse onward again.

Everyone was waiting for them on the front porch with wide grins as the buggy came down the drive. A table had been set up under the cottonwood tree, to the chagrin of the meadowlark family. The adult birds looked as if they were ready to swoop down on the cake that graced the center of the table.

Shannon brought out her guitar, and it turned out that Pharaoh could play the fiddle. With Grace accompanying them on the piano that had been rolled out to the porch, they made a fine band. A makeshift dance floor had been placed on the lawn, and after the meal there was dancing.

Caleb didn't mind. Cat had asked him beforehand if dancing would make him uncomfortable, and he had told her to go ahead with it. It pleased him to see Amanda being whirled around the floor by Cole, Zane, Dan and Randy. Jake grew impatient then and made Shannon come down and dance, and Cole drew Grace away from the piano as Pharaoh slipped into a slow, soft ballad.

"Dance with me, Caleb." Amanda was a bit out of breath with flushed cheeks and shining eyes as she stood before him.

"I can't."

"Yes, you can," she said holding out her arms. "You can do anything."

"More likely I'll fall flat on my face," he said as she led him onto the dance floor. The music was slow, and he soon found he was able to move to the waltz because he led with his right foot anyway. He might not be able to do the reel, but this was nice. Especially since Amanda was beaming up at him and everyone else had quietly moved off the floor to watch the newlyweds. They lost track of time and place as the sweet sounds of Pharaoh's fiddle filled the late-afternoon air.

The last strains of the ballad had just faded and Caleb was turning with a sheepish grin to the applause of his friends when two riders came up the drive.

The sheriff and the circuit judge.

"Time to turn him over, Larrimore," the sheriff said to Cole.

"Who am I supposed to turn over?" Cole asked with a wide grin.

"Are you Cole Larrimore?" the judge asked. "Your reputation as a lawman precedes you."

"I've quit the law," Cole replied. "Especially since some folks around here have no respect for it." He looked directly at the sheriff.

"I understand you're protecting a murderer," the judge said. "Jason Lynch was a friend of mine from way back. I can understand your distaste with a lynching. I don't hold with mob action myself, but the law is the law and the boy must be tried."

"We're not so sure the boy did it," Ty said.

"You saw him do it," the sheriff protested.

"I never said that," Ty replied.

"This man rode up to my office and told me that Jason was shot by Charlie Potter and that you two saw it," the sheriff sputtered as he pointed to Caleb.

"I don't recall saying any such thing," Caleb said. "I didn't even get off my horse."

"Then *you* said it." The sheriff pointed at Jake.

"I can't recall," Jake said, looking at the sky.

"You sound a bit confused, Sheriff," Cole said. "Maybe you ought to sit under the tree and have some lemonade."

"Was Jason Lynch murdered?" the judge asked.

"My father is dead," Cat said, coming up to the judge's horse. "He was accidentally killed while visiting some settlers that were passing through. He's buried up on the ridge behind the house, if you'd like to pay your respects to him."

The judge looked at Cat, and then at Ty, who had come up behind her and placed a possessive arm around her shoulders. "I'd like that very much," the judge said. He dismounted and walked with Cat and Ty through the house.

The sheriff tried to follow, but found himself coming up against several bodies placed in his path.

"I'm not so sure I like what's going on here," he spouted in frustration.

"I'm pretty sure I don't like a lot of things that happen in Laramie," Cole retorted.

"Lemonade?" Shannon offered the man with a sweet smile. "We have some cake, too, if you'd like."

"I know you've got that boy and his family stashed out here somewhere," the sheriff said. "It's just a matter of time before I find him."

"Feel free to look around," Chase said. "I'll be happy to guide you." His dark eyes settled on the sheriff with his typical regal look.

Jenny covered her hand with her mouth. She didn't dare laugh out loud.

"I know my way around," the sheriff said and quickly moved away from Chase. "What's going on here anyway?"

"It's a wedding," Shannon said, shoving a plate into the man's hand. "Caleb and Amanda."

"The crippled one?"

The sheriff got so flustered by the icy look Jake shot him that the glass of lemonade and the piece of cake both wound up in his lap.

"I think now would be a good time for us to leave," Caleb said to Amanda as she ducked her head into his chest to keep from laughing out loud.

"Where are we going? Should I pack a bag?"

"You don't need a thing," he assured her and led her by the hand. He put a finger over his mouth, telling Chance and Fox to keep their secret as he and Amanda ran to the buggy.

"I know where we're going," Amanda said as the buggy turned off the main road and made its way up a small hollow. Soon enough a sod hut came into view. It was the Potters' former home. The garland of flowers that had hung in the trees at the grove was now hung over the door frame.

"Someone's been busy," Amanda commented when she saw the garland.

"We were a bit slow after the wedding," Caleb said as he came around to her side of the buggy. Amanda started to jump down, but he stopped her. "We have to follow tradition," he said and moved his arms beneath her.

Amanda smiled gently and let him have his way and he lifted her off the seat and carried her with halting steps to the hut.

A mattress had been added to the bed frame, and the bed had been moved to the middle of the room to face the doorway. A picnic basket sat on the table along with a broken pitcher containing a bouquet of wildflowers.

"I doubt that there's a flower left blooming on the ranch," Amanda said as Caleb gently lowered her to the floor.

"None of them compares to you," Caleb said as he kissed her.

They took their time, lips tracing across of skin, hair curling beneath fingertips as they lay body to body, merging into one.

They talked of their plans for the future. Amanda's head was so full of ideas that Caleb could hardly keep up with her. They watched the moon move across the open door, and dozed before witnessing the sunrise in the eastern sky.

And when Caleb had to get up, he found one of his crutches close to the bed with a note attached.

For going barefoot. Love, Cat.

It was early afternoon before they made their way back to the ranch. They had to pack. They were going by stage to Laredo to collect Amanda's things.

Ty and Cat greeted them at the big house, although Cat scolded them a bit for sneaking off.

"There are no charges against the Potters," Ty said. "Charlie's a free man."

"Thank goodness it's all over," Cat added. "Now maybe we can enjoy some peace."

"I want to say good-bye to Jenny," Amanda said after she had finished packing.

Caleb still needed to pick up some things from the bunkhouse so he dropped a kiss on her forehead and went to pack.

Amanda found Jenny sitting on the front stoop with Faith, watching the boys play in the yard.

"So how was the honeymoon?" Jenny asked with a wry smile.

"Perfect," Amanda said. "Lovely."

"It reminded me of ours," Jenny said. "Right here in this cabin. Of course, we had to put up with people beating on the walls and offering us advice," she said, remembering.

"Caleb doesn't need any advice," Amanda said.

Jenny smiled at Amanda. "Looks like things are working out for you two."

"Just the way you planned it?" Amanda asked.

Jenny laughed. "I admit it. I had an ulterior motive for sending Caleb up to you to mend."

"I'm so glad you did," Amanda confessed. "I'd still be cowering up in that room, hiding from the voices in my head."

"Voices?" Jenny asked.

"Remember the night of the attack? I heard a voice tell me to get the boys out of the house. And I thought I saw a very tall ghost. I decided that I was going insane after that, but I was afraid to tell anyone."

"Amanda," Jenny said. "I think the voice you heard was Jamie's."

"Jamie?" Amanda looked toward the graveyard on the ridge.

"You said you saw something that night. A ghost. A very tall ghost. I believe that was Jamie. He's protecting us."

"You mean like a guardian angel?"

"Yes. He's saved us all more times than I can tell. Most recently when Zane was so sick. Jamie told Zane it was snowing. I had helped Chase get over his fever when he was hurt by putting snow on him. Jamie just reminded me to do the same thing with Zane."

"That wasn't the only time I've heard him."

"Really?"

"Yes. When Caleb was hurt and I was nursing him, Jamie kept asking me what I was afraid of. It made me realize that I wasn't afraid of Caleb."

"He was watching out for you and Caleb."

"But he didn't even know me."

"But you saved his son," Jenny said, looking at Fox.

"He'll be watching out for you from now on, because of that and because Caleb loves you."

"Yes, he does," Caleb said as he joined them. "Who's watching out for us?"

"Jenny's brother," Amanda said.

Caleb looked toward the ridge. "That's nice to know," he said. He took a moment to look around the small valley that had been his home for so long. It was a safe place. It had sheltered him for a lot of years, and it had been the place he longed for during the war. But he had so much to look forward to now. And it wasn't as if he were leaving the ranch behind. It was home. It was the place where he could come whenever he needed family.

"Are you ready to go?" he asked Amanda.

She put her hand in his. "I'm ready," she replied.

Epilogue

There was cause for celebration in the small storefront in Laramie. The first issue of *The Laramie Chronicle* was coming off the press. Caleb and Amanda had moved into the rooms above, setting up housekeeping with the furniture they'd had shipped from Laredo.

They were lucky enough to have a lean-to attached to the back that was big enough to stable Banner comfortably, which made Caleb very happy. He hated the thought of leaving the horse at the ranch and didn't trust the livery to give him the same care that he himself would. They had also found a half-starved mother cat and three kittens living in the shed, and Amanda had quickly moved the little family into a box behind the stove. The kittens now pounced among the feet of the small crowd that had gathered to watch Caleb turn the press while the mother cat, christened True by Amanda, lay across the desk and washed her paws.

Amanda handed out the one-sheet newspaper as the pages came off the press. It featured her first editorial, a condemnation of the sheriff and his casual acceptance of the lynch mob.

"Looks like you're not wasting any time," Ty said as he perused the article.

"Might as well know who your enemies are up front," Chase added.

"Amanda has decided that it's time for a new sheriff," Caleb explained.

"Don't look at me," Cole said. "I've quit."

Amanda leaned over and kissed her uncle on the cheek. "I love you, Uncle Cole, and I think you were a great Ranger, but I have someone else in mind for the job."

She looked at Jake.

"Wait a minute," Jake said, holding his arms up in protest. "I never said I wanted to be sheriff."

"Fancy that," Shannon commented. "Me married to a lawman."

"You're not," Jake growled.

"Yet," Shannon added, grinning at Amanda.

Caleb encircled his wife with his arms as Jake continued his protests. They all knew he was the man for the job. With time, they felt sure Amanda would persuade the townfolk, too.

Amanda rubbed a smudge of ink off Caleb's cheek. "The power of the press," she said, tilting her head toward Jake, who was beginning to look panic-stricken.

"I think he needs to hear your talk about doors opening and closing," Caleb said as he kissed her.

Windfall
CINDY HOLBY

1864: Jake awakens from months of unconsciousness with his body healed, but his mind full of unanswerable questions. Is there a woman waiting somewhere for him? A family? A place he belongs? Shannon walks away from her abusive father and the only home she's ever known. Can a soldier with no past be the future she's prayed for? Grace tries to be brave when the need to capture a traitor rips her lover from her arms. Will it take even more courage to face him again now that his seed has blossomed within her? Jenny's grandfather's beloved ranch becomes a haven for all those she holds dear, but now the greed of one underhanded land baron threatens everything they've worked for. How can she keep the vision of her murdered parents alive for the generations to come?

Crosswinds
CINDY HOLBY

Ty – He is honor-bound to defend the land of his fathers, even if battle takes him from the arms of the woman he pledged himself to protect.

Cole – A Texas Ranger, he thinks the conflict will pass him by until he has the chance to capture the fugitive who'd sold so many innocent girls into prostitution.

Jenny – She vows she will no longer run from the demons of the past, and if that means confronting Wade Bishop in a New York prisoner-of-war camp, so be it. No matter how far she must travel from those she holds dear, she will draw courage from the legacy of love her parents had begun so long ago.

Dorchester Publishing Co., Inc.
P.O. Box 6640
Wayne, PA 19087-8640

___5279-2
$6.99 US/$8.99 CAN

Please add $2.50 for shipping and handling for the first book and $.75 for each additional book. NY and PA residents, add appropriate sales tax. No cash, stamps, or CODs. Canadian orders require $2.00 for shipping and handling and must be paid in U.S. dollars. Prices and availability subject to change. **Payment must accompany all orders.**

Name: _____

Address: _____

City: _____ State: _____ Zip: _____

E-mail: _____

I have enclosed $_____ in payment for the checked book(s).

For more information on these books, check out our website at www.dorchesterpub.com.
____ *Please send me a free catalog.*

CHASE
THE WIND
CINDY HOLBY

From the moment he sets eyes on Faith, Ian Duncan knows she is the only girl for him. But her unbreakable betrothal to his employer's vicious son forces him to steal his love away on the very eve of her marriage. Faith and Ian are married clandestinely, their only possessions a magnificent horse, a family Bible, a wedding-ring quilt and their unshakable belief in each other. While their homestead waits to be carved out of the Iowa wilderness, Faith presents Ian with the most precious gift of all: a son and a daughter, born of the winter snows into the spring of their lives. The golden years are still ahead, their dream is coming true, but this is just the beginning. . . .

WHITE
DECEPTION
SUSAN EDWARDS

Mathilda's world is changed the day the barn burns, for that day she loses her vision. She can still see what is right, however: continuing to ranch, here in the Dakota Territory. But she needs someone who will fight the men who killed her folks, kidnapped her siblings and aim to drive her off her land. Whom can she trust? The soft-voiced half-breed who promises to protect her?

For Reed, the blind woman means redemption. A terrible mistake has set him on this quest that leads to her property, but her hands on his face, the touch of her lips—everything about Mattie feels right. But first he must overcome his past and the hatred inside, to look beyond, and to find what is valuable: not just redemption, but love.

TEXAS VISCOUNT
SHIRL HENKE

Sabrina Edgewater, teacher of deportment, first encountered her nemesis in a London dockside brawl that earned him the nickname of "Texas Viscount." She never imagines that the lout will turn out to be the earl of Hambleton's heir.

Joshua Cantrell is brash and bold, a self-made millionaire who only agrees to become a viscount to ferret out an international conspiracy. The last thing he needs is to lock horns with a prissy little schoolmarm, even if she is cute.

The stakes are raised when Lord Hambleton offers Sabrina money enough to open the school she's always dreamed of if she'd only take the rough edges off his heir. Does she dare risk her reputation to achieve her heart's desire? Or is her heart's desire the Texas Viscount?

Dorchester Publishing Co., Inc.
P.O. Box 6640   __5243-1
Wayne, PA 19087-8640 $6.99 US/$8.99 CAN